CHOSIN STAR

For Elbert

Jack Smith

CHOSIN STAR

When Hell Froze Over

John Smith

To order additional copies of this book, contact:
Xlibris
1-888-795-4274
www.Xlibris.com
Orders@Xlibris.com
723774

With thanks to

Jenell Brossia, Heather Wolf
and
Anna Smith

DEDICATION

Chosin Star is a historical novel dedicated to my fellow members of the "Chosin Few" and all the other brave men and women from freedom loving nations everywhere who gave their lives and limbs to make it possible for the many North Koreans who fled to South Korea by the thousands to seek freedom from the oppression of a communist dictatorship.

Today, the ongoing Korean War is aptly called the "The Forgotten War" but not by those who lived it and made the ultimate sacrifices for those who survived.

PROLOGUE

"Next!"

The shrill voice shocked the white haired man back to reality. He opened his eyes then rose from his seat and walked slowly toward the empty barber chair. The young man standing before him looked as if he was barely out of high school.

A framed picture on the ledge in front of the giant mirror portrayed the same young man with his arm surrounding a smiling petite young lady holding a very small child.

"I don't think I've met you, old timer. Have I ever cut your hair before?" the young man asked.

'Old timer?' The elder man glanced at his own reflection in the mirror then quickly shifted his attention back to the face of the blue eyed, blonde haired boy. The old man saw a lot of what he once was in that youthful smile.

"Nope, can't say that you have," the old man replied as he settled himself back into the chair."

"How old are you, sir, if you don't mind my asking?"

"How old do you think I am?"

"It's hard to say, sir, but just as a guess," he hesitated while rubbing his chin, "I'd say—maybe in your seventies," he offered slowly and very deliberately trying not to be offensive.

"Nope, sonny, I'm 83 years old."

"Pretty close though, huh pops?

"Yeah, pretty close," the old man agreed holding back a grin.

"I'll bet you fought in the 'big one'?" the young man said smugly as he tied the apron around the back of the man's neck.

"No, I was too young for World War II. I joined the Marines in 1949 and fought in Korea when I was a little younger than you are now, son."

"Oh yeah, Korea, I heard about that war but I never did know much about it."

"I didn't think you did, sonny," the old man replied somewhat sarcastically.

"How do you want it cut?" the barber asked, ignoring the elder mans sarcasm.

"Just trim it up the sides and take a little off the top," the man replied thinking back to Marine Corps boot camp. The barber there had asked the same question before stripping his hair down to the nub exposing his naked scalp.

"Korea, eh, from what I heard that wasn't much of a war - was it?" the young man queried politely.

"No not so much," the older man replied curtly. "Not much at all."

He knew the young man wouldn't understand even if he told him.

The drone of the electric clippers buzzed in the old man's ears as tiny clumps of white hair fell to the floor blending in with the brown and black ones already there.

"What was Marine boot camp like? I've heard it was pretty rough."

"Not so bad if you don't mind getting out of bed at four in the morning just to have someone screaming down your neck all day long."

"Did you join to get into the war, sir?" the barber asked casually.

"No, son, I was stationed on a tropical island in the Pacific when the war broke out. I went from there straight into Korea."

"Sounds like you went from heaven to hell. Where were you in the Pacific?"

"I was in Hawaii."

"Wow, Hawaii, what more could anyone ask for?" The young man queried.

The old man smiled, relaxed, leaned back and closed his eyes again.

"Yes, what more could anyone ask for?" the old man thought, with the hum of the clippers still buzzing in his ears.

PART ONE

HEAVEN

~CHAPTER~

ONE

What more could anyone ask for?

A balmy south sea island adorned with beautiful native dancing girls?; maybe a magical sand strewn beach with an elegant crescent moon shining down as he surveyed a vast array of brightly beaming celestial stars?; or perhaps a backdrop showcasing a bounty of swaying palm trees laden with milk rich coconuts?

Yes, what more could anyone possibly ask for?

A Garden of Eden?; a Land of Enchantment?; a virtual Paradise with a seductive tropical breeze flowing lazily over his sun-drenched body delighting his senses?; or, more conceivably, a feast of fire-roasted kalua pig smothered in island grown pineapples served with coconut rum and fruit breads with melodic ukuleles playing softly in the distance?

But there was no need for him to wonder. It was all there.

It was certainly a wealthy tourist's dreamscape—but not for him. He had heard a lot about this Hawaiian tropical splendor but had seen very little of it - and most of what he had seen he couldn't afford - not on his meager military pay of sixty-eight dollars and fifty cents a month.

Night surrounded the tiny Island of Oahu wrapping its inhabitants in a cocoon of silent trust. With the exception of the select few, those designated guardians of the night, most of its residents were fast asleep.

His aching feet trudged reluctantly, one by one, along the well worn pitted streets of the military encampment. At the start of this four hour watch his legs had moved more willingly but now, three hours into it, he struggled ahead futilely attempting to relieve his incessant boredom. His lips quietly whispered, "*One, two, three, four,*" sending rhythmic cadences to each tired foot.

It was a technique he had devised to humor himself while on watch but, actually, this internalized ritual was meant to help him remain alert and, even more importantly, keep him moving. He had been on duty since midnight and would not be relieved until 0400. For him, this was the most grueling watch of all—starting in the middle of the night and ending much too late to get any sleep before reveille. "*Forty five more minutes 'til sack time,*" he agonized.

Around and around the inner borders of the encampment he walked—then robotically went around and around again covering the same ground. His tired eyes searched frantically for sandy beaches but could only find the same old sights they had seen so many times before. Even in the blackness of night, every boring detail of the road that lay ahead had become indelibly fixed in his mind.

His ears listened intently for ukuleles, but the only sounds they heard were the clip, clop, clip of his boots as they monotonously and stubbornly passed each other as if each was in an endless race to get away—away to somewhere—away to anywhere but here.

His post comprised the entirety of the main camp which included the mess hall, the communications buildings, all of the enlisted men's barracks, the non-commissioned officers club, the camp hospital, and the administrative building. As he struggled with his excruciating boredom, his mind drifted back, through a myriad of reminiscences, always returning to the most desirable thing of all—the sight of his bunk.

The Island of Oahu, though not the largest of the Hawaiian Island chain, was just as he had seen it in *National Geographic.* It was difficult to believe that, only nine years prior to his arrival, fear and terror had visited this peaceful island sanctuary. And even more difficult to believe was that it had happened on a sacred Sunday morning when, without warning, bombs rained down from an azure sky onto the American Naval Base at nearby Pearl Harbor. In that defining moment, the intrusive shock of war had replaced eons of tranquility.

His hand strained nervously at the leather sling that held his rifle firmly to his shoulder. His gaze drifted occasionally to the top of the steep hillside that overlooked the abandoned Army camp. This had been his home since his arrival here just six months ago. Atop the hill that rose high above the camp was a huge dimly lit pink building that looked sinisterly similar to the great wizard's castle in the mythical Land of Oz - it was Tripler Army Hospital. Below the hospital grounds lay an open field covered with wild plumeria bushes that had become more abundant during the rainy season. During the day, they graced the hillside with their beauty and at night they filled the air with their aromatic gift of splendorous fragrance.

The rainy season in Hawaii was comparable in a strange way to the advent of winter in his home state of Michigan. The first snowfall that blanketed the earth back home was always welcomed as the advent of sledding, ice hockey, snowball fights, and a white Christmas. However, the rainy season here was heralded by cascading torrents of rain that went on and on until they saturated everything they touched. The unwelcomed gushes of what the Marines jokingly referred to as 'liquid sunshine' would roll down the undulating slopes from the hospital above, forcing the Marines below to remove their boots and roll their pant legs up just below their knees. He frequently puzzled over the need to have Marines stand guard over dilapidated buildings set up on four foot stilted frames to prevent the rushing waters from swamping their elevated decks. This was not what he had dreamed of when he signed the enlistment papers and pledged to 'serve and protect', he mused.

The bad news was that the rainy season, usually between November and March, was hopelessly unpredictable. The good news was that the warm tropic rains turned Hawaii into a garden of pleasure all the rest of the year. Better still was that spring had arrived and the rainy season on Oahu had come to a close.

Suddenly, an agitated voice pierced the stillness of the night. It was coming from the direction of the abandoned ordnance storage area—a vast enclosure dismally known to the Marines as Post #3.

Both hands went automatically to his rifle as his eyes searched frantically to see through the shadowy darkness. He had to be cautious knowing that the lateness of the hour and the utter ridiculousness of his mission might play tricks with his weary mind.

"Smitty!" the voice was heard desperately calling, "over here." The urgency in that voice warned him that something must be very wrong.

"Who's there?" Smitty replied, as he alertly raised his carbine to port arms.

"It's me, it's me," echoed the strained reply.

"Who the hell is 'me'?" Smitty queried, in an aggravated tone.

"You know—Billy—," the breathless voice exclaimed, "it's me, Billy Hoyt, quick, come over to the fence," the voice pleaded again.

The fence the voice referred to was the dividing line that separated the main camp from the old ordnance area, where Billy was standing his watch.

Smitty's hand went to his flashlight. He quickly scanned the form on the other side of the chain link fence. Sure enough, it was Billy, all five feet nine inches of him. The two had met at Treasure Island in San Francisco while awaiting transfer overseas. Aboard ship they had gotten to know each other pretty well. Since then, Billy had become Smitty's shadow. Billy would jokingly comment to other Marines saying that, "Smitty is always where the action is."

They were quite a bit alike, these two, but from entirely different backgrounds. Billy claimed to be a descendant of some kind of vintage stock—something inherited from the legendary Deep South. He claimed to have been raised in a family that stemmed from an aristocratic background, resplendent with lots of money and lots of leisure time; unlike Smitty's family, who had suffered from hard times during the years of the Great Depression.

Smitty, who was two inches taller and twenty pounds heavier than Billy, was from Detroit. Billy was from Alabama. Both had signed themselves into the military at the ripe old age of eighteen. However, they seemed to be most intrigued by the differences that separated them culturally. Both were brown haired blue eyed boys who agreed that they had joined the Marine Corps seeking adventure and both speculated openly about where this journey in life would eventually take them. Billy would talk endlessly about home, especially going hunting with his father and the great love he had for his mother. Smitty was a great listener and loved to hear the thrilling stories that Billy told about growing up in back woods Alabama.

When the ship left the dock in San Francisco and glided through the foam crested waves, under the Golden Gate Bridge heading out into the vast Pacific, none of the young Marines on board suspected how long the confinement of a five day trip at sea could last. Three days out they experienced a violent storm that sent even the saltiest of sailors hanging over the rails. Just the thought of eating made the entire ship's crew sicker as the world in which they had been thrust spun them around in tiny little circles. The sickness that gripped the Marines made the coastal shores of Hawaii an even more welcome sight than what they had originally anticipated.

When they arrived, late at night, a lighted sign at the main gate glared at them in bright red letters, "Aloha and Welcome to Camp Catlin." Now, here they were, surrounded by an old former Army Base that had probably been an antique even before World War II. Not exactly the romantic image that either of them expected when they enlisted in the Marines.

"Quick, come down to the gate and I'll let you in," Billy stammered in an anxious voice.

"What the hell is this all about?" Smitty queried incredulously.

"You'll see," Billy replied. His voice seemed to throb with nervous anxiety.

"I'd better see and it damn well better be good. I'm not supposed to leave my post. You know that, don't you?"

Billy ignored the question and urged Smitty across the crumbling soil toward Building #1 of the six abandoned ordnance buildings that had been used to store munitions during World War II. With flashlights leading the way, they traversed the dusty interior of the huge structure. All the empty buildings in this area of the camp were double walled wooden relics that even termites would turn their noses up at. Yet here they were, guarding them like they were filled with gold.

"I hate to admit it but I'm really scared, Smitty," Billy exclaimed.

"Scared, scared of what, that this firetrap is going to collapse on top of us?" Smitty quipped as his flashlight momentarily scanned the decaying wooden rafters above their heads.

Billy stopped suddenly and pointed his quivering index finger.

"Look—look over there—in the corner—see?" His lips seemed to quiver in concert with his finger.

Smitty's flash light went instantly to the far right corner of the building. His eyes fought the darkness. Then he saw—but what he saw he didn't believe. At first glance it looked like a kid dressed up for Halloween. It appeared to be half lying and half sitting with its back propped up against the wall. If not for all the blood, one might have suspected that someone was just sleeping. The figure that lay before them was split open from the pelvis to the breast bone. Entrails hung out over the sides of the open cavity like a botched surgical operation. Its face, arms, and chest appeared to have tiny slashes and small shallow stab wounds. Smitty felt a sudden chill that coursed through his entire body. Both young Marines stood there for awhile, transfixed like gawkers at a carnival side show. Smitty's face mirrored his utter disbelief as his brain fought the unreality of what he was seeing.

Tell me this isn't real, he mumbled to himself. *This can't be real. Not even in the movies did anything like this happen. Oh yeah, people got killed. Gangsters riddled other gangsters in a hail of flying lead. Cowboys gunned down cheating gamblers in bar fights. Husbands strangled cheating wives, but nothing as vividly bloody and gory as this.*

An eternity of seconds seemed to pass before either of them spoke.

"Oh my God, don't touch anything," Smitty finally blurted out as he turned his face away.

"I already did—earlier—before—before I found you, Smitty," Billy stammered. "I wasn't sure what it was. I was so shocked I just touched the arm to see if it was real. It was s-such an eerie feeling, Smitty, I'm r-really scared."

By now, Billy was visibly shaking from head to toe.

Smitty grabbed him by his shoulders and shook him violently. "Did you see this happen?" he asked as they stumbled back toward the open door.

"N—no, I heard something. I wasn't sure what. Then I saw a shadowy figure coming out of this building. I shouted halt but he didn't, so I chased him between buildings and over to the back fence. Then I saw him climb over. Before I knew it, he was gone. On the ground I saw a large knife and what looked like a shirt covered with blood. I didn't touch them. I left them there. Then I came back here and went inside to look around. I saw a dim flickering light from a kerosene lamp as it cast eerie shadows across the walls. Then the beam of my flashlight picked up something unusual in the far corner of the room. I freaked out after I discovered what it was. I staggered out the door and over to the fence, looking for you. You know the rest. I don't know what to do now, Smitty. You gotta help me." Billy's voice trembled as if he was reliving the entire event over and over again.

"Are you sure there was only one person, Billy?" Smitty asked, as he nervously shined his flashlight around the area outside the building.

"That's all I saw. It was so dark. Maybe there was someone else. I don't know. I just—don't know."

Daybreak was lurking behind a still darkened sky as the two finally returned to the gate that separated their posts.

"You stay here and pull yourself together, Billy, I'm going to the Corporal of the Guard shack to report this." But before Smitty could get turned around a jeep came rolling up to the gate. Inside was Staff Sergeant Carter, the Commander of the Guard. With him were two other Marines, PFC Thomas and PFC Wilson, who were there to relieve them from their watches. By now it was 0410.

"Where the hell've you guys been?" the surly staff sergeant growled.

Smitty told him what they had seen as Billy stood there in rapt silence. The Commander of the Guard withdrew his .45 caliber pistol from its holster and racked a round into the chamber.

"PFC Hoyt, this is your post, you come with me. You other men stay here," the sergeant ordered as he and Billy disappeared into the darkness.

By the time the rising sun peeked from behind a few rogue clouds on the horizon, the entire area was swarming with government vehicles. Hawaiian Armed Services Police, known locally as HASP were everywhere.

The congested scene looked like Hotel Street in Honolulu on a Saturday night, except that everyone was sober.

Smitty knew instinctively that his eyes would not see the sight of his bunk that morning.

~CHAPTER~

TWO

A brief spring shower had begun, lasting only long enough to prevent the police from gathering much outdoor evidence. The majority of relevant clues, however, were thought to be mainly indoors.

The investigation went on around the clock for days that seemed like months. Nothing like this had ever happened in the Territory of Hawaii before. What soon became both apparent and confusing was that there were actually two crime scenes—duplicates of each other. Another body was found in the far left rear corner of the same huge warehouse. Both victims had their wrists bound tightly behind them with pieces of old rope. The fronts of their pants were unbuttoned. They wore no shirts, and their feet were tied together at the ankles. Both wore abhorrent death masks of extreme fear and apprehension. Their mouths were stuffed with strips torn from their own shirts. Not one, but two knives were found near the back fence. One was a small pen knife the other an inexpensive switch blade. Both had been wiped clean. Any blood evidence or bloody fingerprints that may have been on the back fence had been conveniently washed away by the sudden rain squall that morning. Inside the warehouse, finger prints were found on a lantern that had been recently used but they were determined to have come from the deceased as were the prints on two flash lights.

Investigators ascertained that the victims were very young men—both sixteen. They were local boys whose identities remained anonymous for several days after the incident. Neither of them had a police record and neither were considered to be delinquents. It was concluded that they were just good boys who happened to be in the wrong place at the wrong time.

In the absence of any "smoking gun killers," Billy and Smitty routinely became the primary persons of interest. They were interrogated over and over by several investigating agencies, but they could not find even a minute amount of physical evidence or motive to connect either of them to this heinous crime. The agents periodically dropped less than subtle hints that the person or persons responsible must have been raving lunatics. Since neither Smitty nor Billy fit that description, both were released with a warning not to discuss the matter with anyone.

In their final summation, authorities determined that illegal entry to the restricted area could easily have been accomplished simply by scaling the chain link fence to the east of the camp. And, if so, this was probably not the first time that these boys or others had entered that forbidden area even with all the exterior warning signs on the outside of the fence that read in big bold letters "KAPU", meaning keep out in Hawaiian. A broad search was immediately launched to find the phantom intruder or intruders.

Special investigators were assigned the task of questioning family members, friends, schoolmates, teachers, and the usual array of known sex offenders who might have committed a crime of this nature. The most time consuming chore was in dealing with the comings and goings of a multiplicity of tourists from so many foreign countries, not to mention the other Hawaiian Islands. It soon became an investigative nightmare made even more confusing by false reports and dead end leads.

The tip-line that the Honolulu Police Department set up was swamped with calls from vindictive neighbors, jilted girlfriends, and just plain kooks. They even received confessions from a random minority of the mentally disturbed. All of this added to the already magnanimous task of finding the culprit or culprits responsible for these senseless killings. Some members of the police agencies were already facetiously tagging this overwhelming conundrum as "Task Force Tsunami."

After they found out what happened that dreadful night, PFC Wilson and PFC Thomas approached Smitty and Billy Hoyt in the open barracks.

"We think we know what happened out there," Thomas said in a half whisper.

Billy's ears perked up as did all the other ears in the room.

"Yeah," Wilson added, "we've both been on that same watch from midnight until 0400. I have personally heard noises out there—you know—kinda' like low moaning sounds, and so has Thomas. I looked around but never found anything. I talked to Sergeant Pierce about it before he got transferred to the Marine air station at Kaneohe Bay and he told me a story that knocked my socks off," Wilson dramatically hesitated for a few moments.

"Yeah, and what did he tell you?" Smitty impatiently questioned.

"Well, it seems that him and some of the other guys heard about this Japanese fighter plane that got shot down around here somewhere—you know—during the attack on Pearl Harbor."

"And what has that got to do with anything?" Smitty shot back.

"Easy—easy, listen for a minute and Wilson will give you the whole scoop," Thomas said.

"Yeah, Wilson, give us the whole scoop," Billy quickly interjected wanting to hear more.

Lips went silent as all eyes and ears in the barracks crowded in focusing intently on Wilson.

"Well, the way the story goes is that our guys shot down one of the Jap Zeroes right near Camp Catlin, and when they got to the plane the pilot was missing. Nobody saw him bail out. He just—wasn't there. They searched and searched for him but never found a trace. I guess everyone on Oahu was looking for him after the word got out. It was said that he may have committed Hara Kari—you know—that Japanese suicide where they cut their guts out, but no one ever found a body. Then strange things started to happen around here—so strange in fact that the Army packed up and moved out of this creepy hole. They turned this camp over to the Marines and never told them a thing about what had happened.

Soon after that the guys on watch out at the old ordnance area started seeing things late at night—you know—images that would just disappear when you got too close to them. They were afraid to report it because they figured they'd be labeled psychos." Wilson took a deep breath before continuing. "Well, one night, a guy on watch got real close and said that what he saw looked like a Jap wearing a flight helmet with a bright yellow scarf wrapped around his neck. He was inside one of the old ordnance buildings, and then poof, the Jap was gone. There were several more sightings from then on, but that was all that ever came of it - until now. Spooky, eh?"

"Yeah, spooky all right. Just like you, Wilson, and that dim witted partner of yours," Smitty said, looking over at a smirking Thomas.

"Was the Jap shouting Banzai?" one of the guys in the barracks blurted out.

The laughter in the squad room became deafening.

"Jack asses," Billy mumbled.

Wilson and Thomas could easily have become a comedy team like Abbott and Costello. In the barracks they were politely known as the 'Kings of Scuttlebutt,' constantly making up stories that sometimes sounded good but could seldom be mistaken for the truth. They were unique in the sense that they both seemed to be cut from the same piece of cloth. They were not related, at least not by blood. Wilson was from North Dakota and Thomas was from North Carolina. One unusual coincidence was that they both had been born on the same day, month, and year—though hundreds of miles apart.

In a rambling barracks discussion one day Thomas and Wilson were asked what astrological sign they were born under and they readily admitted that they didn't know anything about Astrology. The matter was finally settled by PFC George Walters, who was considered to be the most well-read member of the group. Walters had become bored by what he felt was a total exercise in futility. He detached himself from the book he was reading long enough to resolve the issue.

"Smitty is an Aries and I am a Pisces," Walters told everyone.

"And what are we?" Thomas asked referring to Wilson.

"You two are Feces," Walters told them with a straight face.

"Is that good?" Wilson asked.

"Oh yes," Walters answered glibly, "the traits of a person born under the Sign of Feces are a tendency toward redundant verbosity. Feces are noted for their great oratorical skills enhanced by the 'Gods of the Perpetual Winds' that constantly rage over the ancient Isle of Dung. They are renowned for their grandiose expertise in the fine art of circumlocution exhibiting frequent discharges of verbal flatulence."

Walters quickly went back to reading his book while Thomas and Wilson scratched their heads.

None of the Marines in the barracks understood a word that Walters had said, but to Thomas and Wilson it sounded very impressive. They bragged about it every chance they got until one day a hospital corpsman explained to them what feces meant. No one but Walters could have told them that they were full of crap in such an eloquent way.

After two weeks of total frustration the police called Smitty in again to speak to another investigator.

"I'm Detective Earl Voss with the Civil Investigation Department, but you can call me Earl if you'd like," the detective said very officiously.

The portly middle aged man with graying hair wore a friendly painted on smile, a wrinkled well-worn suit, a soup-stained necktie, and scuffed un-shined shoes. He spoke in soft, deliberate tones as he extended his hand toward Smitty then politely pointed to a chair in front of his desk. The detective was obviously under a lot of pressure to solve this crime and the stress seemed to be exacerbated by the dark circles beneath his eyes. He sat down and leisurely cocked one leg over the other revealing two large holes, one in the sole of his shoe and the other in the heel of his sock.

"I'd like to ask you just a few more questions about the murders," the detective said calmly, with an all knowing fatherly smile.

Just a few more questions—why not? Smitty thought. *I've already answered hundreds of them. What difference would a few more make if it would help to solve these senseless murders?*

Smitty had rehearsed that atrocious scene inside his mind a thousand times since those fateful early morning hours. Sleepless nights had become his constant companion and walking his post, no matter where he was in the camp, brought back the horror and guilt of not having been able to prevent the deaths of those two innocent boys. He had become overly sensitive to every sound he heard—especially at night when he feared that he would miss another opportunity to save a life.

Answer more questions? Sure, he could do that.

Smitty acknowledged the detective with a nervous smile. "My friends call me Smitty, sir, what can I tell you that would help?"

"Well you could start by telling me who killed those boys," the detective said with a sheepish grin.

"I sure wish I could, Sir," Smitty responded politely.

"I'm sorry, Smitty, I'm sure you do but let's get down to business. I know you've been on that ordnance area post many times yourself—you know---the one PFC Hoyt was walking that night. I know it can be very desolate out there. It's a very large area to cover and it looks like it would be very easy for someone to get into any of those buildings without being seen or heard. Am I right?"

"You're right, Sir, they could, but why would anyone want to? There's nothing in any of those buildings but dust and cobwebs."

"Then you have been inside those buildings—before that night," the detective said slyly.

"Sure I have, but so has everyone else that ever stood that watch. I guess it's just normal inquisitiveness. But once you've seen inside those shaky old shacks you don't go back in again—unless it's raining."

"That's odd because that's exactly what PFC Hoyt said."

"I don't think that's odd. That's what every guy in this camp has ever said. Nobody likes that post. Forgive the expression, Sir, but it's as exciting as spending four hours in a morgue."

The detective smiled. "Did you ever have visitors while you were on watch?" the detective asked tapping the tips of his fingers together in front of his chin.

"Just the Commander of the Guard, Sir," Smitty answered. "He makes random checks of some of the posts at night."

"I have a theory. Tell me what you think of it, Smitty. I think two or three, maybe four people came over the back fence and went into that building that night. I think things got out of control, and two of those people got killed. How am I doing so far?"

"Great, so far, detective, but tell me, why didn't one of those boys scream or run out of the building? Why didn't Billy Hoyt see or hear anything?" Smitty queried.

"Maybe—just maybe—Billy Hoyt killed those boys himself," the detective suggested, tapping his fingers on his desk while staring into Smitty's eyes.

Smitty was becoming very annoyed. He sensed that the detective was on a fishing expedition in a stagnant pond.

"Why didn't I think of that?" Smitty snapped back. "Sure—Billy did it—of course. He's a raving lunatic. He killed them, then he ran back to the barracks, took a shower to get the blood off of him, then changed his uniform and ran all the way back to his post without anyone seeing him—including me. Is that all part of your theory too, detective?"

"I'm trying to be serious," the detective said, squirming in his chair.

"So am I, Sir, so am I, and if you ever have any more theories I'd sure love to hear them."

"You seem to be very defensive, Smitty."

"I apologize, Sir, but I've been down a lot of dead ends myself trying to figure this thing out, and its damned aggravating. I can appreciate what you're doing, and I know how anxious you must be to get to the bottom of this mess, but you couldn't be any more anxious than I am."

The detective seemed to lighten up a bit as he accepted Smitty's apology.

"By the way, Smitty, our department has decided to release the identity of the two victims. They were classmates at the same local high school - nice kids. One was named Paulo, the other they called Tedi. It will be in all the papers tomorrow, just thought I'd give you a heads up," the detective smiled.

"Thanks Detective Voss. Is there anything else you want to ask?"

"Maybe later, Smitty. If you think of anything else that might be helpful you'll let me know, won't you?"

Smitty nodded affirmatively then shook Earl's hand.

"Oh yes, just tell me one more thing if you would, Sir."

"Of course," the detective replied with the same smug smile he had greeted him with earlier."

"Do you honestly think PFC Hoyt killed those boys?"

"Not really. It's like you said, Smitty. The person who did this crime would have been covered with blood. So the answer to your question is no. And for that same reason I don't suspect you either. However, both of you guys were there that night and one of you might be able to provide us with a clue that would help us find out who did. Think about it, Smitty."

"Think about it? Oh I do, Sir—believe me—I truly do," Smitty replied as he exited the detective's office.

Two weeks later Smitty was transferred from Camp Catlin to Pearl Harbor without knowing why.

~CHAPTER~

THREE

It wasn't really much of a move. Pearl Harbor was only a few miles down the road from Camp Catlin but, to Smitty, the change of venue seemed long overdue. As he passed through the main gate, he knew that this duty station was going to be more in line with his adventurous view of military service. Months before, when they first arrived at Pearl Harbor it was late at night as all the travel weary Marines hurriedly disembarked, were loaded onto buses, and transported to Camp Catlin.

Pearl was a different sight now and a very welcome one for a young Marine who, as a youth, had experienced World War II vicariously through movies and newspapers.

Pearl Harbor, he recalled, was the final resting place for the men and ships that had been sunk at the onset of the war. This was the place where world defining history had been made in December of 1941.

The excitement of standing right where it had all happened made his heart beat a little faster.

As he walked up the steps of the Marine barracks, he heard a familiar voice calling out his name.

"Smitty!" the sound reverberated under the overhang of the huge deck on the tri-leveled brick building.

"CJ!" he responded joyously.

The two had not seen each other since graduation from boot camp. CJ was from Toledo and probably because of it's proximity to Detroit the two had become very good friends. Smitty often referred to him jokingly as a 'Marshmallow Marine' because CJ was so soft hearted. He was always eager to help a fellow Marine but, in reality, CJ was far from being soft. He

---

was both physically and mentally tough and often encouraged Smitty to keep going when the rigors of boot camp were wearing him down. CJ was a strikingly handsome young man and a poster boy for the Marine Corps in his immaculate khaki uniform, mirrored in the spit shined shoes that glinted brightly in the sunlight.

"Gee, it's good to see you again," Smitty exclaimed.

"Yeah, I thought you were going to the Second Division at Camp Lajeune," CJ remarked.

"Just a little change of plans; you know how the Marine Corps is, CJ."

"And now you're under the command of the infamous Colonel "Chesty" Puller. God help you, jar-head. How long you been here?"

"Just arrived—here, that is—I was at Camp Catlin just down the road."

"Oh no, I've heard of that place. Welcome aboard. Let me show you around the base."

The two walked side by side, laughing and joking about the boot camp experiences they had shared.

"Remember the first day we arrived at Parris Island and those two stone-faced DI's climbed aboard the bus as it rolled up to the main gate and told us to give our souls to God because our asses belonged to them? And remember how we nudged each other and smiled because we thought for sure they must be kidding?"

"Yeah," Smitty acknowledged. "And remember when Corporal MacDonald caught Johnson smoking out at the rifle range and he made him sit on the deck with a bucket over his head. Then he handed him his pack of cigarettes, covered him completely with his blanket and made him smoke the whole pack before he could come back out again?"

"Yeah, and he came out from under that blanket looking like he needed to be embalmed. I don't think he ever smoked another cigarette after that."

The laughter became contagious as they each took turns relating little anecdotes about common experiences even to the point of expanding on them occasionally.

It was a new found excitement for both young men as CJ pointed out Ford Island and the spot where the USS Arizona was memorialized. They walked around the base that whole day, jabbering away like a couple of little old ladies at their bridge club.

Finally, they had come full circle and wound up back at Marine barracks. Smitty went inside and was immediately assigned to Brig Detachment in the same duty section as CJ.

His first day on the job, Smitty learned that, while these prisoners were offenders, most were only guilty of minor infractions under military law. Sailors who somehow missed their ship after it sailed on to other ports, victims - in many instances - of too many girls, too much booze and too little time in port. Most were good guys who would be released to their ship when it returned to port or they might be reassigned to the next ship leaving Pearl for who knows where.

By the time he got off duty at midnight, most of the other Marines had gone on liberty, so Smitty carried an unused mattress from one of the empty bunks out the window of the second floor onto an extended ledge, then up a rung ladder to the flat roof atop the barracks. From there he could get a full view of the southern sky. It was a typically quiet Hawaiian moonlit night and, for Smitty, an opportune time to be alone for a while with his thoughts.

Smitty was, in reality, Jay Smith, an only child born to a poor family during lean times. His mother taught him how to read and write when he was only five years old. She became ill about that time and went to stay in a tuberculosis sanatorium on the outskirts of Detroit. She died a year later. That was the first time that he was forced to deal with the permanency of death.

He went to live with his grandmother and grandfather and, though he grew to love them, it was not quite the same as the bond he had had with his mother. His father remarried when Smitty was eleven and he introduced his new wife to him saying, "Jay, this is Ellen, she is going to be your new mother."

"*The hell she is,*" he remembered thinking, so he went back to live with his grandparents. Jay was the name he had been given at birth, but in school all his friends had called him Smitty. Jay was only twelve years old when his father died.

Looking for adventure, Smitty joined the Marine Corps when he turned eighteen years of age. His romantic desire, during WWII, was to be able to fight for his country someday, but the chance of that happening became pretty bleak when the war ended in 1945.

Lying on his back, he watched the vista of stars moving ever so slowly overhead as they twinkled out little messages in secret code telling him what he wanted to hear and reminding him of a few things he didn't really want to remember. Smitty had a girlfriend back home who had not written him since he left Detroit. He thought about the last time he had seen her. It was right after he had returned home on leave from boot camp.

"*Oh, Smitty, I love you so much,*" she told him, *in the heat of passion, the night before he left to go overseas. Yes, Smitty was thinking, I love you too.*

"*Oh God, Smitty, you are the only man for me,*" she breathed passionately *into his ear.*

Yes, Yes, Yes, Smitty thought while his arms surrounded her firm young body, his heart beating rapidly. "I love you Carol," he murmured as she ran her fingers through his boot camp haircut. "You are sexier than…than…" she coughed nervously, "than anyone I've ever seen in the movies, she finally concluded."

At that moment Smitty thought she might have a certain name on the tip of her tongue. A name—not his—but one that he might easily have recognized had it slipped out.

"I want to have your baby," she sighed again.

Whoa, Smitty, whoa, he thought, as he backed away from her. This intoxicating moment was going way beyond what his plans were for his future. It wasn't that he didn't care about her. He just felt that things were happening much too quickly to suit him.

He lay there, looking up at the tropical moon, wondering in his youthful lust if—just perhaps—she was looking up at the same moon at that very moment. "No," he quickly answered himself, chuckling, "that is just romantic foolishness."

Smitty continued reminiscing about home—just scattered memories of boyhood friends, favorite places, special things, and his grandparents.

Earlier that day, Smitty desperately tried to put together a letter to his grandmother and grandfather, just to keep in touch as he had promised them he would. He strained to think of something to say that he hadn't already said in previous letters and finally settled for the old standard: I'm fine, how are you?

Could he possibly tell them, he thought, that two boys were killed late one night in the camp while he was on guard? Could he say that he had joined the Marines to protect and defend and had failed in his first opportunity to do so? Could he bare his soul and tell them of the guilt he felt at not being able to save those boys from whomever it was that ended their young lives? Could he tell them that he felt that he should have seen or heard something that surely would have changed their fate? Could he say that that singular moment haunted his sleeping and waking hours and that he could not escape the vision of one of them lying in front of him so very innocently and yet so very dead?

His reverie was abruptly halted.

"Hey, Jarhead—doki-laki-hoki-pau." It was CJ.

Smitty looked up puzzled by what he had just heard.

"What does that mean?" Smitty asked inquisitively.

"What does what mean?" CJ answered with a huge grin.

"Doki laki hoki pau—is that Hawaiian?"

"Oh hell no, I just made that up. Pretty good though, huh?"

"Yeah, you're a real linguist, CJ."

"What did you call me?" CJ's hair bristled on the back of his neck.

"Oh, forget it," Smitty replied. "How did you find me?"

"Walters told me you were out here. He said he saw you going out the window carrying a mattress over your shoulder and thought you were nuts. I told him he was right and then I grabbed a mattress and went out the window too. No telling what he's thinking now."

"Where did you go tonight, Honolulu?"

"No, Smitty," CJ stammered, "Jimbo, Corporal Tyne and me went to Waikiki and had a blast. We found this nightclub called the China Doll that had a lotta pritty women there, and the beer was reasonable. I tell you it was a blast. It's the first bar I've ever been to where they told a bunch of Marines to come back again sometime. By the way did I tell you that it was a blast?"

"Yeah, I think I remember you saying that." Smitty smirked.

"We're all going back again next payday and you're going with us. It was a blast Smitty. I tell you it was a blast."

"CJ, you are without a doubt totally blitzed."

CJ ignored him and rambled on and on, aimlessly, in his drunken stupor until he finally passed out but not before telling Smitty that it was a blast at least a dozen more times. Smitty didn't want to wake him. He figured that eventually the sound of reveille would do that for him.

Smitty's gaze reverted back again to the southern sky overhead. It was as peaceful and tranquil as the night he remembered back at Camp Catlin, the night of the death of those boys. His thoughts reflected further back to when he was a boy, just after his mother died.

He recalled the time that one of the neighbor boys was building a tree house with his father while Smitty watched. He thought about how great it would be if he had a place like that where he could go to be alone with his thoughts. He talked to his father about it and his father assured him that when he got older they would build one too. It never happened.

Smitty sought solace elsewhere, mostly in his bed at night before he drifted off to sleep. Sometimes he would hide in the attic of his grandmother's house and stare dreamily out the gabled front window into the silent sky high above him. He would seek out a single point of light off in the distance – a bright and shining star that would become his friend—and his alone. It would become his respite – his place of safety when the world crowded in on him – his haven that shielded him from fear and inner pain. There, he could visit with his mother and tell her how much he missed her tender touch and quiet understanding. From time to time he revisited his new-found haven with the star that shielded him from the sometimes unfair world until one evening he fell asleep, putting his grandparents into a panic when they could not find him in the morning.

It had been what he called 'His Place' and for years afterward he sorely missed it.

On his way to Hawaii, he created his own space as often as he could on the farthest deck aft of the ship, a place that sailors referred to as the fantail. There, he could be alone in his own quiet world.

And now he had found another – at least semi-private place – with a warm and friendly star above the roof at Marine Barracks, Pearl Harbor.

~CHAPTER~

FOUR

Payday arrived as always, with great fanfare. Marines were pressing their khaki uniforms and spit shining their dress shoes as if a visiting general was coming from stateside for a base inspection. This, however, was not the case. Every Marine not on duty was headed for town; CJ, Smitty, Jimbo, and Corporal Tyne among them.

Tyne and Jimbo went way back. They had served together in World War II, fighting jungle battles from Guadalcanal to Iwo Jima. Both had been awarded the Purple Heart, and both had earned Bronze Star medals for gallantry. Jimbo, whose real name was James Terp, hailed from New York City – the Bronx to be exact, Jimbo would add. Andrew Tyne was a Texan. Dallas, he would proudly state. The two could well have been born of the same mother. They were like brothers who had been bonded together in the heat of battle. They argued but never fought, at least not each other.

Private James Terp got his nickname from Tyne, who had grown tired of hearing the two joined-at-the-hip buddies laughingly referred to as Terp and Tyne. Many good men had gotten awfully bloodied using that wise crack—thus 'Jimbo' had been born. Those who didn't know them well often wondered how a Texan could ever be best friends with a Yankee – especially one from New York City.

Nevertheless, Tyne often remarked that if you had a choice of who you would want to have in a foxhole with you, Jimbo would be that man.

Jimbo could easily have been a sergeant or at least a corporal by now if not for the fact that, as great as he was in combat, he was a royal screw up in a peacetime civilian world. When he was sober he was fine, but he would frequently get drunk and fight at the drop of a hat. That was why he was still a buck-ass private. Except for the pay cut, he didn't seem to mind. He repeatedly bragged that being on the bottom of the pecking order was a lot safer and hell of a lot less aggravating.

"After all," he would say, "they can't bust me any lower than I already am, and as Private Terp I ain't responsible for nuthin."

The liberty bus lurched forward taking them straight from the main gate into Waikiki. CJ and Smitty decided to cruise the beach for a while to bide some time before going to the China Doll. Jimbo and Tyne had other plans, so they all agreed to meet in front of the Royal Hawaiian Hotel at nine o'clock that evening.

Smitty and CJ removed their shoes and began walking along the beach, squishing sand between their pale white toes, while boyishly kicking at waves that stealthily crept up at them along the shoreline.

"Check out those chicks lying on the beach at twelve o'clock," CJ said.

"I see, I see," Smitty responded exuberantly. Their bronzed bodies and dark hair told them that the girls were more than likely local wahines.

As they got closer, CJ started to limp a little and hop on one foot. He stumbled over to the dry sand near the blanket where the girls were sunning themselves and abruptly sat down.

"Ouch," he exclaimed while holding his foot and slyly winking at Smitty at the same time.

What a make out artist, Smitty thought.

One of the girls asked if he was all right. The other mockingly asked if the big strong Marine had hurt his little pinky. Smitty and CJ laughed, and soon the girls joined in. Before they knew what had happened they were like old friends.

"Your necklace says Lani, is that your name?" CJ asked.

"Yes, but it is pronounced Lon-Nee," she replied, and my sister's name is spelled N-a-n-i pronounced Non-Nee."

"My friends all call me CJ. It's pronounced C-J and my buddy here is Smitty, pronounced....?"

"Never mind, CJ," Lani said laughing. "We get it."

As if by fate, Lani took to CJ immediately while Nani and Smitty were busily exploring each other's eyes.

"Do you girls come here very often?" Smitty asked.

"We live here," Nani swiftly replied with an impish smile.

"No, I mean here—to the beach," Smitty said with downcast eyes, a little embarrassed.

"I knew what you meant and I apologize," Nani said, chuckling. They all laughed again, and the laughter became the glue that held their budding relationship together.

Lani, it turned out, was seventeen and Nani was eighteen. Both were black-haired beauties, who seemed to be highly intelligent. Their mother, the girls told them, was a teacher at the local high school. The girls went on to say that they were very intent on going to college though they hadn't decided where. It was, for all practical purposes, just idle chatter but it broke the ice and helped them get to know each other a little better.

The foursome left the beach that day only long enough to get something to eat from a local street vendor, then they went back and walked and talked some more. Up ahead, they saw a huge lighthouse in the distance. It looked, in all respects, like a fine expensive painting hanging on a backdrop of sand, water, mountain, sun, and sky.

"The Diamond Head Lighthouse has been here for many years to warn ships that the waters near it are very shallow and that they could run their ships aground if they got too close. Many years ago, it was used as a land mark to guide outrigger canoeing parties back to Oahu at night," Nani explained.

Smitty loved listening to her talk and intently watched her lips as she told more stories of their visits to the lighthouse with their mother when the girls were very young.

Smitty was star struck from the beginning but felt a little tense in this new relationship.

"I don't know if I told you this or not, girls, but I am from the state of Michigan which is made up of two peninsulas that jut out into the Great Lakes. The lakes are not quite as huge as the Pacific Ocean, of course, but they are quite vast. Much of the shipping of iron ore and automobiles is conducted along those waterways, and we have many lighthouses all around our state to guide the ships. It is truly a beautiful state but not quite as beautiful as Hawaii," Smitty added in a feebly boyish attempt at making intelligent conversation to impress Nani. Luckily CJ, jumped to his rescue saving Smitty from any further embarrassment.

"Why do they call this volcano Diamond Head?" CJ asked.

"Some sailors supposedly found what they thought were diamonds in the rocks on the steep slopes of the volcano. They turned out to be just calcite crystals, but I guess the name stuck so my people have called it Diamond Head ever since," Lani answered.

Before they knew it the day was gone. At that moment had you asked each of them privately, they would have told you that they were in love. Not an ordinary love, mind you, but that very special love that only young men in their teens could comprehend.

They all agreed to meet back at the same spot the following afternoon. The guys promised to bring some swimming trunks and towels and the girls would bring a very special Hawaiian treat for lunch.

Smitty and CJ had another appointment to keep, so they reluctantly bade the ladies goodbye.

At 2200 Smitty, CJ, Tyne, and Jimbo strolled into the China Doll like they were plank owners on their own private yacht, with CJ leading the way. Smitty wanted to order one of the fancy Hawaiian cocktails that were advertised on the card display but knew their meager funds would dictate otherwise.

"Beers all around," Smitty told the waitress.

When they became more accustomed to the dimmed lights, their eyes searched the smoke filled room for young wahines but the only ladies there were older ones and most were tourists escorted by older men.

"Too early," Tyne said, "the younger ones will be here later. Hey Smitty, are you listening?"

Smitty's train of thought was elsewhere. His attention was fixed in the direction of the bar. CJ shook his arm.

"What do you see?" he inquired.

"I thought I saw a familiar face."

"Guy face or girl face?"

"Guy face—see that Marine with the corporal stripes sitting at the bar with his back to us? Do you know him?"

"Not really," CJ replied after puzzling the matter for a while. Why don't you go over and check him out?"

"No it's not that important. Besides the show is about to start."

The band began to play, but it wasn't anything any of them recognized from back home. The music had a Hawaiian flavor and the singer sang words that sounded like CJs when he was drunk. Smitty became absorbed in the music while the others laughed and joked about the last time they had been here.

"Smitty, is that you?" A voice came from over his shoulder.

Smitty turned and looked up. He immediately recognized both the voice and the face of Billy Hoyt.

"How you been?" Billy sputtered.

"Sit down," Smitty insisted as he pulled a chair over from another table. Smitty looked around to see if there was anyone with him.

"Look at me, I'm a corporal already," Billy said, pointing to the chevrons on his sleeve.

"How did you do that? Did you steal some noncoms shirt?" Smitty smiled sheepishly.

"No, Smitty, the CO at Camp Catlin called me in. I was scared. I didn't know what he wanted to see me for. Seems he admired what I did that night. You know goin' after that guy in the dark then checkin' out the building and all. He wanted to give me a medal but I guess he decided this was just as good. I don't know though, I think I'd look pretty good with a medal don't you?"

"I think the CO should have been there that night," Smitty replied with a look of amazement.

"You're jealous aren't you, Smitty? Go ahead, say it—you're jealous. Am I right?"

"No, Billy, I'm not jealous. I'm happy for you, really, I am."

"Can I buy you a beer?" Billy asked.

"No, let me buy you one," Smitty said as he waved to the waitress.

Smitty introduced Billy to the rest of the guys, never mentioning the incident at Camp Catlin.

As they talked, some soldiers came in and sat at a table nearby. All four of them looked like they had already had a few too many before they had arrived. They had just gotten seated when the dance floor came alive with hula dancers. Drums beat from backstage and grass skirts swayed to a throbbing Tahitian rhythm. Brightly colored lights shifted from one dancer to another as all eyes focused on the movement of the skirts. For some reason the words "*what a blast*" echoed in Smitty's brain. When the hula show abruptly ended, the MC announced the main attraction.

"On our stage tonight we have the exotic, the gorgeous and renowned island temptress Mai Ling—give her a warm Hawaiian aloha!" he shouted.

Wolf whistles echoed from the walls in every corner of the room. Mai Ling was a knockout by any standards, dressed in an oriental skirt with slits all around that revealed her long slender legs and emphasized the movements of her hips with every step she took. Her face appeared smooth and soft and her body from her neck to her toes exuded carnal sexuality. She glided around the dance floor in short rhythmic strides on her naked feet with her long black tresses dancing on her graceful shoulders.

The four soldiers seated nearest the dance floor were coming unglued. She smiled an impish 'come hither' smile, swishing her head from one side to the other. The soldiers reached out to touch her exposed legs as she coquettishly shimmied past their table. Then she slyly skirted away, leaving them with only a handful of air.

When her performance concluded to seemingly endless applause the band started to play slow dance music and encouraged patrons to come out on the floor. Mai Ling appeared again from behind the curtain and was moving tauntingly through the clusters of dancers. The male singer crooned out romantic lyrics. One of the soldiers weaved his way across the floor occasionally bouncing off of annoyed couples, altering their rhythm. Soon, he was seen proudly escorting Mai Ling back to his table.

After buying her a few very expensive drinks, the soldier led her precariously out onto the dance floor, looking like he had just won the jackpot on a slot machine. The song the band was playing was very beautiful, the dimly lighted setting was very romantic, and the love struck lonely soldier was very drunk.

Corporal Tyne, humming along with the melody, leaned back in his chair and smiled a sheepish all knowing grin as the singer mesmerized the couples on the dance floor.

> *The night is like a lovely tune,*
> *Beware my foolish heart.*
> *How white the ever constant moon,*
> *Take care, my foolish heart.*
> *There's a line between love and fascination*
> *That's hard to see on an evening such as this.*
> *For they both give the very same sensation,*
> *When they're lost in the passion of a kiss.*

"Oh my God," Jimbo exclaimed, "do you guys see what I see?"

The soldier had one hand on her breast, while the other traced its way down her slender back onto her firm buttocks. From Smitty's perspective, it appeared that the soldier had his tongue located somewhere near her tonsils. CJ and Jimbo were roaring with laughter to a point where Smitty would have sworn he heard CJ say, *"What a blast."*

"What's so funny, CJ?" Smitty asked.

"Yeah, what's so funny?" Billy Hoyt chimed in.

"You don't know—that's right you, guys don't know. That ain't no woman that's a female impersonator—and that dogface—he don't know that yet either."

"You mean Mai Ling is really a guy?"

CJ couldn't respond. He just kept laughing and shaking his head up and down affirmatively.

Mai Ling's hand slid down the soldier's hip then crossed over to the front of his trousers as the singers words echoed across the room, *"there's a line between love and fascination."*

To everyone concerned, the soldier appeared to be in a moment of supreme ecstasy as Mai Ling's hand moved in a circular motion between his thighs.

Suddenly the soldier's hand glided slowly around from Mai Ling's tailbone to her belly then plunged deep down into her crotch.

Then, just as suddenly, the soldier let out an epitaph that could be heard back in the states.

"Beware my foolish heart," were probably the last conscious words she heard before a fist flew in her face and Mai Ling went skidding across the floor on her back. She did not get back up again. After a few more epitaphs more fists went flying around the room. Many of the unsuspecting male patrons believed that they were justifiably defending a lovely lady's honor.

"Let's get the hell out of here before HASP comes," CJ shouted, but he couldn't help grinning from ear to ear. "What a blast," he was very audibly heard mumbling on the way out.

Jimbo muttered all the way back to Pearl Harbor too. "First chance I've had since Frisco to get into a good fight and CJ wants to leave. You meathead, CJ," he stammered.

~CHAPTER~

FIVE

His feet were moving down the old company street. He urged them to go faster but they only dragged along — l e f t, r i g h t, l e f t — ever so slowly. He struggled to increase his speed, but his legs felt heavy as if they were slogging through mud. Finally he reached a chain link fence with sharp pointed spikes protruding from the top. Through the openings, he observed the shambles of an old decaying barn. His hand pulled at the gate, but it resisted. He urgently pulled harder and harder straining with all his might, but it still wouldn't move. He reached up to grasp the tiny openings in the ten foot high chain link fence that separated him from his undefined mission. In desperation he began to pull himself skyward hand over hand. He looked up and saw the top of the fence just beyond his grasp. He reached again—then again—helplessly and ever so hopelessly, but it was still out of reach. His arms were weary but, with another determined thrust, his fingers curled tightly around the metal bar at the top. He pulled his weight up until his legs finally straddled the fence. Then he looked down at what now appeared to be a deep, dark chasm on the other side. He frustratingly began his hand over hand, foot after foot agonizing descent into darkness, but the ground seemed to get further and further away instead of closer. In desperation, he finally let go and began tumbling and floating in spiraling turns for what seemed like an eternity before he fell to the ground below. He slowly picked himself up and staggered toward the huge barn door ahead of him. His hand reached up to grasp the huge handle. He pulled hopelessly with all his might to open it, then, using both hands, he pulled again. The door responded gradually and reluctantly to his demands, creaking as it barely crawled across the dust and dirt that blocked its path. With one more weary thrust, the door crashed back toward him and fell from its rusty hinges almost crushing him. He picked himself up again and stepped inside to almost total darkness. There, in front of him, was an eerily illuminated, indistinguishable face. His eyes strained to recognize the owner, but all he saw were two hollow dark pits where the eyes should have been and a long drawn chin with lips that harbored the cunning smile of a demon. Looking up, he saw two raised arms with gnarled fists that clung tightly to a knife the size of a bayonet. The blade glistened in the dim light. The phantom was straddling a tinier figure in front of him while slowly guiding the point of the knife toward a naked chest. He looked down and saw the tender face of a young boy—fear and terror radiating from his eyes. The knife continued its downward arc. His arms reached out and grabbed the phantom's wrists. The boy's eyes shifted to his as he pleaded—please, please, please! He strained against the power, but the knife continued to inch its way closer and closer to the boy. He desperately tried to scream, stop-stop-stop! His lips moved, but the words never came. The struggle continued in an effort to suppress the will of the phantom. Suddenly, he looked up again into the void face and saw the features begin to transform themselves into something recognizable. It was Walters. It was Walters. Then just as swiftly it contorted and it became CJ, then Jimbo, then Billy, then Tyne, then Thomas, then Wilson wearing a yellow scarf around his neck, then back to the void again. The demon laughed with delight louder and louder, assaulting his ear drums. He trembled at the powerful force exerted by his adversary until he finally succumbed to the power of the demon. He began screaming—help me—help me—someone help me—please........

Smitty was suddenly sitting bolt upright on his bunk staring blankly into space, his fists clenched and his forearms tight and aching. He cleared his eyes with the backs of his hands and noticed that everyone else in the squad bay appeared to be asleep. It was about 0300. He walked into the head and stood at the urinal for a while, then walked over to the wash basins and stared at himself in the mirror. He washed his hands and splashed water on his face to rinse the perspiration from his brow before returning to his bunk. He heard a voice in the darkness. It was Walters. Obviously, not everyone had been asleep.

"You must have been having one heck of a dream," Walters said in a whisper.

"Yeah, I guess so. Did you hear anything?" Smitty asked.

"Nothing intelligible, just a word here and there—sounded something like, help me—I think."

"Was that all?" Smitty asked.

"Yeah, basically, that was it, but it sounded pretty desperate."

"Just a nightmare I guess," Smitty said, "I'm sorry I woke you."

Smitty laid his head back down on the sweaty pillow case. The dream did not return again that night.

A bugle suddenly pierced the morning air.

All four Marines jumped out of their racks, shaved, showered and headed for the mess hall. Another full day of liberty awaited them. Smitty and CJ headed to the Post Exchange where they bought swimming trunks and Aloha shirts with the multi-colored flowers of the islands brightly imprinted on them. As they rode the liberty bus toward Waikiki, Tyne and Jimbo teased them about how cute they looked in their new shirts worn in combination with their khaki uniform trousers.

"No one will ever guess that you're Marines," Tyne said winking at Jimbo.

"Never! Not in that disguise," Jimbo added sarcastically.

"Not with those khaki pants," Tyne chimed in. "You guys are definitely incognito. Everyone will think you are wealthy tourists on vacation in Hawaii. There probably aren't more than 500 other guys wearing khaki pants like those—and the shoes? How many tourists out there are wearing Government Issue spit shined shoes?"

"Probably all of them," Jimbo snickered, but Smitty and CJ ignored them both, pretending to stare out the window of the bus.

A newspaper lying on the seat beside him caught Smitty's eye. The headlines were about a fight at the China Doll in Waikiki the night before. Smitty picked it up and read aloud, "A female impersonator known as Mai Ling, alias Lee Polonius, was taken to the hospital in Honolulu last night, but he is expected to recover from a fractured jaw. Four soldiers were arrested in the incident and are being held in the stockade at Schofield Barracks."

"That might have been us if we hadn't got out of there when we did," Smitty interjected.

"Yeah," Jimbo agreed.

"Listen to Jimbo," Tyne chimed in. Jimbo shot a terse glare at the corporal.

Lani and Nani were waiting at the beach when Smitty and CJ arrived.

Nani was just as Smitty remembered her. Her eyes appeared to twinkle with excitement and her demure smile revealed a pleasing personality that he had never seen on any girl before. She is unlike anyone I have ever known, he thought.

"Wow, look at those shirts," Lani exclaimed, "if I didn't know you were haoles I would swear that you were one of us."

"Hey, what's this holys stuff," CJ blurted out defensively.

"It's how-lees, CJ, not holys," it means white person or foreigner in our native language," Lani explained as Nani laughed.

"Well, CJ, that settles it we got to get working on our image," Smitty said as he began to remove his shirt to expose his pale white torso to the sun.

"No don't do that," Nani said, "not yet, we've got a surprise for you. We have our mother's car and we are going to give you a tour of the rest of our island. First, we're going to head along the south shore toward Koko Head then to the Halona Blow Hole. You'll love it."

"Whatever you say," Smitty said, shrugging his shoulders.

~CHAPTER~

SIX

The scenery was breathtaking. The ocean view to their right was as vast and awesome as Smitty had remembered from his shipboard journey to Hawaii. The mountains and cliffs to their left were nothing short of spectacular combining rich emerald green landscapes brushed with earthen tones that faded in and out with sunlight and shadows. The two state-siders soon realized that the natural colors of Hawaii were, in reality, even more brilliant than their new Aloha shirts.

They stood in awe at the Blow Hole as waves rushed to the shore congesting an underwater, lava formed cavern beneath that catapulted its engorged contents upward through a small opening at the top of the cliff. The towering water funnel burst eagerly skyward, pausing only momentarily at its apex then, in a cloudy haze, returning to earth in mists of glistening white, showering back onto the sun drenched magma below—only to repeat its awesome wonder again and again.

"How beautiful!" Smitty exclaimed. "By the way, Lani, what is the Hawaiian word for beautiful?"

"Nani," she replied.

"What?" Smitty wrinkled his brow.

"Nani, is the word meaning beautiful in our language," Lani said.

"Yes, and Lani, in Hawaiian, means heavenly," Nani added.

The young Marines glanced at each other and smiled.

"Your mother really knew what she was doing when she named you two," Smitty said.

The girls blushed.

"Tell us more about your mother," CJ asked inquisitively.

34

"Our mother is just a simple island girl who met a handsome young Air Corps pilot from the United States before the war. He was stationed at Hickham Air Field at the time. She fell in love and they got married."

"What is your mother's name?" Smitty asked.

"Kalea, it means 'bright' in Hawaiian, but we just call her Lea," Nani said. "We want you to meet her soon."

"What does your father do?" CJ asked.

Both girls fell silent for a moment waiting for the other to answer.

"Our father was killed in the war when we were both very young," Nani said, feeling obligated to answer. "His name was John Tyler just like one of your American Presidents only he was a Captain. Our mother once said he was like no man she had ever met before. He was brave and strong but kind and gentle and loving at the same time. She called him her "Mauna" which means mountain in Hawaiian. He was her tower of strength she often said. We know that she loved him very much. Many men have asked, but she has never married again."

Now it was CJ and Smitty's turn to fall silent for a while.

The next stop was a scenic overlook that opened its view onto two bays bordering the vast Pacific Ocean. One was Kailua Bay and the other was Kaneohe Bay where the Marine Air Station was located at Mokapu Point on the east side of Oahu. From their perspective, it did not matter in which direction they looked because each new scene was even more spectacular than the one before.

Jutting out of the ocean along the way was a weird looking cone shaped island clearly visible from the shore.

"What is that?" CJ inquired.

"That is Mokolii Island. We sometimes call it 'Chinaman's Hat' because of its odd shape," Lani said.

"We are going to stop at Kualoa Point. There is a park there where we can eat lunch and get a better view of it from the shore," Nani added.

The young men watched as the girls unloaded the cooler.

"Our mother is a stickler for good health," Lani said. "She thinks our people eat way too many carbohydrates and fatty foods, so most of this lunch will be honey chicken, vegetables, pineapple and poi."

The purplish colored poi attracted the attention of CJ and Smitty.

"Do I dare ask what this is?" Smitty enquired cautiously.

"We call it poi. It is made from mashing and baking the taro plant. Some people say it tastes like paste but the flavor is very delicate and sometimes it takes a little getting used to. Once you do, you will probably like it. Try some," Nani urged.

"How do you eat it?" CJ asked.

"Use your fingers," Lani answered as she scooped some up on her middle and index fingers and put it into his mouth.

"Have some more," she urged.

Dipping his fingers into the gooey substance CJ ate more, then said with a childish grin, "It tastes a lot sweeter when it comes off of your fingers, Lani."

"Ooooh," Smitty cooed teasingly.

"Where next?" CJ quickly asked, to change the subject.

"Sunset Beach," Nani replied.

The remainder of the trip to the beach was spent comparing life in Northern Ohio and Southern Michigan to life in the South Pacific. The girls had never seen snow before and the guys had a hard time explaining snowball fights, ice skating and walking to school on frosty winter mornings.

"It would be fun to make a snowman together," Lani said delightfully.

"Perhaps someday," CJ uttered in response, "perhaps someday."

The four were as excited as kids in a candy store as they chattered away about the possibilities of things to come.

Nani drove further along the coastal shoreline, finally making a turn into a parking area. She abruptly interrupted the conversation, "This is it, Sunset Beach, everybody out."

The golden sandy beach was warm and replete with rolling waves and lots of skimpy bathing suits. It appeared to be a surfer's paradise. The four strolled along the beach and watched as sun tanned surfers were mercilessly driven back toward shore by a relentless wave—then, the same bodies would masochistically turn back to do it all over again. Smitty and CJ felt like they were the only white men out there as the heat from the afternoon sun seared their virgin skin.

"Are you guys OK?" Nani asked.

"Oh yeah, we feel as comfortable here as a couple of nudists at a Sunday school picnic," Smitty tersely replied.

The foursome walked back to their spot on the beach, where Smitty and CJ put their shirts back on and put a towel across their legs. The girls apologized, but the guys assured them that it was OK. Soon the conversation shifted back to family.

"CJ and I are looking forward to meeting your Mom. Do you think she'll like us?" Smitty asked.

"Maybe," Lani teased. "But, before that, you will meet another person that we dearly love—a wonderful woman who has always been like family to us."

As they turned off the main highway onto a winding dirt road, Nani pointed to a small house near the jagged rocks along the shore that was decorated with palm leaves.

"These are our friends CJ and Smitty," Nani told Mama Ahue as the stout barefoot lady, wearing the flowing blue and gold muumuu approached the car.

"Aloha," Mama beamed an amiable smile.

Mama Ahue was a close family friend of the Tyler's. Her grandsons went to the same school the girls attended.

"We brought these haoles here to see where the pearl comes from," Nani announced.

"Mama Ahue is considered to be the resident expert on the pearl culture and its historical value to Hawaii," Lani added.

Mama told the young men about the difference between salt water and fresh water pearls. Then she elaborated about white, black, blue and chocolate colored varieties. She told them everything about diving for undersea pearls and oyster farms, where pearls were formed in man made oyster beds. The boys were fascinated by her wisdom and especially her command of the English language.

"Let me tell you boys about the oyster," Mama Ahue began with a twinkle in her eye. "The oyster is one of God's most amazing creatures."

"A slimy oyster?" Smitty grinned. "You're joking, aren't you?"

"No, Smitty, I'm not. Mama Ahue knows the oyster. She has lived with them for years. Just listen carefully and you will learn," she smiled. "The oyster copes with nature by taking something ugly and turning it into something magnificent. When a coarse grain of sand invades its private world and becomes an irritant, the oyster begins to build a protective seal around it, and after many months of repeating this process a wondrous thing of great natural beauty replaces the offensive intruder—a thing that we have come to know as the pearl. We humans can learn a lot from a slimy oyster, Smitty."

Smitty and CJ stood in quiet wonder amazed by Mama Ahue's stern confidence.

"Are these kanes very good friends?" Mama asked Nani slyly.

"Very," Nani answered glowingly smiling into Smitty's eyes.

"Then I have something very special for them. I am sure they will know what to do with them," Mama Ahue said with a wink.

She went inside and brought out two pearls, each in a single setting, suspended from a gold chain. The pearls were exquisitely beautiful and obviously mounted in their settings with expert care. Mama's eyes beamed with delight as she watched the four admire her craftsmanship.

"These necklaces will look very pritty on the right wahine's neck," Mama said winking at the boys again.

"Thank you very much for everything Mama Ahue. We enjoyed the pearl lessons and the pearls very much and we know that these have great value. How can CJ and I ever repay you?" Smitty said with great humility.

"You will repay me someday with something you do for me or for someone that I love. You may do it without even consciously knowing that you have done it, but Mama Ahue's spirit will know."

"She is quite a lady," Smitty said as they were leaving. "But I do have one question. She called us 'kanes,' is that good or bad?" Smitty asked.

The girls laughed. "'Kane' is pronounced kon-nee and it means man in our language," Nani replied then laughed again.

"Before we leave here this kane wants to say I love you, Nani," Smitty said as he hooked the clasp around her neck then turned her back around. "This pearl is almost as beautiful as you," he said as he looked deeply into her eyes.

"And I love you," Nani said before she kissed him.

A similar ceremony was being conducted on the other side of the car.

Nani then pointed the car toward Wahiawa, where the pineapple groves are located on Oahu.

"This will be our last stop today," she said. "After this, we will drop you guys off at the main gate at Pearl Harbor."

The ride took them through the center of the island. Nani and Smitty were talking about her open house party, which was coming up soon, and Smitty was assuring her that he would be there if Uncle Sam would let him.

Suddenly, Smitty picked up on a word coming from the back seat. The word was 'murder' and, just as quickly as he heard it, he tuned Nani out and listened to the conversation behind him as Nani rambled on about her school and her mother's future plans for her and Lani.

Lani was telling CJ about some boys at her school who were murdered and wondered if CJ had heard about it. He hadn't, so she went on to tell him how close they were to the murdered school chums.

"One of the boys, Tedi, was the grandson of Mama Ahue," she told CJ. He listened intently as she told about the effect that the whole incident had on her mom and everyone at the school. Smitty smiled and looked at Nani as she spoke, continuing to pretend that he was listening to her while he was still straining to hear Lani from the back seat.

CJ knew nothing. *Thank God*, Smitty thought. Smitty had never told him. In fact, Smitty never told anyone after he left Camp Catlin and now he knew that he was going to have to tell Nani about his role in the matter—but not today.

"Well, what did you think?" Nani asked Smitty whose mind was in the back seat.

He appeared to be startled. "About what?" Smitty asked.

"About what I just said—about today. Did you enjoy this trip?"

"Oh yes, just being with you is very special, Nani," Smitty said, feeling like the boy who got caught with his hand in the cookie jar. He hadn't heard a word she'd said.

Nani seemed a little perplexed by his inattention but dismissed it.

The visit to the pineapple plantation was the climax of the wonderful day that had slipped by much too quickly for the young Marines. Smitty delighted in seeing how pineapples actually grew. In the groves, Nani showed CJ and Smitty how to select a ripe, ready to eat, pineapple.

"My mother says that this spiny yellowish brown fruit, when properly picked, is one of the most delicious and nutritious foods you can eat, and the juices are very delightful too," Nani said.

They bought two pineapples; one to take home to their mother and the other they cut up to eat on the way to Pearl Harbor. Though it seemed like a good idea at first, and the pineapple was delicious, it created a sticky situation that forced Smitty to feed pieces of the sweet fruit to Nani as she drove. They arrived at the main gate at Pearl laughing and licking their fingers and lips incessantly.

"I really am sorry if I seemed to be disinterested at times. It was a wonderful tour, and this was truly a fulfillment of my fanciful image of what Hawaii would be like." Smitty said.

"I'm glad you enjoyed it," Nani smiled.

Nani gave Smitty her phone number and asked him to call when he found out when they would be free to see them again. Smitty leaned over to Nani and looked into her eyes. He felt a sudden chill. A fear that was never there before gripped him. He saw his own image in her deep brown eyes. It was an image he didn't want to erase. He kissed her gently then he licked his lips and kissed her again. With a smile he whispered, "Soon."

"See if you guys can get liberty on Memorial Day. We have special plans and it will give you an opportunity to meet our mother," Lani called out to them. They nodded in acknowledgement and waved as they walked backwards toward their barracks.

~CHAPTER~

SEVEN

When Smitty got back to Pearl he found a letter lying on his bunk. The envelope had a current postmark but the letter inside was dated four months earlier.

My Dearest Smitty,

Sorry I haven't written but I've been very busy. I'm taking a night-school class that I can apply toward college credits. I can't believe that it was September when I last saw you. It has been so lonely here without you. Sometimes I cry myself to sleep at night thinking about what our lives might have been like if we had a baby. My girlfriend Marie is going to have her baby soon. She plans to name him Tom after her boyfriend—if it's a boy.

I saw your friend Bill the other day. He says he is going to go away to some engineering school and told me to say, hi. Otherwise, everything is pretty much the same here except that it is snowing. I got a job at the drug store and I work behind the soda fountain making sundaes and ice cream cones. I get to see a lot of people so I really enjoy the job. You know me, I like people. I like ice cream too and I get to eat as much as I like when the boss isn't watching.

Your old buddy Ray just now stopped by and wants to take

me to a movie. He knows how lonely I am without you and he wants to look after me while you are gone. I'll get back to this letter a little later.

The letter stopped there then continued on - much later.

Sorry Smitty I almost forgot about this letter. I must have been awfully tired that night. Ray and I saw a really good movie though and it reminded me a lot of you. Ray wanted me to tell you, "Semper Fidelis," whatever that means. Marie had her baby early. She named him Steve because her and Tom broke up before the baby was born. Ray and me have been going out a lot and I want you to know that being with him does help me a lot to not be so lonely or miss you too much. Spring came early here this year, so Ray and me went canoeing around the canals on Belle Isle then went picnicking with some of his friends.

By the way, I know I haven't told you this. How silly of me. I haven't written you before so how could I. My mom thinks I might be pregnant. I'm so excited, but we're not sure yet.

More later. Take care of yourself and remember I truly love you.

Faithfully,
Carol

Smitty began laughing hysterically as he handed the letter to CJ. PFC Walters, who had been busy reading a book, looked over at Smitty.

"What's so funny?" Walters asked, but Smitty was laughing so hard he couldn't answer.

Finally CJ said, "He just got what looks like a 'Dear John' letter." Then, he too, began laughing.

Walters shook his head. "Now I know those two guys are nuts. The guy gets a 'Dear John,' then they laugh about it. Figure that one out." He went right back to reading his book.

Private First Class George Walters was a laid back guy who spent a lot of time reading, running, and working out. He was six foot two, weighed about two hundred pounds, and was - by Marine Corps standards - unquestionably physically fit. His chiseled countenance portrayed a man of great strength and determination. He appeared to be self educated. He never got in any trouble that anyone knew about. He didn't drink or smoke and seldom went on liberty. When he did go, no one ever saw anyone with him, and he never talked about where he had been. As a matter of fact, no one knew much about him at all, except that he was from Pennsylvania and he seemed to be a pretty nice guy. But no one could really attest to that either.

Someone once asked him about the beautiful large gold ring that he wore on his right ring finger. "My dad was in the Marines. He wore it during WWII and he gave it to me when I graduated from boot camp," and that was all he said. The ring was the one thing he seemed to really treasure. On the face of it was mounted the famous eagle, globe and anchor that was symbolic of the Corps.

Still, Walters was a mystery. Everyone who tried to figure him out would give up soon after trying. Almost everything Smitty knew about Walter's had been learned aboard ship coming to Hawaii. In addition, Walters had been one of the Marines who transferred to Pearl from Camp Catlin with Smitty. During that time Smitty had come to respect him as a no-nonsense guy who loved the traditions of the Corps and expected all Marines to perform to their best at all times.

Walters knew about the murders, but never spoke about them. In fact, he never spoke much to anyone about anything, even when prodded to do so. He was truly a man of few words, but when he did speak people listened.

Over at the bulletin board, someone was posting a notice that got everyone's attention. Basically, it read that certain Marines were going to Barber's Point for annual qualification with the M1 rifle then over to a Military Reservation for two days of field training. The list of names included Tyne, Jimbo, CJ, Walters and Smitty. It was signed by Colonel Lewis Puller, and that made it very official.

"That shoots our weekend liberty in the ass," CJ commented.

"Yeah, and that's Memorial Day weekend too," Smitty sighed.

Colonel Lewis Puller, if measured, would have been five feet ten inches tall with a barrel chest that earned him the affectionate nickname 'Chesty,' but no one dared call him that to his face. To every Marine who was fortunate enough to serve with him he stood ten feet tall and got taller every year. His face was rugged and swarthy. He was often described as looking like a bull dog. To all who knew him he was a Marine's Marine—a living legend who had been awarded countless decorations for bravery in battle, which included four Navy Crosses, the second highest award given by the Navy Department. It was frequently rumored that if you dared to follow him you would certainly find a battle and, if you stuck with him, you would probably win—or die trying.

The Marines arrived at the rifle range at Barber's Point with full pack and field gear. They unloaded from the trucks and were shown to an area where they could stow their gear.

Smitty watched as two other trucks rolled in from Camp Catlin. Thomas, Wilson and Smitty's old buddy, Corporal Hoyt, were among the familiar faces.

"How is everything at the haunted woodpile?" Smitty quipped.

"We're still livin'," Thomas grinned.

"You guys haven't let the enemy infiltrate that strategic military installation, have you?" Smitty asked facetiously.

Sergeant Allen barked out a stern order for everyone to fall in. Then, he marched them over to the rifle range. They each took a numbered station, facing their target and were issued a pre-loaded eight round clip of 30 caliber ammunition. The range officer instructed everyone very precisely to load the clip into the breach of their M1 rifle.

"On my command, everyone will fire one round. We will then check to see where that round hit. Then, you will adjust the windage and elevation knobs accordingly, then fire another round into your target until you are satisfied that you are hitting where you are aiming. Is that perfectly clear?" He quickly commanded, "Ready, aim, fire," not waiting for an answer.

The air suddenly vibrated as it collided with the impacting sound waves of multiple explosions. Ears popped and shoulders rebelled against the violent recoil of the rifle's butt. The pungent smell of gun powder permeated the nostrils of the Marines—and that was only the beginning.

"We have two hits on target 24 and no hits on target 25," the range officer announced. "One of you meatheads is firing into the wrong target," he bellowed.

"The meathead he is referring to would be you," Sergeant Allen shouted over the din while pointing at PFC Thomas at station 25.

"Oops," Thomas responded.

If anyone laughed no one heard it through the intermittent reports of gun fire all along the line.

On the way to the chow hall for lunch, Billy caught up with Smitty and the two talked and laughed recalling that infamous night at the China Doll.

"Have you ever gone back there again?" Billy asked.

"No," Smitty said. "CJ and I met two nice local girls and we plan to see more of them in the future. How about you, Billy, what have you been doing?"

"I've been going to Honolulu, hanging out at the bars and getting drunk with strangers, but it ain't much fun anymore. I kind of miss going on liberty with you like we used to in Frisco, remember?"

"Yeah," Smitty chuckled, "we had some good times. We should get together again but, not being in touch anymore, I don't know when you got liberty."

"It makes it rough, but I heard some scuttlebutt that they're going to shut down Camp Catlin soon and most of us will be moving to Pearl. I sure hope so," Billy sighed.

"Have you heard anything more about that night?" Smitty asked.

"Not much, but sometimes the police ask more stupid questions and act like they know more then they're telling."

"Do you ever think about what happened?" Smitty asked, thinking about his dream.

"Yeah, but I try not to. It was just too scary—do you?"

"Yeah, sometimes I do, but I don't talk about it. Maybe I should, but you ain't around anymore, and you're probably the only one who could possibly understand."

After chow, they all returned to the range.

"We are about to begin firing for qualification," the range officer bellowed. "We will all start from the standing position, then the kneeling position, then the sitting position all from 200 yards. When we finish that we'll all move back and fire from the prone position at 600 yards. Just make sure that all of you 'ladies' fire into your own targets, he added sarcastically. Now, commence firing."

By late afternoon they had completed marking and scoring targets and headed back to the chow hall. The plan was to spend the night at the range and head for a military training site near the Waianae Mountain Range for jungle training.

"They must be preparing us for WWIII," CJ quipped.

"Sure they are," Billy Hoyt responded. "What country in their right mind would want to mess with us after the whipping we gave to Italy, Germany, and the Japs? Not even Russia, as big as they are, would want to take us on."

"You got that right, Corporal. Ain't nobody ever gonna' mess with ole Jimbo again," Jimbo chimed in with a gleeful grin.

~CHAPTER~

EIGHT

The next morning the Marines rose early, ate chow, and loaded back onto the trucks. The convoy headed toward an unknown destination somewhere at the base of a mountain that half of them couldn't pronounce and the rest only thought they could.

"This is pretty typical of the military," Wilson announced. "They pack us off to somewhere we never heard of, to do something we don't really want to do and then they tell us we're going to enjoy the opportunity to help preserve our democratic way of life. So, I ask you, what's democratic about this? What do you say we take a vote on whether this trip is really necessary?"

The sounds of laughter soon replaced all the complaining and the incessant ringing in their ears.

At the base of the mountain they met with special teams of World War II vets who would be leading them through a military exercise. They were formed into six squads of thirteen men each. Three of them were appointed to head fire teams within the squad. When they got to Tyne and Jimbo some of the vets recognized them from prior service in the Pacific.

"You two guys ought to be training us," one of them said.

The Marines were then split into two sections and, despite their rank, Tyne and Jimbo were immediately named section leaders for purposes of the training. Corporal Hoyt was made a squad leader in Jimbo's First Section and CJ, Smitty, and the always quiet, unassuming Walters were among those to serve in Billy Hoyt's squad.

Much of the day was spent climbing up steep precipices. When they would reach the top they would climb down the other side then up the

---

next slippery slope. They were taught to build rope bridges to cross wide crevasses and descend from higher elevations. They would stop occasionally for a break and would fill their canteens from mountain streams. They were ordered to add chlorine tablets to purify it—despite the fact that the mountain water was probably purer than the tap water they were accustomed to drinking at their home base.

Smitty could only imagine what it must have been like on those treacherous Pacific Islands during World War II. He had seen the documentary films in movie theaters during the war but, even then, he couldn't feel the clinging grip of the stifling jungle humidity; nor could he experience the chilling fear that a determined enemy might be lurking behind a palm tree with his sights trained at his head; he could not hear the cawing sounds of the island birds mocking the Marines with every step they took; even in his wildest imagination, he could not envisage the sting of sudden loss when a fellow Marine was mortally wounded by an unseen enemy; and, try as he might, he could not conceive killing another human being with just the simple squeeze of his trigger finger.

The first man to reach the plateau was Walters—way ahead of everyone else. He was proving to be quite physically fit.

"Show off!" Hoyt gasped at Walters as he finally struggled to the top of the next ridge, out of breath.

"Who are you calling a show off, Corporal pokey-ass?" Walters volleyed back.

"I'm the fire team leader here, Walters. You're supposed to follow me."

"No, you got that wrong, Corporal. What you mean is that you're supposed to lead and you can't do that if you're always dragging your sorry ass up from behind. When you lead, you're supposed to do it from the front."

That was the first sign of anger or emotion that anyone could remember hearing from the ever calm and cool, PFC Walters.

They found a fairly level area on one of the mountain's many plateaus and decided it was a good spot to bed down for the night. No tents could be used on the rolling slopes but that did not bother Smitty or CJ. The squad members all huddled near each other. Smitty was the first to break the silence that was born of the exhaustion that gripped them all.

"Jimbo, what's it like to kill a man?" Smitty asked very tentatively.

"Why are you asking me?" Jimbo queried, taken by surprise.

"Because I'm sure you have—I mean, killed somebody—haven't you?"

"Yeah," Jimbo answered matter-of-factly.

"What did you feel?"

"Well, if you must know, it was a kind of a relief. You know, when you do something that you know is going to be difficult, but you also know that you have to do it anyway. Then you do it, and you're relieved to find out that you could do it after all," Jimbo spoke slowly, as if he were weighing every word. "Does that make sense to you, Smitty?"

"Um, yeah," Smitty lied. He really didn't understand a jumbled word that Jimbo said.

After a long pause Smitty broke the silence again. "What I really wanted to know was how did it make you feel inside? You know, to take another person's life."

Smitty waited for an answer that never came. Jimbo had already rolled over and, by then, was sound asleep.

Smitty, who was lying on his back, anticipating an answer, finally whispered to CJ, "I hope he wasn't offended by my question," but CJ too had fallen fast asleep. And Billy, with his back to Smitty, appeared to be asleep as well.

Walters was taking advantage of the remaining light of day by reading a book. Smitty glanced over at him and noticed that the title of the book was <u>Animal Farm</u> and the author was a guy named George Orwell.

Oh no, Smitty thought, this guy even reads children's books. What a character.

Smitty lay there for a while thinking about Nani and soon, he too, was asleep.

They awoke abruptly at dawn to the sound of Sergeant Allen's voice. "Wake up, Devil Dogs, and get into the showers. We'll be moving out soon."

"What showers?" someone shouted.

"What showers?" Sergeant Allen boomed. "The only showers that you're ever going to see out here—unless it rains," Sergeant Allen growled. "And that ain't likely to happen today, so get your sorry asses movin'."

"Why do I get the feeling that I'm back in boot camp?" CJ muttered to Smitty.

Breakfast, field training style, consisted of a small sample sized box of dry cereal from C-rations left over from WWII. The Marines washed that down with a few sips of water from their canteens. No coffee—no milk—that was it. The grumbling became contagious and lasted well into mid-morning, when they found something else to grumble about.

Their lunch that afternoon wasn't much better. More C-rations with a choice of ham and limas, pork and beans, or spaghetti and meat balls all crammed into a twelve ounce can.

"Eat it and like it," Sergeant Allen responded to the new wave of grumbling.

"We'll eat it, but we don't have to like it," someone shouted.

After chow they fashioned stretchers from their rifles and blankets and with four Marines—two on each side—they carried selected Marines up and down the hills, simulating the evacuation of wounded from a combat area. Many Marines, understandably, volunteered to be one of the wounded but soon discovered that even that could be a less than comfortable ride.

Eventually, they arrived at a very steep crevasse that appeared to be 50ft across. The near side was a gradual downward slope, but the opposite side was concave and appeared to be impossible to climb. The problem was that it blocked them from advancing any further west. They stopped there to rest and to decide what to do next. Studying their map and compass, it became obvious that they would need to go south and west to reach their base camp. Second section had already turned left, heading south, and was moving out at a rapid pace.

"We need to cross over to the ledge on the other side or head south with them," CJ said.

Billy Hoyt groaned, "If we could get over there it would cut at least an hour, maybe even an hour and a half, off of this sorry-ass torture training."

"Good luck with crossing over to that plateau," Sergeant Allen quipped. "Nobody's ever been able to do it before. You can get down the slope on this side and it's impossible to get back up on the other side unless you have someone already stationed there with a line to help you up, and we don't have anyone here who can fly, so that's out."

The Sergeant turned south and struck out alone to catch up with the other group.

"Better hurry," he shouted back, "or you'll miss chow."

The exhausted Marines shouldered their field packs again, heeding the sergeants warning. Hot chow sounded like the motivator they needed to get them going again.

"Wait! We got it," Thomas shouted. "Wilson and I figured it out."

"Figured what out?" Billy asked.

"How to get across," Wilson replied.

"OK. I'll bite, how we gonna' do it?" Billy asked anxiously.

"It's easy," Thomas replied. "All we gotta' do is radio back to base camp and have them send the Army Corps of Engineers to build us a bridge."

"They never fail to fill me with pride," CJ grunted, "ever wonder how those two ass-holes made it through boot camp?" he sighed, as Sergeant Allen called out to them again, waving his arms and urging them to hurry.

While First Section prepared to move out to the south behind Second

Section, they suddenly heard a voice calling from a distance. Looking up, they saw a Marine waving his arms, shouting, "Throw me a line." It was Walters. He was standing above them on the other side.

"How the hell did you get over there?" Jimbo shouted back.

"Never mind that right now, just throw me a line."

After several failed attempts that fell short, Walters caught the weighted end of the narrow line. CJ tied it to the heavier line and Walters hauled it across the ravine. He then tied it securely around the base of a sturdy tree on his side and instructed the Marines on the other side to do the same. One by one, the Marines wrapped their legs over the line and, hand over hand, pulled themselves across to the other side.

First Section was waiting patiently, eating hot rations, as Second Section straggled into the base camp, scratching their heads at the sight of them. Sergeant Allen seemed to be the most perplexed but never uttered a word.

Smitty leaned over and whispered to Walters, "How the hell did you get over there?"

"Later. I'll tell you later," Walters smiled.

The ever mysterious Walters had just become even more of an enigma, Smitty thought.

The only real enemies the Marines had encountered that day were the heat, the muscle cramps and the annoying mosquitoes. Adding to that was the unforgiving mountain that seemed to have taunted them as they senselessly scaled an endless series of ridges and peaks in an attempt to conquer her. By the end of the day, even though they had finally reached her highest point, they knew in their utter exhaustion that she had ultimately prevailed.

Smitty arrived back at Pearl Harbor tired, aching, hungry and grubby but feeling good about himself and his fellow Marines. Toughness was, after all, one of the reasons he had joined the Marines in the first place.

Another letter was lying on his bunk.

Dearest Smitty,

Just a line to let you know that I'm still missing you. My mom is excited about meeting you after hearing so much about you— from me, of course. I told her that I care about you a lot. I hope you don't mind. We have plans for Memorial Day, and we hope that you and CJ can be here. You have my phone number. Please call as soon as you can.

Love, Nani

Smitty checked the duty roster to discover that both he and CJ had duty on Saturday and Sunday. That was the bad news. The good news was that they had liberty on Monday, Memorial Day. Smitty went to find CJ and together they headed to the lobby of the barracks where Smitty picked up the phone. The decision was made that Lea, Nani, and Lani would pick them up at the main gate early Monday morning.

From the phone, they both headed to the showers.

~CHAPTER~

NINE

The drive from Pearl Harbor with Lani, Nani and Lea on Monday morning gave CJ and Smitty an opportunity to get to know the woman they had heard so much about—a woman who had entrusted her daughters to two young American Marines sight unseen. She was charmingly different than the woman they had anticipated. She was very young in appearance with the same creamy bronze skin tones that she had bestowed on her daughters. Her stature and self-confidence made the two young men feel a little uncomfortable at first, and they both strived to be on their best behavior.

"My daughters told me all about you two—how you met and where you are from. I trust their judgment. I always have. I raised them. They probably told you that I teach school, history as a matter of fact, and I coach girl's athletics.

I attended college on the mainland and returned to Hawaii to complete my Masters Degree in Education. I love teaching, and I love young people. I don't consider teaching to be a job, in fact, I call it a vocation. I have a great passion for good health, proper eating and exercise, so if I sometimes sound boring maybe that will be the reason."

"You don't bore us Mrs. Tyler. In fact we belong to an organization that emphasizes some of the same philosophies," Smitty interjected.

"And sometimes to extremes," CJ added quickly.

"Oh, and one more thing," she said, "please call me Lea."

It was early when they arrived at their destination with the morning sun rising on a calm new day. Punch Bowl National Cemetery near Waikiki was an awesome sight to behold for a first time visitor. Lea turned into the driveway leading to the newly dedicated War Memorial. Ahead of them the American Flag at half staff danced lightly on a soft spring breeze.

"This is where my husband lives inside my mind," Lea hesitated briefly, "he and all the many other brave men and women who gave their lives for our freedom." The words rang with sincerity, coming from a woman who had sacrificed so much.

Silence hung suspended in the air as she found a place to park.

The statue of Lady Columbia etched in stone looked down at them from her place on high above the massive acres that surrounded her. Rising thirty feet above them on her ship's prow pedestal, she stood her endless vigil over the resting place of those who made this place so sacred. The words carved in stone along the base of the statue told it all: "THE SOLEMN PRIDE THAT MUST BE YOURS TO HAVE LAID SO COSTLY A SACRIFICE UPON THE ALTAR OF FREEDOM."

Smitty and CJ realized that this family understood that phrase so much better than they could.

"It is so fitting that this beautiful edifice be here in the land where it all began in 1941," Lea said. "It was newly dedicated in 1948 into the Pu'owaina Crater. Pu'owaina means 'Hill of Sacrifice.' An appropriate place, isn't it? It was formally dedicated this past September. War is such a painful waste and I pray that we have seen the last of it with all its devastation, injustice, and human suffering."

They walked the fertile green grounds, admiring the well kept graves with row on row of grave markers illuminated in a serene Hawaiian setting.

Banyan trees stood here and there like sentries guarding the multiple stations where mourners could pay homage to their sleeping warriors.

Lea stopped, standing motionless for a moment, then turned to Lani and CJ and asked if they would return to the car and bring the flowers she had left in the trunk.

Lea gestured to a spot a little ways ahead then stopped again. "This is where his body rests, and this is where it will be for eternity." She dropped down to one knee followed by Lani, CJ, Nani, and Smitty. She bowed her head and vocalized her tribute to John Tyler in Hawaiian words that neither CJ nor Smitty understood.

Lani, Nani, CJ, and Smitty rose to their feet and slowly walked back to the base of the memorial edifice to allow some private time for Lea to spend with her beloved husband, John.

She seems to be so fully in control of her life, Smitty thought.

With Lani and CJ leading the way, they began to ascend the rising staircase toward Lady Columbia.

"Let's climb to the top," Lani said.

"You guys go ahead. Smitty and I will wait here for Lea," Nani responded.

Nani and Smitty sat down on a nearby bench, where Smitty finally broke his solemn silence.

"By the way, what was it that Lea said at the grave site?" he asked Nani.

"I knew you would ask."

"How did you know?"

"Because of that inquisitive mind of yours, Smitty."

"Well, what did she say? Please don't tease me."

Nani laughed mischievously and Smitty smiled.

"Lea was speaking in our native language and she said, 'Just as you have always been here for us, we will always be here for you.'"

"Wow, how eloquent." Smitty exclaimed.

"Mom is like that. Give her time and you'll see."

Nani and Smitty looked up. Lea was about to rejoin them.

"It is a shame that we devote so much beautiful space to death isn't it, Smitty?"

"Yes it is," Smitty agreed, "and that reminds me of something I have wanted to tell you for some time now. I hope this isn't a bad time, but it is the first chance I have had."

Smitty began by telling Nani about overhearing the conversation in the back of the car on the way to the pineapple plantation, then he went on to tell them both about what happened that night at Camp Catlin.

"I was warned not to speak of the matter to anyone, so I have never told even my friend, CJ. It was an ominous night and I can't even begin to tell you how horrifying it was. When I learned how close you were to those boys I knew I would have to tell you about this sometime. I feel very badly for you and all your friends and family."

Lea listened intently then said, "This appears to have been as difficult for you as it has been for us, Smitty. We appreciate your caring and sharing these unsavory details with us—especially today."

Smitty felt a heavy burden drop from his soul, cushioned by Lea's very understanding heart.

Nani sat quietly while Lea spoke. "The police have been in constant contact with everyone at the school, and especially with me, wanting to know if the boys had ever said anything about prior visits to Camp Catlin. I have racked my brain but I haven't remembered anything that would be of help to them though I wish I could. Sometimes I wake up late at night and, in a foggy dream state, I reach out to put my finger on something elusive that I just can't seem to touch."

Smitty could definitely understand that sentiment.

Lea went on. "To appreciate these fine young men you would need to know them as I did and the best way to describe them would be to say that they were boys–just boys. I know how absurd that sounds, but they were typical of almost all the young men I have ever known—full of life and adventure and a great desire for exploring the unknown. And yet there was something more there. Paulo and Tedi were very generous with their time and their money—what little they had. In grade school they put together fund raisers to help build this place of honor at the Punch Bowl. They were always dedicated to the veterans of WWII. They came here with us to the opening dedication ceremony. They were so proud and they cried with me when my husband's name was read aloud."

Nani knew that the whole nightmare had agitated her mother since the boys were killed. She knew that Lea had changed and become more introspective. Nani also knew that nothing would be the same until this mystery was solved.

"Do you think the police will ever catch the person who killed those boys?" Smitty asked Lea.

"I'm not sure, Smitty. My neighbor, Captain Haikoa, is an investigator with the Honolulu Police and he told me that they have decided that the killer is probably a sociopath."

"Forgive me for asking, but what is a sociopath?" Smitty inquired.

"Simply stated, it is a person who has absolutely no feeling for others. They are filled with anger and are usually very good at disguising it. Captain Haikoa said the police are looking for someone who is bitter about life and blames everyone else for the way they feel inside," Lea said.

"In my thinking, that could be just about anybody," Smitty said.

"Yes," Lea agreed, "but the difference is that these people enjoy exhibiting power over people and killing them just to satisfy they're sadistic urges."

"It sounds like it might be very difficult to find this killer—unless, of course, they do it again."

"You're right, Smitty. Unfortunately, you are very right and I'm sure that Captain Haikoa would agree with you," Lea said.

When CJ and Lani returned, the four of them ascended the staircase toward the awesome Lady Columbia.

The day ended as calmly as it had begun and Smitty felt pleased that he had made a new friend whose values were much the same as his.

"We all hope to see you both next Sunday for Nani's graduation from high school," Lea said, as they pulled up to the gate at Pearl.

The first Sunday in June arrived and Nani's Graduation Day was welcomed by another glorious Hawaiian sunrise.

CJ and Smitty had agreed to meet the Tyler family at the high school. They were wearing their immaculately pressed khaki uniforms at Lea's request. The front of the high school looked like any other that you would see in the United States, except that the face of the building was almost entirely white. They didn't have to wait very long before Lea and her daughters showed up. Nani seemed nervous and Lani wore a proud smile for her big sister. More people began to arrive and soon the principle guests took their places in front of the building. As the students paraded one by one across the oval lawn in front of the school, the crowd exhibited their pleasure with intermittent applause.

"These are Hawaii's finest," the speaker was saying. Then the Valedictorian was introduced to the deafening crowd. Smitty went instantly into shock mode. It was Nani and she had never said a word to him about it. He listened intently but was so consumed by her presence that he hardly heard a word until she said that the senior class was dedicating this day to Paulo and Tedi. The audience seemed dumb struck for a few moments, then erupted into a resounding clamor as the graduating class raised placards with pictures of the two boys along with signs that read: 'We love you guys.'

CJ and Smitty felt lost in the throng as everyone was congratulating everyone else. Finally, Nani signaled to Smitty to come over to her. A large, handsome young man was hugging her tightly. Her feet were off the ground as he spun her around in circles. When he finally set her down Nani introduced him to Smitty.

"This is my boyfriend, Smitty," Nani said, "and this is, Kileona. It means strong fighter, but we just call him Kee."

Smitty held out his hand and Kee grabbed it, squeezing it very tightly.

"I'm impressed," Smitty said facetiously, not hesitating to count his numbed fingers.

The look Kee gave to Smitty was cool and anything but friendly.

"Kee is the captain of our football team and I think he plays linebacker, don't you Kee?" Nani asked.

Smitty was waiting for Kee to say "ugh," but all he got was a smug smile and a taunting stare. He had seen that look before and it usually spelled trouble.

After Kee removed himself from the scene, Nani told Smitty that Kee's last name was Ahue and he is the grandson of Mama Ahue. He is also Tedi Ahue's older brother.

"I didn't like the way he looked at you, Smitty. It's not really like him to be rude. Please promise me you won't get in a fight. Today is very special to me," Nani pleaded.

"I won't. I promise." Then he thought, who in hell would want to get in a fight with that bulldozer?

Nani excused herself to mingle with her friends for a while.

"Find Lea and I will catch up with you a little later," she said, giving Smitty a parting hug.

Smitty felt very alone now, in the unfamiliar setting. CJ and Lani were lost in the crowd and Lea was busy talking to some of her fellow teachers. Smitty wandered toward the school building and went inside. He got a drink from the water fountain then walked further down the hall. Eventually he found the door labeled 'MEN' and entered. Smitty stood in front of the huge mirror, reminiscing for a moment about the first time he met Nani. He turned to leave when three young men came boisterously through the door. Two of them stood blocking his exit, the other was Kee. They had a celebratory bottle with them from which they each took a drink. Smitty wasn't surprised that they didn't offer him any.

"You must be pretty tough, being a Marine and all, aren't you?" Kee taunted him.

"Not really...," Smitty replied. He wanted to tell Kee that he had met Mama Ahue and that they had become good friends, but Kee didn't give him a chance.

"I'll bet you played football back home, didn't you?" Kee said in a mocking tone.

"Yes, as a matter of fact I did...," Smitty acknowledged but was interrupted again.

"On the girls' team?" Kee chided him mockingly.

His friends all laughed.

Oh no, Smitty was thinking. I'm not going to be able to get out of this one.

Smitty watched as Kee menacingly advanced toward him. When Kee stepped forward on his left foot Smitty stepped into him and broadsided him with his best right hook. With a look of total surprise, Kee took two staggering steps backward and went straight to the floor. His eyes were glassy. He moaned a little and, though he tried, he couldn't get back up on his feet.

Expecting some form of retaliation, Smitty slowly walked toward the other two with a look of intimidation and asked, "Alright, which one of you tough guys is next?"

He got no response as they moved to the sides, away from the door, to let him pass.

Smitty calmly walked between them and out through the doorway.

It didn't take long for the word to spread among the student body—after all, no one had ever conquered their school hero before. Everyone who heard about the incident was in total shock. Nani, too, was in shock with tears rolling down her cheeks. Smitty knew he had disappointed Nani. He wanted to explain, but he felt that nothing he could say was going to change anything. He was right.

"You promised me," Nani said. "You promised that you wouldn't get in a fight."

"That wasn't really a fight," Smitty fumbled with the words.

"Then what was it?" she asked angrily.

"Well in the Marine Corps we like to refer to it as evasive action," he said, knowing that she wouldn't understand. He tried to embrace her, but she would have none of it.

"Leave," she said, "please—just leave."

With his heart aching, Smitty backed away and CJ started to follow. "Stay here CJ, they will need you—especially Lani. Please stay and I'll see you back at the barracks. I'm sorry I screwed things up. I'll explain to you later."

Smitty found his way back to Honolulu and walked down Hotel Street, directly to the YMCA. He was hoping to meet someone there that he knew—someone he could trust or maybe just someone who might understand his dilemma.

~CHAPTER~

TEN

Hotel Street in Honolulu was known as the most popular hangout for servicemen on the Island. Besides the GIs, con artists, pimps, thieves, homosexuals, prostitutes and winos, the infamous Hawaiian Armed Services Police, known as HASP, patrolled the streets during the after hours—seven nights a week. Trouble was available around every corner and, if you didn't find it, it would eventually find you. Hotel Street was not Smitty's favorite place but, under the circumstances, he thought, what the hell.

The YMCA at the far end of Hotel Street was different. It was more like a U.S.O. and to GIs it served as a veritable oasis in the middle of a decadent desert. They served free coffee and a lonely serviceman could find some relaxation and decent company there. Smitty surprisingly found both. There, seated on a sofa near the front entrance, was Walters—reading a book, of course. Walters seemed to be mesmerized by whatever he was reading. Smitty studied him for a while; Walters never looked up.

"Surprise," Smitty said.

"Well if it ain't the barracks nut case," Walters exclaimed. "No windows to crawl out of here," he added with a grin.

"You aren't going to let me forget that are you?" Smitty exclaimed.

"I'm just kidding, Smitty. Thanks to you I discovered a new way to escape the insanity," he confessed. "I've been going up there to find solace at times myself."

He and Walters sat there for a while, just talking, and Smitty discovered a slightly more amiable personality than what he had previously known. Smitty attributed Walters' more trusting demeanor to the fact that they were in a more relaxed, one on one setting, away from the earshot of all the other Marines. Smitty wanted to share his pain with Walters but, after the 'Dear John' incident at the barracks, he wasn't sure that he should. It would require far too much explaining.

"Wanna' go get a beer somewhere?" Smitty asked.

"I'll pass," Walters said, smiling, then went back to his reading.

It was getting late, so Smitty headed back again along Hotel Street to the Kahuna Bar. The smell of stale cigarettes, the dingy lights, and the odor of rancid beer made Smitty's eyes and nose burn. He turned to walk back outside but there on a stool near the door sat Corporal William Hoyt, already half in the bag.

"The action has arrived," Billy grunted. "Let's get drunk."

Smitty joined him.

"You're way ahead of me, but I'll try to catch up if you'll slow down," Smitty said as he ordered a shot and a beer.

"Pain killer," Smitty announced for all in the bar who would listen, but no one seemed to care. Everyone there seemed to have their own personal pain. Looking around, Smitty saw the dregs of humanity—people who had definitely seen better times. One derelict, sitting at the far end of the bar waved and beckoned Smitty to come and sit next to him. Smitty ignored him.

"Put some money in the juke box," someone called out.

Smitty wasn't there to socialize or make new friends. He just wanted to mourn the loss of his newest best friend. After another shot and a beer, he shared his sad story with Billy.

"I don't blame you for punching him, Smitty, I would have done the same thing," Billy said.

Smitty chuckled inside at his bravado. Billy hadn't seen Kee. Smitty went on to inquire about the rest of the old buddies he had left behind at Camp Catlin—especially Thomas and Wilson. Billy was a little buzzed and he rambled on for a while about the police asking everyone on the base about any previous instances of trespassing in the old ordnance area. Billy told him that the police were always acting like they were onto something—like maybe some new evidence, but Billy didn't know exactly what.

Suddenly, they were interrupted by a voice coming from over Smitty's shoulder.

"My name is Gerald Needham and I served in the big one, WWII," the voice explained. "My friends all call me Jerry—oddly enough."

The crusty appearance of the man was a turn off. He was lean and gaunt and his grizzly face, that had rarely seen a razor, was old beyond its years. But, behind his forehead, there seemed to be a story that explained his apparent irrelevance. His smile and quick wit told Smitty that he was more than likely in his thirties. His eyes twinkled when he spoke.

Billy looked at Smitty incredulously.

"A friend of yours?" Billy asked sarcastically.

Mr. Needham just stood there at attention saluting Smitty.

"I take it you were in the Army?" Smitty replied as he returned his salute, noting that Jerry's arm pits didn't smell any better than his beer breath.

"That I was, young man, that I was. I served at Normandy and the Battle of the Bulge with good old George 'Blood and Guts' Patton," quickly adding an old cliché. "Yep, it was his guts alright, but it was our blood."

"Where are you from originally?" Smitty inquired, guessing from his appearance that he was not a native Hawaiian.

"New Jersey," Jerry shot back without hesitation.

"Could you buy an old soldier a beer?" Jerry implored.

Smitty had been around long enough to have expected that.

"Hey, bartender, do you serve any food here?" Smitty asked.

"Just burgers," was the stunted reply.

"You eat a hamburger and I'll buy you a beer to wash it down with, OK?"

"OK," Jerry answered as he bellied up to the bar.

The bartender placed a hamburger and a beer in front of Jerry. Smitty watched while he wolfed it down.

"Do you work, Jerry?" Smitty asked.

"Not if I can help it," Jerry answered without even cracking a smile. "I'm just homeless, and most of the time, I enjoy it. You see that scar on my shoulder? I got that at the Bulge and a Purple Heart too but I don't know where it is now. I think my sister has it back home."

Jerry pulled up his right pant leg and showed him a withered leg with several scars. "I got some other scars too, but they're inside my head where no one can see them. I got to see the internment camps where Hitler stored the Jews until he could murder them or work them to death. It was a God awful sight in those camps. Men and women herded into barns not fit for cattle and starved until their bones protruded from their flesh. I'll never forget it if I live to be a thousand. It made me wonder where justice was hiding and, to this day, I still haven't found it. If there ever was any justice in this cock-eyed world, it suffered a lonely death a long time ago."

Smitty was fascinated by Mr. Needham. He bought him another beer.

From the end of the bar, another voice was heard. He was a shorter man with a dark complexion who appeared to be quite physically fit, but was a little unsteady on his feet as he ambled his way toward the trio.

"I'm Kona, me and him is pals," the voice was saying as he pointed at Jerry.

Smitty took one look and realized that this was about to become a party—like it or not.

"Let's move to a table," Smitty suggested.

Kona, it turned out, was a local who didn't smell much better than Jerry. Billy reluctantly bought him a beer.

Smitty found Jerry to be very interesting and more articulate than he had originally thought.

"When I got discharged from the Army, I came back home. All my friends warned me not to get mixed up with my old girlfriend, Sally, again. They said she had been sleeping with every guy she met while I was gone. She didn't seem interested anymore anyway, so I started college on the G.I. Bill. During the first semester, my uncle died. He left me a big chunk of dough—and you know what?—Sally was back, quick as a fly on a pile of horse shit. She told me how much she loved me and how desperately she wanted to have my baby."

"Sounds vaguely familiar," Smitty said with a grin.

"Well, anyway, like a jerk, I married her and after a few months the marriage started to sour. One day, while she was out somewhere, the police came knocking at my door and asked me if I had a gun. I told them that I did, and I asked them what they needed it for. They told me that my wife had reported that I had threatened to kill her with it. I asked them if she was dead. They said no, so I assured them that I must not have threatened her or she would already be dead." They took me downtown and booked me overnight. I told the judge that I had never threatened her, but she had some slick shyster for a lawyer who must have been pals with the judge.

And the judge, well he was an old buzzard who should have retired years before. If that dowdy old reprobate was able to hear, he sure as hell wasn't hearing me, but he definitely listened to her and believed every lying word she said. He reminded me a lot of a bronze statue in a City Park just sitting there motionless staring into space. At one point, I would have sworn that I saw a pigeon land on him and crap all over his shoulder. Pretty soon I was divorced and Sally, her lawyer. and probably the judge wound up with most of my money.

Oh, I thought about fighting back, but I knew I didn't have a chance of winning. I always referred to it later as a daring daylight robbery conducted in a court of law. I took what little I had left and booked passage on a steamship headed as far away as I could get, and here I am."

"Wow, you sound pretty bitter about the law, Jerry."

"Law! What law, Smitty? There ain't no law, and there sure as hell ain't no justice either—only politics, corruption and scam artists. And I spent my young life fighting for them so they could get away with this kind of crap. I don't trust lawyers, judges, or cops and I stay as far away from them as I possibly can. I learned a long time ago that if you ain't got nothin no one can take nothin away from you."

"What do you live on Jerry?" Smitty asked.

"The government sends me disability compensation for my wounds once a month. It ain't a hell of a lot, but I get by."

Smitty found Jerry's story very absorbing but beer wise, it was becoming a very expensive evening and, by now, Billy and Smitty were feeling no pain themselves.

Across the room, an argument was getting out of control as a woman was heard calling the guy with her every rotten name Smitty's mother had warned him not to say. The man was now on his feet swaying from side to side as the woman rose to curse him again.

Suddenly the man smacked her across the face with an open hand and, without a moment of hesitation, Billy darted across the room. He grabbed the guy and struck him with a single blow to his face. He reached back to hit him again, but the man's knees buckled, and he slumped to the floor. The woman immediately took a swing at Billy, but missed. She dropped to the floor on her knees, kissed the guy's face and wiped the blood away from his mouth. She looked up at Billy and called him a war criminal.

"You military bastards are all alike," she screamed.

Smitty held Billy by the shoulders to keep the altercation from escalating any further.

"You behave yourself, Ruth, or I'm going to have to toss you out of here," the bartender said as he placed another beer in front of her.

"That should shut her up for a while. Sometimes you got to fight fire with fire," the bartender whispered to Smitty.

Smitty apologized to the bartender. "We didn't mean her any harm," he said.

"It's OK, Marine, she gets so drunk in here every night that by the next day she can't remember what happened the night before anyway," the bartender added.

"I'm so sorry Ruthie, baby," the man was slobbering as she helped him to his feet.

Billy and Smitty nodded to each other, then they said goodnight to all.

"Let's have one more drink just for old times," Kona said.

Smitty bought Jerry and Kona one more beer. Billy and Smitty downed another boilermaker, raising their glasses to 'old times' before they left.

Then, they struggled to get out the door through all of the friendly adulations.

"I tell you they're all alike," Billy mumbled as they were leaving. "I go to her rescue and she calls me—hell, I don't remember—what did she call me? Anyway, it makes no sense. A guy thinks he's doing something right and what does it get him?"

"Don't worry about it, Billy. You're a hero in my book."

"Am I really, Smitty?" Billy's face lit up, even on the darkened fringes of Hotel Street. "Gee that means a lot to me," he drunkenly added.

"What made you do it? That wasn't like you. You really surprised me."

"I don't know. I guess it reminded me of…." Billy halted.

Smitty suddenly nudged him, signaling that a jeep on other side of the street bore the words "Hawaiian Armed Services Police." They hesitated only long enough to notice that a burly Army Sergeant was beating another soldier mercilessly with a night stick.

"That guy's on the ground and he's still hitting him."

"Shut up Billy and keep moving. If he does that to one of his own, imagine what he'd do to a baby face Marine like you."

Back at the barracks, all that Smitty could be heard vaguely murmuring before he passed out, was something about regretting that he had let Nani down.

~CHAPTER~

ELEVEN

The warm water beat down on his throbbing head, cascading across his shoulders, slowly trailing along the contours of his body. He turned his face upward, toward the showerhead, allowing the pelting stream to batter his face and forehead. He stood there for a long time feeling some of the trapped agony escape through his pores.

"Not feeling too good this morning eh, Smitty?" It was CJ.

"You got that right partner. I feel like Mauna Loa is erupting inside my head."

"I went out looking for you last night, but I couldn't find you anywhere. Nani wanted to see you," CJ said.

"She did? Come on, you're jerkin my dog tags, aren't you, CJ?—did she really?"

"Scouts honor, Smitty."

"What did she want?" Smitty urged.

"She wanted to tell you that you're a jackass," CJ chuckled.

"I know that, but seriously what did she want?" Smitty asked, forgetting for a moment about his self inflicted anguish.

"How do I know? You'll have to ask her," CJ exclaimed.

In the mess hall, Smitty downed several cups of coffee, trying to quench his insatiable thirst and extinguish the fire that raged in his gut. He filled his tray several times, gulping down at least a dozen scrambled eggs with toast.

"Never gonna do that again. If I live through this I swear I'll never take another drink as long as I live," Smitty muttered.

"Sure, sure, how many times have you said that? As a matter of fact, how many times have I said that?" CJ cajoled.

"So tell me again, CJ, what does Nani want to talk to me about?"

"I told you, Smitty. She just wants to talk to you. She didn't tell me why. I suggest you call and ask her. I don't want to get in the middle of this."

Smitty nervously dialed Nani's number from the phone in the barracks lobby; it seemed to him like an eternity between rings.

"Hello."

"Nani?" Smitty responded anxiously, anticipating her voice.

"No, Smitty this is Lea. Nani and Lani are at the home of a friend who is helping them plan Nani's open house. Will you be coming?"

"I haven't exactly been invited. Do you think Nani will want me to come?"

"I'm sure she will, but you'll have to talk to her about that. A lot of things have changed since you last saw her."

"For the better?" He begged.

"Yes, for the better Smitty" Lea said reassuringly.

Smitty felt like he was twelve feet off the ground. He just stood there, hanging tightly to the phone while enjoying the altitude.

"Hello, hello—Smitty are you still there?"

"Oh, yes, Lea," he seemed startled, "I'm here. I was just thinking. I'm going on duty right now. Do you think I can call back later this afternoon—say about four?"

"I'll tell her, and I'm sure she'll be here waiting for your call."

Smitty snapped on his duty belt, slid a magazine into his 45 caliber pistol, and reported for duty at the brig.

A new prisoner had arrived the night before and Smitty had been assigned to him. Smitty read the report, it listed the prisoner as Petty Officer Third Class Erwin Blake, Medical Corpsman; duty assignment USS Midway; arrested by HASP in Honolulu; the arresting officer was listed as Sergeant First Class Lucian Urbino. At the bottom it described the offense as 'drunk and disorderly.'

"Drunk and disorderly—my, my, if we aren't careful, we'll have a regular crime wave going on right here in Honolulu," Smitty whispered under his breath.

The military ID card contained in the file showed a young man 5 foot 11 inches tall, weighing 180 pounds with a crew hair cut.

"Hey sailor, how you doin' in there?" Smitty shouted through the cell door.

The sailor sat up on the edge of his bunk. "Are you talking to me?"

"I don't see anyone else in there," Smitty said, smiling.

"Where the hell am I?"

"You're on a Caribbean Cruise sailing to Jamaica."

"No kiddin', am I really?"

"Hell yes. I'm the ship's steward, is there anything I can get for you?"

"I'd like a shower and two aspirin," the sailor muttered trying to steady himself as he rose to his feet. "And please stop rockin' this damn boat."

Smitty led him to the shower room and handed him a towel.

"I see you got some bruises on your back and shoulders. Did you get in a fight, sailor?"

"You might say that, but I got the worst of it. I ran into two guys from HASP and this Sergeant kept goading me, trying to get me to fight him. I wouldn't, so he started hitting me with his stick. I curled up into a ball on the ground. Some other guys from HASP came along and said they were headed to Schofield Barracks and would drop me off at Pearl along the way. I saw the name tag on the shirt of the guy who was wailing on me. It was Urbino. I'll never forget it. Have you ever heard of him?"

"Not by name, just by reputation. He's Sergeant First Class Urbino United States Army. They jokingly refer to him as the 'White God of Honolulu,' but he's really just a first class son-of-a-bitch. They also tell me that even his own soldiers hate his guts, but there isn't much anyone can do about it. Here take these aspirin, Blake, and remember you won't feel any worse later than you do right now."

"You know my name?"

"That's my job, sailor. Now, you get into this prison garb. I'll sign you out and hustle you over to the galley for some good ole Navy chow and strong coffee."

"My name is Erwin Blake, Petty Officer Third. My serial number is 1104644 and, under the articles of war, that's all I'm required to tell you," he said with a huge grin as he struggled to stand at attention.

Smitty laughed. "You're not a prisoner of war, Petty Officer, and I ain't Sergeant Urbino, so relax."

"Relax? Tell that to my throbbing head," Blake grunted.

"I know how you feel, sailor, I think I drank out of the same bottle that you did last night."

Blake wolfed down some eggs and toast, then he washed it all down with copious amounts of coffee.

"You'll feel better now. I know from experience," Smitty assured him.

"You're not such a bad guy, Jarhead," Blake said.

"Tell that to my girlfriend," Smitty responded. "Seriously though, what do your friends call you? Do you have a nickname?"

"Most of my friends just call me Doc—Doc Blake, but sometimes people call me Red because of my hair. I answer to both. What do they call you?"

"Just Smitty," he answered. "Where is home, Doc?"

"West Virginia but, actually, I was a transplant. My dad moved there to take a job as a pharmacist when I was a boy. He encouraged me to go into a medical field, so I went off to college and, after two years, I ran out of money and joined the Navy, but I still call West Virginia home."

When they got back to the brig, the Commander of the Guard presented Blake with the news that his ship had sailed during the early morning hours. "You are being reassigned for duty at the hospital here at Pearl Harbor, awaiting the return of the Midway from its Pacific cruise.

"Smitty," the Commander ordered, "you take the Petty Officer over to Captain Corwin at the base hospital, and be sure to get these release forms and reassignment papers signed, then bring them back to me. Good luck to you, sailor. Try stay out of trouble while you're here. We don't want to see you back in the brig again—do you understand?"

Smitty rendered a proper salute and took Blake back into the cell area to change into his Navy uniform.

At 1600 Smitty was dialing the phone again. Nani picked it up on the first ring.

"Is that you, honey?" Nani asked.

Honey? He thought. She called me honey. Lea was right—things had changed since Smitty last saw Nani.

"Yes it's me," Smitty said, "and I just want you to know that...."

"Please, Smitty you don't have to say a word. Kee told me everything that happened. He admits that it was entirely his fault. He wants to apologize to you. Kee really feels bad about what he did. Believe it or not, I think he likes you. When can I see you again?"

"Slow down, sweetheart, you sound like you're out of breath. You have no idea how much better I feel, just hearing your voice. I had a rough time last night and I want to see you soon, but I have duty again tomorrow. I can get liberty Wednesday night, but then I have duty again on Thursday morning."

"We could have dinner at my house, then I'll take you to a movie and drive you back to Pearl Harbor. Just one minute, Smitty, Lani is trying to tell me something. Yes, she says she wants you to ask CJ to come too. What time should we pick you guys up?"

"Four thirty at the main gate would be good. What's the name of the movie?" Smitty asked.

"It'll be a surprise, but I'm sure you'll like it. Trust me."

"I trust you and I love you, Nani"

"I love you too, Smitty—very, very much."

CJ came walking by, just as Smitty jumped into the air, clicking his heels together.

"I don't know what you were drinking last night but I gotta' get me some of it." CJ said.

The Tyler house was a single level home with four bedrooms, situated in a middle income neighborhood. The interior was decorated in somewhat of an oriental style that Smitty had never seen before. The rear portion of the house disclosed a huge family and recreation room surrounded by glass on three sides that faced a very spacious well kept back yard. Lea was in the kitchen, preparing something that smelled very tempting.

"Don't come in here. This room is full of surprises. Go into the family room. Kee just called and he'll be here very shortly with his girlfriend, Joi."

Smitty sat up a little straighter when he heard the doorbell ring. He knew it must be Kee and, although he felt no guilt, he did find some discomfort in knowing that there were some very awkward things that would need to be discussed.

Lea entered the room first, with her guests following close behind.

"This is Joi," Lea began. "She is like a daughter to me. Her family and ours have been very close. It is traditional. We live together, grow up together, and stay together. It's one of the benefits of living on such a small island."

Smitty rose to his feet and extended his hand to Joi who smiled sweetly at him.

"It is a pleasure to meet you, Smitty. I have heard very good things about you and, of course, you've already met my boyfriend, Kee."

Smitty appeared a little bewildered by her statement as he extended his hand to Kee. The hand shake was firm and friendly—not threatening. He looked straight into Kee's eyes and couldn't help but notice that his left jaw was a little bruised and swollen.

Everyone sat down as Lea spoke. "Kee has something he wants to say to you, Smitty."

The room went suddenly silent. Looking down at the floor, Kee cleared his throat and began to speak very slowly.

"I have already apologized to the Tyler family and now I want to apologize to you, Smitty. First of all, I must admit that I ruined a day that was expected to be filled with happiness for all of us. I don't plan to make any excuses for my behavior, but I will try to explain what happened as best I can. I grew up with these girls and I always saw myself as their protector, especially since they had no father to fill that role. I started drinking early that day and then more as the day went on. We had all waited a long time to celebrate our graduation and I kind of over did it. I guess I saw you as an intruder. I was jealous too, that someone might be taking my place. I didn't know you and I should have waited longer to see what you were really like. Since then, Nani has told me a lot about you. I realized afterward that you were probably a really good guy. Anyway, I hope you will forgive me."

"Of course I will," Smitty said, "and I'm really grateful that this family has had someone around to look after them. I also want to ask you to forgive me for hitting you so hard. You're a pretty big guy and I was hoping I could quickly end what might have become a very nasty situation."

"Oh, and another thing," Kee added, "I really feel bad about the 'girls' football team' remark. That was really stupid. Anyway, I guess I found out that I'm not really as tough as I thought I was."

"None of us are, so let's just put the whole thing behind us and get to know each other better," Smitty said.

The dinner was full of wonderful surprises. It was like a Luau without the music and dancing. Smitty and CJ were both overwhelmed by the amount of food served. Roast pork and chicken with pineapple and honey, sweet potatoes, steamed vegetables, sweet breads, and a delicious Hawaiian fruit punch.

The conversation was light-hearted and friendly, with CJ and Smitty asking a lot of questions about life in Hawaii and Kee asking about military life. Then it shifted to Nani's open house. Lea insisted that CJ and Smitty try to be there and told them that they could invite some of their friends.

"It will be better if you have some people here that you know since Lani, Nani, and I will be tied up with other guests much of the time," Lea explained. "And, look at the clock, you guys better get going if you want to get to your movie on time."

Smitty stared for a moment at the theatre marquee that read 'Sands of Iwo Jima.' The movie stars were John Wayne and John Agar. Smitty smiled at Nani.

"So, this is the surprise, a Marine Corps movie," he said.

"Yes, and Lea insists that we pay for you and CJ."

Two familiar faces were seen in the crowd outside the theater, although they were not together. Billy came over to say hello while CJ signaled to Walters to join them. Smitty introduced everyone to his Marine buddies and told them that they were both invited to Nani's open house. The three girls, CJ, and Kee excused themselves and told Smitty that they would meet them in the lobby.

"I was reading in the paper that they are going to shut Camp Catlin down very soon and the article mentioned that the police are going to conduct another search of the old ordnance area as soon as the Marines leave. I guess they feel that there might be some evidence out there that they may have overlooked," Walters said.

"Yeah, they've been hinting about that for a long time, but searching through that dump would be very dangerous, and the only thing they would ever find in there is evidence of neglect—and lots of that," Billy added.

"You walked that post yourself didn't you, Walters?" Smitty asked.

"Many times, and it was the most boring watch I ever stood—especially at night. It was too remote, too quiet, and too dark to read. It was four hours of murderous torture—please excuse my choice of words."

"Did you ever see anything out there?"

"Nothing but a lot of field mice," Walters answered. "I haven't had that watch again since the murders and I thank God I transferred to Pearl when you did, Smitty. If it was up to me I'd have that place exterminated with a blow torch."

"I gotta' catch up to my group," Smitty interjected. "I'll see you guys later and don't forget about Nani's open house. The food will be great. I guarantee it. Nani says she will pick us up at Pearl on Sunday."

In the lobby, Nani was juggling a big box of popcorn and two soft drinks. Smitty took them from her and they proceeded cautiously down the aisle to find seats. They had just gotten seated when the silver screen lit up and the previews of coming attractions came on. When the feature film began, the Marine Corps Hymn began to play. Smitty and CJ jumped to their feet and very soon several men in the audience including Billy and Walters stood at attention too.

"Marine Corps tradition," Smitty whispered to Nani. "I'll bet all of those civilians who stood up are former Marines."

The movie was a typical Hollywood World War II hoorah film. John Wayne played John M. Stryker, a highly disciplined Marine Sergeant, dedicated to the men under his command.

Nani squeezed Smitty's hand tightly and whispered, "I'm glad the war is over. I would worry a lot if I knew you were in danger of being killed."

"You need to remember that John Wayne is the hero and he always rides off into the sunset at the end of his movies," Smitty chuckled softly.

"And you are my hero, but I would worry if you ever went into harm's way like that," Nani sighed. "Now that I've found you, I could never let you go."

As the movie came to its conclusion and the Marines prepared to raise the flag on Mount Suribachi, Sergeant Stryker was killed by a Japanese sniper. Nani squeezed Smitty's hand more tightly than before while glancing at him in the dimly reflected light of the movie screen. He quietly avoided her glance and was careful to change the subject on the way out of the theatre.

"Nani, I never met anyone like you before. I was so proud of you at the graduation ceremony." He spoke quickly before she could. "The way you mesmerized that crowd reminded me of your mother. You captured your audience and made them love you. I knew then that you were the girl for me—forever. I will never leave you Nani, I promise."

At the main gate, Smitty kissed Nani, thanked her for the movie, and told her that he would see her at the open house.

"Do you think it would be OK with Lea if I invite Jimbo and Corporal Tyne too? They are both World War II vets, you know?"

"Sure," she nodded affirmatively and, with a wave of her hand, she drove away.

~CHAPTER~

TWELVE

It was Sunday morning, June 25th. The car with Kee behind the wheel had just picked up Smitty, CJ, Jimbo, and Corporal Tyne at Pearl Harbor and was cruising down the highway to Camp Catlin. Kee parked beside the main entrance and Smitty got out. An old friend of his, PFC Graham, was standing guard at the gate.

"Hey, Graham, how you doin'?"

"Smitty, you sentimental old jarhead, you're back. Don't tell me you're lonesome for this place already."

"No, Graham, I definitely won't tell you that," Smitty answered, with a chuckle. "Actually I'm just here to pick up Billy Hoyt. Have you seen him?"

"Not recently, but most of the guys are down at the far end of the camp watching some work crews get set up to tear down one of the old munitions buildings in the restricted area. The cops are down there too. We figure they're looking for some evidence or something—you know, about those kids who were murdered back there. Starting tomorrow morning they're going to tear down Building #1, where it all happened. It's in all the newspapers, so it's been quite a circus around here lately."

"Is it OK if we drive down and see if we can find Hoyt?"

"Sure, but you can't get down the road next to the fence. You'll have to park near the communications building and walk over from there."

"That's fine. If Billy shows up, hold him here and tell him we'll be right back. OK?"

CJ joined Smitty as they walked a path that was all too familiar to Smitty.

"What a pile of crap," CJ exclaimed as Smitty pointed out the six

72

buildings that he had once guarded so religiously. "It's no wonder you were glad to get reassigned to Pearl Harbor."

Up ahead of them, Smitty spotted Wilson and Thomas staring through the holes in the chain link fence. They appeared to be arguing about something.

"Hey guys what's the beef?" Smitty asked.

"It's Wilson," Thomas smiled back at Smitty. "He's already mourning the loss of his home away from home. He doesn't think they ought to tear it down. He claims this is a historic landsite and that it needs to be preserved for posterity."

"That's crap, Thomas. It's you that's worried. He thinks they're gonna' find his Hula skirt hidden in there. The one he practices with at night while he's on watch. He's afraid that it would reveal his true identity," Wilson shot back.

As Smitty and CJ walked away they could hear Wilson saying, "What about your yarn and your knitting needles, Thomas? They might find them in there too."

"It's good to see those guys chipping away at each other, for a change," Smitty told CJ.

As they walked along the fence, Smitty briefly reminisced, replaying the fateful night that haunted his dreams and left him with remnants of guilt. He still harbored the feeling that he should have been able to see or hear something—just anything that would have allowed him to prevent those murders.

Looking ahead, he saw Billy standing alone by the fence with a somber look on his face. His fingers were wrapped tightly around the open links in the fence as his face was pressed against it. His eyes seemed to be focused on the void between himself and the buildings on the other side. Smitty had not spoken to Billy about the murders in a long time, believing that he must be feeling the same way he did. And now, with all this ruckus Smitty hoped that maybe there would be some answers to the mystery that shrouded his already tainted memories of old Camp Catlin.

"A penny for your thoughts," Smitty said, sneaking up behind Billy.

"Oh my God, you scared the hell... out of me... I thought....", Billy responded breathlessly.

"Yeah, I know what you must have been thinking Billy, I feel the same way. Are you ready to go? Everybody's back in the car waiting for us."

"Yeah, yeah..., I, I'm ... ready." Billy stammered.

When they got back to the car, Billy's eyes searched its interior, "Where is Walters?" he asked.

"He was back at the base reading the newspaper when I left. He apologized, saying he had other plans. I told him he was going to miss a good time, but he said maybe later. I gave him Nani's phone number and address. Hopefully he'll show up or call us at Nani's house to get a ride. You know Walters."

"Where do we go from here?" Kee asked, starting the car again.

"One more quick stop in Waikiki, if you guys don't mind. I need to buy some flowers for Nani," Smitty answered.

The sign on the front of the house read: 'CONGRATULATIONS NANI TYLER' in big, bold letters. People were already starting to arrive, so Smitty introduced his buddies to Lea and went to find Nani.

"These are for you, Nani, with all my love on your very special day."

Nani beamed with delight as she very carefully opened the box, which was held together by a large gold ribbon with a bow. Then, an even bigger smile spread across her face. Inside were a dozen red, long stemmed, American Beauty roses. In the middle, was a single yellow rose.

"Nani, please accept these roses as a symbol of my love for you—not just for today but for every month throughout the year. The yellow rose symbolizes our special friendship—a friendship that will last forever."

The words were awkward for him to say. He had said words like these before, but this was the first time he really meant them. Even in the movies, he didn't go very much for romantic slobber, but these words and his feelings were very genuine and sincere. He had practiced this moment for a long time and wanted to get it just right.

The next few moments found them alone in a room full of people. They embraced and kissed, then kissed again until the applause startled them back to reality.

"I will always love you, Smitty, and I will always be your friend," Nani said.

Nani had rehearsed that moment as well, except in her version the moment lingered much longer. Her obligation to her guests dictated that the rest of that moment would have to wait until a later time.

Smitty spotted Mama Ahue standing off to the side of the room, in a brightly colored muumuu, wearing her usual cheerful smile. He excused himself and walked over to greet her.

"I see Nani is wearing her pearl necklace today," Mama Ahue said, beaming with delight.

"She loves it very much, Mama Ahue, thank you," he added.

"She loves you too, Smitty," Mama said with a twinkle in her bright, brown eyes. "And I have something for you too. It will protect you in times of danger, and I feel you will be in need of that protection very soon. Trust me, Mama Ahue knows these things. Since the death of my grandson I have been given a very special gift. Sometimes I know things—things about danger, for sure. Don't ask me how I know. Mama just knows."

"Are you saying that this is something that will ward off evil spirits, Mama Ahue?" Smitty asked as he carefully opened the small box she handed him.

"You might say that, but you must promise me that you will wear it at all times so that God's Grace and Mama Ahue will be with you wherever you go."

Inside the box was a silver cross that glistened brightly as it dangled from its sturdy chain.

"You are too good to me, Mama," Smitty said softly as he gratefully gave her a hug.

"I know," she said with a devilish grin as they strolled off to find Nani.

"How beautiful," Nani exclaimed, "that cross looks very masculine on you, Smitty. Thank you, Mama Ahue. You are very special," Nani added.

The guests began to swarm in on Nani, so Smitty wandered off to rejoin his friends. He kept fondling the cross between his fingers, still wondering what Mama could have meant by her remarks about danger and needing protection soon. He found Tyne and Jimbo engrossed in conversation with Kee, who prodded them about the Marine Corps and their experiences during World War II. In the back yard, Billy was laughing and joking as he shared his disdain for Camp Catlin with anyone who would listen. Everyone seemed to be enjoying themselves while drinking Lea's delicious, but punchless, punch.

Smitty's eyes wandered over to the bookcase in the front room. There, he saw a picture of Nani and Lani in their younger years. Lea walked over and remarked, "Weren't they cute when they were young, Smitty?"

Smitty smiled affirmatively and then, picking up a book from the shelf, he asked Lea if that was one of their children's books.

"No that's mine. As you can see it's called Animal Farm," Lea answered with a smile. "Actually, it's one of the finest books I've ever read. It has a lot of insights into power and politics. You should read it sometime."

Smitty wanted to ask her what animals and farms had to do with politics, but thought better of it.

The party wound down by evening, phasing into a group discussion out on the patio. Jimbo and Tyne excused themselves, saying that they had to return to Pearl. Both of them would be going on watch at four in the morning. The few guests who still remained all listened intently as Mama Ahue spoke of her grandson, Tedi, and his friend Paulo.

"They will always be greatly missed, especially at celebratory times like this, when everyone is gathered together," Mama spoke in gentle tones. "Those boys were like Siamese twins. They spent a lot of time at my house working and playing. Adventure was their passion; they were always looking for new ways to perform feats of daring. They were truly good boys with no malice in them—just an eager desire to help whenever and whoever they could. I have missed them a lot, as has their entire family and all of their close friends. Whoever killed them will not escape justice. Mama Ahue knows these things."

Kee spoke up, adding, "Those boys always talked about joining the Marines someday. I never knew exactly why, but now I guess it was their spirit of adventure and the feeling that someone needed to protect the good people from the bad ones. I also know that they loved to hear stories about war. I am certain that they would have loved to have met Jimbo and Corporal Tyne."

Time slipped away quite rapidly, surrounded by gaiety and laughter with interspersed reflections on the trials and tribulations of growing up—mostly aimed facetiously at Nani and Lani.

Smitty glanced at the clock. It was getting late and Walters was still not heard from.

"We better get going back to the base soon. CJ and I have to go on watch early tomorrow morning, and I know you must be very tired. It has been a long day for you, Nani," Smitty remarked.

The guys all helped by putting away tables and chairs, while the ladies put away the food and cleaned up the kitchen. Kee and Joi volunteered to drive the Marines back to their home base.

By the time they left the house, it was just a few minutes before midnight. Kee drove and Billy rode up front next to Joi, since he would be getting out at Camp Catlin. Nani's open house had been a fabulous success and everyone in the car joined in by praising the food and good company.

Billy, from his vantage point, was the first to spot it. He nervously pointed out the front window to a glow of light in the night sky that seemed to be directly in line with Camp Catlin.

"It's probably just a reflection from the lights at Tripler Hospital," Joi said. But, as they got closer, the light got brighter and larger. Ahead of them on the road, they saw flashing red lights.

"I think it's more likely police and work crews at the restricted area preparing for the demolition at Camp Catlin tomorrow morning, but I don't know why they would be working this late on a Sunday, do you Billy?" CJ asked.

The traffic ahead, what little there was at that late hour, was slowing down and police were guiding cars over to the left lane. Suddenly, a police car went speeding past them on their right. As they approached the side road, leading to the main gate at Camp Catlin traffic stopped momentarily.

"It looks like a fire," Billy stammered. "I'm going to jump out here, see you guys later."

By now, the light in the sky was beginning to glow a crimson red and was reflecting more radiantly off the face of the hospital far above. The car inched along slowly for a moment. After they passed the entrance, Kee sped up at the urging of the traffic control officers ahead. To their left, more emergency vehicles were approaching at high speeds as the air began to reverberate with the wail of sirens. By the time they got to the main gate at Pearl Harbor, emergency vehicles and fire trucks were coming straight toward them, then dashing out through the main gate, heading back toward Camp Catlin.

"I haven't seen so much excitement on this island since I was a kid and the Japanese were bombing this place," Kee said.

CJ and Smitty opened the car door. "We'll get out of the car here. Good luck getting back," Smitty said to Kee.

After running all the way from the main gate to the Marine Barracks, Smitty and CJ went directly up onto the roof of the brig to get a better view. What they saw from there made it appear like all of Oahu was ablaze. Burning embers were shooting up into the air and floating off in every direction. It was an awesome sight. Looking over the side of the building, they saw four military transport trucks pull up in front of the barracks. Sgt. Allen was shouting that all Marine personnel, not on duty, should get into their dungarees and boondockers and report to the trucks immediately.

Not a word was spoken in the back of the truck. Outside the vehicle, Smitty could hear the Fire Chief telling the driver to take them over to the far side of the fence that separated the old ordnance area from the vacated field that led up the hillside to the hospital. As they hastily emerged from the rear of the truck, they were ordered to man the hoses that were connected to the fire departments transportable water tankers. The firemen wasted no time before informing the young Marines of the urgency of keeping the fire contained inside the camp enclosure.

On the other side of the camp, personnel from Camp Catlin were fighting desperately to keep the fire from spilling over the fence into the main camp. With the fire surrounded, the fire fighters hoped to be able to keep it contained allowing the core to eventually burn itself out.

The heat was intolerable and Smitty soon realized that there was no way to advance the hoses any closer to the blaze. The only hope they had was to lay back and keep the water flowing to prevent the fire from advancing any closer. The Marines on the front end of the hose were required to drop back occasionally, allowing the men behind them to rotate to the front while they went to the rear of the line to get a little respite from the searing heat and suffocating smoke.

Smitty began to fear that there wasn't enough water on the entire Island to quench this raging inferno, as more tankers kept rolling in from other fire departments on the island. Smitty rotated back to the head of the hose again. Precious minutes seemed more like hours to the exhausted firemen and Marines.

Soon, more help arrived in the form of soldiers from Schofield Barracks and airmen from Hickam Field. They took over the hoses as the Marines dropped further back to rest and drink water to keep from dehydrating—but not for long. More men were needed to sweep around to the back of the camp, where the fire seemed to be gaining ground. Smitty and CJ joined those ranks.

Trained Navy firefighters from some of the ships at Pearl Harbor had been on the scene for an hour but were steadily losing ground to the cannibalizing flames. The Marines stepped in to relieve them and soon discovered that the fire was still very much in control. More men were brought in, along with more equipment. They were followed by bull dozers used to dig trenches between the firefighters and the back fence in the hope that they could halt the advancing firestorm. The battle plan was succeeding, but not before some of the firefighters collapsed from the extreme heat.

Because the wooden structures were so tinder-dry, it was a fast burn, lasting only five hours. With nowhere else to go, the fire finally fell back upon itself and lay there, smoldering. Sporadic bursts of flames were still erupting here and there, but they were quickly doused by the new crew that arrived that morning. Nothing was left inside the compound that remotely resembled what it had been before. By early morning, it appeared that a small volcano had erupted then become dormant again leaving behind only cinder and ash. The important thing was that, because of the courageous actions of the local fire departments and the military, the main camp and Tripler Hospital miraculously survived.

Men lay on the ground on the periphery of what was once a storage place for an arsenal of war. Some were transported to nearby hospitals.

Smitty slowly opened his eyes. "Where the hell am I?" he asked.

"You're on a Caribbean Cruise sailing to Jamaica," the reply came.

"No, am I really?" Smitty answered, without thinking.

"Hell yes. I'm the steward, is there anything I can get for you?"

"Oh my God, Blake—Doc Blake—what am I doing here?" Smitty said, as he tried to raise himself to an upright position on the table.

"Lay back, Jarhead, you're going to be fine. You just ate a little too much smoke before you passed out. Your buddy CJ saw to it that they brought you here. I'm going to put this oxygen mask back on for a while longer and I'll put some ointment on your face. You look like you were out in the sun too long.

Oh yes, and you mumbled something earlier about having to go on duty at the brig this morning. I can get you out of that if you'd like."

Smitty shook his head from left to right, signifying 'no' to the generous offer.

~CHAPTER~

THIRTEEN

At 0800, Smitty reported for duty at the brig. He had just been on the phone with Nani. He knew she would be worried about him. Smitty assured her that, although he had been treated for smoke inhalation, he was feeling fine and was ready to report for duty.

The morning newspaper was lying on the desk next to Walters. The front page report jumped out at Smitty, displaying numerous reports and pictures of the blaze. The rest of the newspaper was equally as dedicated to stories about the fire from various angles, depending on the perspective of the reporter.

The story that caught Smitty's eye was the one with the caption, "Police Suspect Arson." The article read, "Fire Inspectors were immediately dispatched to the scene and concluded that, because of the fire pattern and rapidity of its spread, the fire appeared to be very suspicious. Spokesmen from the fire department further indicated that if there had been any wind at all—even a slight breeze—the fire would have spread and caused a major disaster on the Island. Spectators applauded the fire fighters who were able to confine the burn to the empty warehouses at Camp Catlin. Many Islanders seemed pleased that an eye sore had finally been removed from an otherwise beautiful area of Oahu. Three firemen were killed fighting the blaze. One of them died from a heart attack, while several military members were taken to the hospital for smoke inhalation and heat exhaustion."

"If you're done with the paper, I'd like to read that article on the back page," Walters told Smitty.

Smitty handed him the paper and went back with CJ to check on the prisoners. When they returned, Walters was mumbling something to himself that didn't seem to make much sense.

"What's up?" Smitty asked Walters.

"This article says that the North Korean Army crossed the 38th parallel into South Korea yesterday."

"Is that a big deal?" CJ asked.

"It could be very big before it's over. Anytime the Soviets are involved, it's big," Walters answered.

"What is Korea and where is it? I've never heard of it," Smitty said, looking over at CJ.

"Korea is a peninsula. Being from Michigan, you know what a peninsula is. This one juts out into the Pacific Ocean right near Japan," Walters explained.

"What's so important about that?" CJ asked.

"Are you sure you want to know, CJ?"

"Sure, I'm sure. I never heard of the place."

"Korea has a population of about 30 million people and, actually, about 10,000 persons of Korean descent live right here in Hawaii, so someone you have seen here might actually be a Korean. Do you want to know more?"

"Yeah, sure, tell us more," Smitty said.

"For twenty five years Korea was a colony of Japan, which never endeared the Korean people to the Japanese. During World War II, the Japanese invaded Korea again and used the southern most part as strongholds for American prisoners of war. At the end of the war in 1945, Korea was repatriated, and then divided into two occupation zones; the Russian zone was to the north and the American zone to the south. The dividing point became a very arbitrary line at the 38th parallel. It was supposed to remain that way for five years and, after that, both the Soviets and the Americans were supposed to leave the Koreans to govern themselves.

That five year period ends this year, but it looks like the Russians don't intend to keep their bargain. They want it all and they don't think the U.S. will do anything to stop them. The Soviets have been heavily arming the North and organizing them militarily. The head of North Korea, Kim Il Sung, is said to be a megalomaniac whose regime is controlled from the North Korean Capital of Pyongyang. That's the short version; would you like to hear the long one?" Walters jokingly asked.

"No, not really, but what's all the fuss over a little place like that?" CJ asked Walters.

"That's a good question," Walters replied.

"Is it a question of justice?" asked Smitty.

"Another good question," Walters smiled.

"You know, when I was in school I wondered a lot about where all those idiot dictators came from and why they always rose to the top. We got rid of Uncle Adolph and Benito Mussolini and even Tojo. Now we got Joe Stalin and this guy in North Korea. What did you say his name was?" Smitty asked.

"Kim Il Sung," Walters responded.

"Well, what happens now, does the U.S. go to war over all this or what?" CJ asked.

"That all depends on the United States and the United Nations. We can only wait and see."

"It doesn't seem all that important if it's on the back page of the newspaper," Smitty concluded.

"I'm sure that it got relegated to the back page because of the fire here last night. Otherwise, it would be front page news, and I'll bet it is back in the States. Wait until tomorrow, and I'll bet it will be big news here when more facts come out."

"What a guy. In all the time I've known him he hasn't said more than ten words a day and now he suddenly sounds like a college professor," Smitty said, after Walters went back to check on the prisoners.

"Do you think he knows what he's talking about, Smitty?"

"Well, if he doesn't, he's a damn good actor, but it was good to finally hear something from him after all this time."

Sure enough, Walters was right. The next day's paper carried the news of the invasion by the North into South Korea—and it filled the front page. A story about the arson investigation was relegated to page three. The headline about Korea was big and bold.

NORTH KOREA ROLLS INTO SOUTH KOREA

In a daring Sunday morning attack, well-trained and well-equipped North Korean troops, shielded by Russian made tanks, rolled across the 38th parallel toward Seoul, the capital city of South Korea. The northern forces have been slaughtering innocent civilians, as well as members of the armies of the south, as they progress nearer and nearer to the capital. Just seven days ago, the U.S. Ambassador to the United Nations, John Foster Dulles, told a very anxious audience at the South Korean National Assembly: "You are not alone, you will never be alone." American President, Harry Truman, has taken immediate action by sending American troops on occupation duty in Japan to Korea to stall the attacking forces, while more troops are being called in from other regions in the Pacific area. The South Korean Army known as ROK's which stands for Republic of Korea has been crumbling and falling back steadily under the pressure of the larger and better equipped Communist forces. Experts are predicting that, if they are not stopped soon, the South Korean Capital will in the hands of the enemy within days. It appears that the attack was planned well in advance and that the Communists intentions are to seize the entire Peninsula.

"It sounds pretty serious," Smitty said.

"Yeah, but once we get some American troops over there things will change," CJ answered confidently.

By the end of the week, life on the Island of Oahu had changed dramatically. The Asian populace was in a dither over Korea, the Fire Department was in a full scale investigation of a suspected arson, the Police Department was combing the ashes of Camp Catlin looking for any evidence they could find regarding the killings, the military was preparing to send soldiers and Marines to Japan to fortify troops in Korea, and the Marines had decided not to close Camp Catlin after all.

Orders had come from on high that the existence of the camp would be necessary in order to temporarily house more troops being sent in from the states. Some of the Marines who were going to Korea were from Pearl Harbor and others from Camp Catlin. The shortages that were created by their departure meant that many Marines would be performing longer and more frequent watches.

CJ, Smitty, and Walters decided to pay a visit to Camp Catlin to see what was going on over there and, being naturally inquisitive, they were anxious to see what the place looked like since the fire.

"Wow," Walters exclaimed, looking at the vacant skyline. "I never realized that..." Walters was again at a loss for words.

"Yeah," was all Smitty could say.

Smitty stood there, almost hypnotized, staring at a place where a bad dream had once stood; a place that was now a vast wasteland. And he knew in his mind that, with all that had happened here, this place would forever remain a place of bad memories.

For him, it was a mystery that, consciously or subconsciously, would need to be resolved and, now that that ominous building was gone, the mystery had deepened, making it even more difficult to understand.

Teams of police dressed in special clothing roamed through areas that were marked off in six distinct grids, defining the places where the warehouses once stood. Some carried rakes and others appeared to sweep special rigs, with magnets attached, across the surface of the ground. The task seemed dauntless, especially since there was so little left after the fire.

Standing in the middle of the devastation, somewhere near where Building #3 had once been, was a steel skeleton of what appeared to have been a very old farm tractor—no paint, no tires, no leather seat, not even any sign of rust—nothing but a steel skeleton. The entire area was a ghostly sight that spoke volumes about how completely thorough the fire had been in eliminating all traces of an undesirable historic landmark.

Investigators remained busy, gathering every item that had endured the flames and the extreme heat generated by the fire. They placed charred rubble into canvas bags that were slung over their shoulders.

"That's one hell of a lot of wasted effort if you ask me," Walters said. "How do they expect to find anything of value in that mess?"

"Yeah, if any evidence of the murders was ever there it surely ain't there now," CJ concurred.

The young Marines decided to eat lunch at the mess hall at Camp Catlin before returning to Pearl Harbor.

The chatter at the mess hall was all about the bewildering new conflict in Korea. The fire at Camp Catlin had been totally eclipsed by the possibility of Marines going into battle once again. Those who hadn't read a newspaper since they left home were now devouring every nuance of the growing menace in a land they knew very little about. To them, it had nothing to do with Korea itself but everything to do with the defiance of the Soviet Union against the free world. Words like "bullies" and "tyrants" were being bantered about in the lower courts of Marine Corps justice.

"I'm going to volunteer to go over there and kick some ass," Thomas said. "That's why I joined this man's Marine Corps in the first place."

"Be sure to take Wilson with you," Smitty told him. "Maybe you guys could scare the crap out of the North Koreans with your ghost stories."

Billy was too busy laughing to even comment, but he did manage to squeeze off a quick, "Gotcha' Thomas."

The other Marines laughed too, but most of them concurred that if they were asked to volunteer they were ready and willing to go. Just then, Captain Colson entered the mess hall and apologized for interrupting their lunch.

"I have an important request to make of you men. There are a number of ships arriving at Pearl Harbor from California as I speak. The men on those ships, sailors and Marines, are on their way to Japan and will be sent into Pusan, South Korea to help stabilize conditions there. They will be allowing the men on those ships to go on liberty this weekend before they set sail again on Sunday morning. All of you know what that could mean. We are being asked to provide four of our off duty men for MP duty Friday night in Honolulu, and Marines from Pearl will provide four personnel for Saturday night. I will expect to get volunteers before you guys leave the mess hall or I will have to select the men myself. I know I can count on you to make this job easy for me."

The day after he got back, Smitty found a letter from home lying on his bunk. It was postmarked "Air Mail, Special Delivery" and it was from his grandparents.

Dear Jay,

With this news about the possibility of war in Korea, we are all very worried about you. When you joined the Marines I didn't worry because the war was over—or so we thought. Now, out of the blue, comes more unrest in the world. I know we must do something about it but it seems so unfair. Mothers here are concerned that they might reinstate the draft. I'm sure that this thing will be ended soon, but we have suffered enough in this country because of selfish dictatorships in other parts of the world. I hope you have made some nice friends over there, but please don't do anything foolish. Remember that you plan to go to college when you get back. Your grandfather wants me to tell you to be safe and, if you do go to war, keep your head down.

Love, Ma and Pa

Smitty checked the bulletin board and, sure enough, he, CJ, Jimbo, and Walters were scheduled for shore patrol duty in Honolulu from 2000 Saturday night until 0600 Sunday morning. Smitty sat down and wrote a letter home, assuring his grandparents that he would be very cautious but that he might have to go to Korea.

That night Smitty made another visit to his sanctuary on the roof.

~CHAPTER~

FOURTEEN

The early morning edition of the Honolulu newspaper dated June, 1950, carried an update to the rapidly escalating conditions in South Korea.

UNITED NATIONS INTERVENE IN KOREA

Korea, known as the Land of the Morning Calm, has gone from cold war status to being the focal point of a very hot war. As 150 Soviet-made T-34 tanks rumbled through the South Korean Capital of Seoul an emergency session of the U.N. Security Council was demanding the cessation of hostilities ordering the North Korean withdrawal of troops back to the 38ᵗʰ parallel. Members of the council have called this an act of war against the United Nations and warned that they will take action by sending troops from member nations. This warning has yet to be heeded. The NKPA (North Korean People's Army) is now plunging further south into weakly defended South Korean territory. Reports of casualties are very high and murders and atrocities to soldiers and innocent civilians have been witnessed in violation of the Geneva Convention. General Douglas MacArthur has assumed full command of all U.N. forces. President Harry Truman, wanting to avoid the use of the term war, has dubbed this the "Korean Conflict."

"Hey guys, looks like this war's gettin' really serious," Smitty commented.

Walters asked Smitty to hand him the newspaper. He noticed a small article at the bottom of the back page that attracted his attention. The article appeared to be treated very insignificantly by virtue of its length and inconspicuous location.

It was the headline that first captured Walters's attention.

BODY FOUND ON BEACH

During the early morning hours, the dead body of a homeless street person known only as Kona was found lying nude on the beach near the lighthouse at Waikiki. He appeared to have been disemboweled and stabbed repeatedly. Further investigation determined that he had consumed a large amount of liquor before his death. Floating at the water's edge near the victim's body was an empty Scotch bottle. Further back from the beach Kona's unwashed clothing was heaped in a pile. They smelled of smoke and gasoline. Police will not disclose any additional information at this time.

Walters handed the paper back to Smitty and suggested he read the article.

CJ, Smitty, Walters, and Jimbo were dressed in their pressed khaki uniforms with shoes that shined back up at them like mirrors. They wore their flat topped barracks caps mounted so the brim was almost covering their eyes. Around their ankles they wore white leggings with the bottoms of their trousers bloused over the top. On their left sleeve they donned a white armband with MP emboldened in black letters to confirm their authority. As if that wasn't enough, they each carried a .45 caliber pistol and an equally menacing night stick in a holster that was attached to their white webbed duty belt.

Hotel Street in Honolulu had become an element of dark history during World War II. It had become a place where GI's and sailors would stand in lines for hours to relieve their hormonal frustrations. Young men who had been away from home for long periods of time, especially during their teens and early twenties were drawn to this atmosphere of virtually uncontested freedom. It was certainly a staging area that invited all kinds of antisocial behavior. If you asked any of the locals, they would tell you that Hotel Street in Chinatown was a haven for hedonism that solved a few problems while creating many more. It would be the daunting task of these young Marines to control and referee these events—at least for this one night.

The sights, sounds and smells of the street even in the early hours of the evening defied imagination. Hotel Street consisted of two narrow traffic lanes but, to the eye, it gave the appearance of being much narrower than it really was. The two story wood-framed structures had been built very close to the road. The buildings were attached to each other by common walls, giving the entire length of the street a cavernous appearance. Most of the store fronts came replete with hustlers who made a living by urging passersby to come in and sample their wares, whether they were drugs, sex, booze, or tattoos—all reasonably priced—of course. The smells that emanated from within the shops and bars almost required that you condition yourself with a couple of shots of Jack Daniels before entering. All four of the Marines had been on that street before but not for the same reasons they were here on this evening.

They wisely decided to split into pairs and patrol opposite sides of the street, being careful to remain within sight and earshot of each other.

"I don't know about you, Walters, but 'people-watching' has always been one of my favorite pastimes," Smitty commented.

"Then you should really have an enjoyable evening," Walters shot back, in somewhat of a mocking tone.

"This really isn't your thing is it, Walters?"

"No, not really."

It was still early, but they were already seeing little glimpses of things to come. The streets were gradually becoming congested by masses of humanity, unloading from liberty busses and taxi cabs, as they converged on the hottest spots in Honolulu. Smitty nudged Walters and pointed out two local gentlemen holding hands as they sashayed down the street through the midst of the white and khaki uniforms that had begun to dominate the scene.

The later it got, the worse it got. Up ahead of them, they watched a drunken sailor struggling with the thirteen buttons on the front of his trousers. As his right hand searched inside the unbuttoned flap, he tried to steady himself with his left hand by holding tightly to a lamp post. Then, as he rocked back and forth like he was still aboard ship, he accomplished his mission, but not without peeing all over his shoes. His shipmates beckoned to him to hurry, as they looked back impatiently, watching him struggle to refasten the same thirteen buttons.

"Makes you wish you'd joined the Navy doesn't it, Smitty?" Walters snickered.

It was still early and fairly quiet on the street, so Jimbo and CJ crossed over and joined them, suggesting they go to the YMCA to get a cup of coffee before the action got started.

"I'm all for that," Walters said.

The YMCA was one of Walter's favorite places when he was on liberty. No one knew what his other favorite places were.

The "Y" was at the far end of the street, in a more subdued and less populated part of Hotel Street and Walters appreciated the opportunity to visit a quiet place. They took their coffee and went up the stairs to the second level of the ornately designed structure and peered out from one of the tiny balconies. From that vantage point, they could see back down the street from whence they had come.

"Oh crap, we gotta' go. There's a fight down there already. Looks like Navy versus Army," CJ said.

By the time they arrived and pushed their way through the crowd to get to the drunken pugilists, some other GIs were already trying to separate them, which only added to the confusion.

"Alright guys, let's face it, we aren't the enemy. They're over in Korea – we're all on the same team, so let's save our energy for the real fight, OK?" Walters implored them.

"Are you going to arrest us?" one of the drunks asked.

"No," CJ assured him. "Not if we don't have to. That'll be up to you."

After they dispersed the remainder of the crowd, Smitty breathed a sigh of relief, "That was a pretty good line you used PFC Walters. You're just a budding diplomat. We need to send you to Korea to talk sense into those people on both sides and then maybe we wouldn't have to go to war."

"You guys did it again," Jimbo butted in. "You ruined my whole evening. I was hoping to kick some ass out here tonight—just kiddin'," Jimbo added quickly.

"That really was some piece of talkin' though," Jimbo agreed, patting Walters on the back.

"Don't worry, Jimbo, from the looks of this mob you may get your wish before this night is over."

They split up again and headed back toward the seedier end of Hotel Street. As they walked they noticed the street getting even busier.

"Must be every swab that floated into Pearl Harbor yesterday came here," Smitty commented, "as if this place wasn't bad enough before."

"Being bad is obviously why they're here," Walters added as he and Smitty cruised over to the other side of the street again.

Smitty peered into every whorehouse and tattoo parlor along the way. The bars were so crowded that patrons were spilling out into the streets with glasses and beer bottles still in their hands. It was definitely against

Hawaii's laws, but there weren't enough jails on the island to hold the entire crew.

"Hey!" a voice came from out of the crowded streets. "You guys are two of the handsomest MPs these beautiful brown eyes have ever seen."

Standing before them was what appeared to be the original fat lady from Barnum and Bailey's circus, and every ounce of her wiggled as she walked. She was stone drunk.

"Hi, gorgeous, who are you?"

"They call me 'Boom-Boom,'" she blurted out with a breath that would have stopped a speeding freight train.

"'Boom-Boom,' how romantic," Smitty replied. "How did you ever get a name like that?"

"I thought you'd never ask," she said as she pulled up her blouse.

"Oh no, you had to ask didn't you, Smitty," Walters said shaking his head from side to side as they watched her weave her way down the street, parting the crowd as she went.

"Her breasts looked like twin ski slopes," Smitty snickered, choking on his own words.

"Yeah—after an avalanche," Walters chimed in with a disgusted tone.

They laughed as they watched her stagger across the street, almost wrecking a moving vehicle that stopped suddenly to avoid totaling his car. Smitty and Walters stood dumbfounded continuing to watch as she approached Jimbo and CJ. They waited and, sure enough, up went the blouse.

Smitty and Walters roared with laughter.

"I wonder which one of those two idiots had to ask," Walters chuckled.

"Look ahead of us at 12 o'clock, the pee pole is being revisited. This time by a puker and his aim ain't any better. Check out the shoes on that swabby," Smitty chuckled.

"Let's talk about something else, Smitty. This place is wearing me down. I'd hate to have this as permanent duty."

"Yeah, it must take a special kind of person to enjoy this line of work."

As they walked, Walters talked more and Smitty felt that he was getting to know him better.

"I've wanted to tell you that I was sorry I didn't make it to your girlfriend's open house, but I had some important business to take care of that evening."

"Like I said before, you missed a super party but, knowing Nani's mother, you'll get another chance."

"Stop for a minute, Smitty. I've been watching that girl across the street. She's been stopping sailors and trying to get them to go between those two buildings. See there—she's pulling on that sailor's sleeve."

"She's probably just a prostitute," Smitty said. "Yeah see, she's hugging him now."

The girl was probing and squeezing the back of his tight fitting white sailor pants with both hands, as if she were searching for pockets she knew weren't there. The drunken sailor didn't appear to be protesting very much. She was gradually turning him around until his back was next to the small opening between the two buildings. Suddenly, two men stepped out of the opening and, grabbing him by his neckerchief, pulled the sailor out of sight.

"Let's go!" Smitty shouted.

Night sticks in hand, the two Marines rushed across the street into the darkened alleyway. Walters grabbed one of the men and spun him around, shoving him into the wall. Smitty clouted the other man across his face before an arm reached across his neck, choking him. He felt a hand trying to remove his 45 from its holster. Smitty bent over at the waist, shifting his weight forward, then quickly spun his body to the right, freeing himself from the man's grip. He suddenly became aware that there were not just two but actually four of them, and the fourth man was attacking Walters. Smitty heard two distinct thumping sounds and heard two men groan as they slumped to the ground.

"The cavalry to the rescue!" he heard someone shout. It was Jimbo, with CJ right beside him.

Smitty stepped behind Walter's second assailant. He shoved his night stick under his chin and across his throat, dragging him, choking and sputtering back into the light of Hotel Street. The four men were now subdued and the girl was fleeing down the street into the arms of an awaiting Honolulu Police Officer.

The four Marines took a few moments to assess the damage. The sailor seemed bewildered and confessed that he didn't even know what had happened. Smitty's gun was still in its holster. Walters and CJ were standing over their captives, who were lying on the ground. Jimbo was smiling from ear to ear as he continued to slap his nightstick into the palm of his hand.

"Well, we finally got to arrest some real criminals," Jimbo blurted out gleefully.

"Look at the size of those animals. They didn't look that big in the alley," Smitty sighed, catching his breath.

The Marines helped the Honolulu police load the prisoners into the back of their paddy wagon. Smitty signed some papers and watched as the police cars disappeared from view. They turned the sailor over to two of his blurry eyed buddies, who had wandered back looking for him.

"What a night. I'm ready for the sack," CJ said.

It was 0300 and the action on Hotel Street had slowed considerably; a stray drunk here and there was all that could be seen.

"It's time we headed back to the 'Y'," Walters said. "Even the crazies know when it's quittin' time, besides I could use another cup of coffee."

The streets were filled with litter and broken glass from that eventful night of debauchery. Lying on the sidewalk was a neatly folded piece of paper. Walters picked it up and unfolded it. It was a five dollar bill.

"How did anyone miss this?" he said. "And how are we going to split it four ways? Do the math for me, Smitty."

Seated on a flower box full of dead flowers was a left over orphan of the night. He claimed to be Private Woodrow Philip Jackson the third, United States Army. He went on to say that he was from Columbia, South Carolina. He was very homesick and, by his own admission, very drunk. His badly soiled uniform appeared to have taken quite a beating during the night.

"The third?" Smitty repeated, winking at Walters.

Where are you stationed Private Woodrow Philip Jackson the third?" Walters asked.

"Schofield Barracks, Sir," the young man answered smartly.

"I'm not an officer. You don't have to call me sir," Walters assured him.

"Yes, Sir," the young soldier answered.

"How old are you?" Walters asked shaking his head.

"Eighteen, Sir," he answered.

"You're coming with us," Walters said.

"I'm under arrest, am I right, Sir?" the private said as he struggled to his feet and tried desperately to stand at attention.

"No, soldier, we're going to get some coffee and you could use some too," CJ said.

"What army are you guys in?" The soldier asked staring at their uniforms.

"We're Marines."

"Oh yeah, I've heard you guys are pretty mean, and you don't like soldiers. Am I right?"

Just then, a jeep rolled up to the curb and stopped. An army sergeant stepped out and introduced himself.

"I'm Sergeant First Class Urbino of HASP," he announced officiously.

"Yeah, we've heard of you," Jimbo replied.

"Who've you got there?" the sergeant snapped.

"This is Private Jackson," Jimbo answered.

"What's he done?"

"We haven't figured that out yet," Jimbo said.

"Put him in the back of my jeep. I'll figure out what he's done in a hurry."

"No, I think we'll keep him. Thanks anyway," Jimbo said.

"Have you placed him under arrest?"

"We haven't decided that yet either."

"Do as I tell you, Private, and put him in the back of my jeep," the sergeant admonished Jimbo sternly.

"You have no authority over us, and this man is staying right here," Jimbo told the angry sergeant.

"Have it your way for now, boy, but this night ain't over and he'll be mine before it's done. And those ribbons you're wearing, private, where'd you get them, in a Cracker Jack box? I'm sure you didn't earn 'em."

"You better leave while you still can, Sergeant," Jimbo cautioned him firmly.

The sergeant pointed a menacing finger at Jimbo and warned that he wouldn't forget him. Then he mumbled something inaudible as he punched the accelerator, squealing his tires as he drove away.

"Do you think he's going to get me?" Private Jackson asked.

"Not if we can help it," Walters answered.

"You Marines aren't as bad as I've heard."

"Oh we're bad alright, soldier. Luckily you caught us on a good night," CJ chuckled.

The nice lady at the "Y" welcomed them and said that she had just made a fresh pot of coffee.

"My kinda' woman," Jimbo smiled at her.

The coffee tasted especially good and worked wonders for Private Jackson.

"How much money you got, Jackson?" Jimbo asked.

The soldier reached into both front pockets turning them inside out. They were empty. Walters went out front and flagged down a cab.

"How much do you charge to Schofield Barracks?" Walters asked.

"About four bucks," the cabby replied, shrugging his shoulders, "maybe a little less."

He handed the cabby the five dollar bill he had found in the street and told him to take Jackson to Schofield Barracks. Walters turned to Smitty, shrugged his shoulders and said. "Easy come, easy go, and besides it's for a good cause."

"Yeah, we couldn't have divided it four ways anyway," Smitty agreed.

"I think a dollar twenty five each would have done very nicely, PFC math major," Walters said sarcastically.

When the Marines got back to Pearl Harbor, all four of them headed straight for the showers to rid themselves of the noxious odor of the street.

~CHAPTER~

FIFTEEN

Several weeks had passed since the great debacle on Hotel Street. During that time, more troops had been sent to Korea and more Marines were itching to get involved; especially Jimbo, who admittedly lived to find 'causes' to fight for.

The North Korean People's Army had pushed down to the southernmost tip of the Korean peninsula to the seaport town of Pusan. The NKPA were squeezing American and South Korean ROK troops into defensive positions in an area that was being referred to as the 'Pusan Perimeter.' General MacArthur was advising President Truman that we must hold on or be pushed permanently out of South Korea and lose that country to Communism—perhaps forever.

The police in Honolulu filed a report that efforts to find any tell-tale evidence in the ashes at Camp Catlin were fruitless. Among the items they found were metal door hinges and handles, Coke bottles, metal pipes, six water faucets sticking up out of ground next to where each of the buildings had once stood, and numerous metal buttons that remained from the burned coveralls left behind by warehouse workers. They also found screws and nails by the thousands.

The only good news was a rumor that there had been a recent break in the case that might result in an arrest in the very near future.

Smitty, CJ, and Walters were grumbling because they had been assigned an extra shift at the brig, which wouldn't have been so bad but for the fact that it was from midnight until 0400. The only other good news was that more Marines were on their way to relieve the personnel crisis in Hawaii and free up some of the Marines who would be shipping out to Korea from Camp Catlin and Pearl.

Walters was carrying a book under his arm when he arrived at the brig.

"Looks like it might be a long night," he said to CJ.

The activity log showed that the prisoners had been in their racks since lights out at 2200.

"It looks like it's going to be a quiet night," CJ was saying, when suddenly the phone rang.

Walters took the call.

"Come on, Smitty, that was the guard at the main gate, seems that somebody from HASP is holding a prisoner there for us to pick up."

They pulled up to the gate and, sure enough, it was their old friend, Sergeant First Class Urbino, sitting behind the wheel of his jeep with a satisfied look on his face like a cat that had just swallowed a canary.

"Where's the prisoner?" Smitty asked.

"Right here behind me," the sergeant answered gruffly.

Walters and Smitty looked into the backseat and saw the slumped body of a Marine with his forehead resting on the back of the passenger's seat.

"Just a minute," the sergeant announced as he proceeded to unlock the handcuffs from the restraining bar across the back seat.

"He may need some medical attention. Looks like someone had to work him over a little when he tried to resist arrest," the swaggering sergeant smirked.

The prisoner appeared to be only semi-conscious as Smitty and Walters helped him out of the jeep.

"Are you OK, Marine?" Smitty asked.

It took a moment for Smitty to recognize him, despite the fact that it was a face he saw every day.

"Oh no, Walters, its Jimbo," Smitty said incredulously, "let's get him to the hospital fast."

"Just a minute, you got to sign for him before I can let you take him anywhere," the sergeant barked.

Smitty ripped the clipboard out of Urbino's hand and scrawled his name across the page. The sergeant very ceremoniously handed Smitty a list of the charges being brought against Private James Terp.

When they arrived at the base hospital Walters called CJ at the brig and told him what had happened and that he would have to hold the fort until they got back.

The nurse carefully removed Jimbo's uniform, revealing bruises across his back and along the rib cage on his right side. She was mostly concerned about the multiple head injuries. The Marines were informed that they would be keeping him overnight and that they would assign a hospital guard to his room.

When they returned to the brig and told CJ, he went into a tirade about Sergeant Urbino. Walters casually went back to reading his book.

On the way to the hospital the next morning, Tyne told CJ, Walters, and Smitty that he had been on liberty with Jimbo the night before.

"We had just come out of the bar and I couldn't find my cap, so I went back inside to get it. When I came back I saw Jimbo riding away in the back of a HASP jeep. I waited there for a while, but the jeep never returned. I roamed all over town looking for him, but never found him. I came back to Pearl and he wasn't here either."

"Had Jimbo been drinking a lot?" Smitty asked.

"Two beers, that's all, and that's just mouthwash for him. You know Jimbo."

Jimbo was sitting upright on the bed with his head braced against the pillow behind him.

Tyne looked at the Marine guard who was sitting on a chair in the corner.

"I leave him alone for ten minutes and he gets busted," Corporal Tyne sputtered.

The guard laughed, but the nurse gave Tyne a dirty look as she left the room.

"Smitty and I have read the list of charges against you, Jimbo, and the Commander of the Guard informed us that you're going to be court-martialed."

"For what?!" Jimbo bellowed.

"You tell us, Jimbo. What happened last night?" Smitty asked.

"I was standing outside the bar waiting for Tyne to return. A jeep rolled up and Urbino ordered me to get in the back seat. He started asking me a lot of questions about what I was doing and where I had been. He asked me if I was alone and I told him I was waiting for Tyne to come out of the bar. Then he asked me if I was drunk and I told him hell no, and if I was drunk I probably wouldn't have gotten into the jeep. Then he asked where Tyne and me were headed. I told him we were going back to Pearl Harbor. Then he takes off in the jeep with me in the back seat. I asked him where he was going and he says he's taking me back to Pearl, so I asked him what about my buddy Tyne and he says he radioed his partner to pick him up and bring him to base. So, then I told him that that was a waste of gasoline and I asked him why we couldn't ride together, so he says that was no problem since they were both headed that way anyway. It all sounded like a lot of crap to me but, by then, I didn't have much choice."

Walters was shaking his head from side to side and CJ was leaning forward in his chair with his head in his hands.

Jimbo let out a deep sigh, as if he were searching his brain to remember what happened next. Then he continued to pour out the details of his nightmare encounter with Sergeant Urbino.

"Along the way, he pulled off to the side of the road and said he was going to wait for his partner to catch up. He got out of the jeep and next thing I know I felt a thud on the back of my head. When I could open my eyes again, my wrists were handcuffed in front of me. The chain on the cuffs was looped through a metal bar on the back of the passenger's seat; I couldn't move. He started whacking me on the back and shoulders, poking me in the ribs with the point of his night stick. I called him a few names like 'liar' and 'coward.' Then, I felt another whack on the back of my head. I don't remember much after that until I woke up here."

"Tell me something, Jimbo, and this is very important. Did you try to fight him or try to resist arrest?" Smitty asked.

"Well, first of all, he never did say I was under arrest and, secondly, I would have fought him if I could. I believe that yellow belly bastard knew that. That's probably why he blindsided me with his club and put the cuffs on me," Jimbo answered.

"The plan is to court martial you and I have the list of charges with me," Smitty said.

"What are they?" Jimbo asked.

"I'm going to read them to you, Jimbo, but you've got to promise me that you won't come flyin' out of that bed, OK?"

Jimbo nodded his head affirmatively.

"You, Private James Terp, are charged with drunk and disorderly conduct, resisting arrest, and assaulting a non-commissioned officer."

"Bullshit!" Jimbo screamed, which brought the nurse running into the room.

"You people are disturbing my patient and I want all of you out of this room—now!"

"I got work to do on your case, Jimbo", Smitty said, "but I'll be back to see you later."

Smitty spotted Captain Corwin at the nurse's station.

"Sir, I don't mean to interrupt, but can you tell us how Private Terp is doing? I mean, is he going to be OK? I brought him here last night and he's a friend of ours, Sir."

"He's not my patient," Captain Corwin answered, reaching for Jimbo's chart, "but his record indicates a slight concussion and a rib separation;

however, there was no damage to his spleen. With some rest and light duty he should heal and be good to go in a couple of weeks."

"Thank you, Sir, for the good news."

Glancing to his right Smitty saw Jimbo's nurse. "And I want you to know, Sir, that you have some wonderful nurses working here," Smitty said, smiling at her.

The doctor shot back a cordial smile while the nurse threw him a scornful scowl.

Smitty knew that he didn't have much time before the court martial, and he also knew that he had never done anything like what he was about to do now. He stopped at the gift shop and bought a small note pad and a pencil.

"I'm going to need your help," he said to Walters.

Smitty was busy writing notes from all the things that Tyne, Jimbo, and Urbino had told him.

"What can I do?" Walters asked.

"I need close up pictures of Jimbo in his skivvies, front and back, and I need to have some research done on court martial procedures and military law," Smitty said, "but that should be easy for you."

"Why are you going to all this trouble?" Walters shrugged. "You know they're going to hang him anyway. It's Jimbo's word against the word of the big bad sergeant. You know it will be kind of—he said, he said—and Jimbo's just a buck private, so who's word are the high muckity mucks going to take?"

"I know it doesn't look too hopeful, but it's Jimbo, so we've got to try," Smitty answered.

The next day, Smitty was back at the hospital. Jimbo seemed to be back to his old cantankerous self again.

"How do liars like him get away with this crap?" Jimbo asked.

"It's really quite simple, Jimbo. Some people take a defeatist attitude and let things slide, or maybe they just don't know how to fight back."

Jimbo looked Smitty in the eyes and said, "You know I'm a fighter."

"Good, so am I, Jimbo, and I'm on your side—remember that."

Just then, the nurse stepped into the room. Smitty smiled and said, "I'm awful sorry about yesterday, Ma'am, but all his friends are kind of worried about this guy."

"I'm sorry, too," she said, going back to her job of changing the bandages on the back of Jimbo's head.

"How's the war in Korea going, Smitty?" Jimbo asked.

"Not so good. I think they're waiting for you to get there so they can start winning, Jimbo. And get this, they're not calling it a war, they're calling it a 'conflict.' Isn't that what they call a squabble between a man and his wife?"

"That's the world of politics for you, Smitty," Jimbo laughed, "and please don't make me laugh again, my ribs still hurt like hell."

"Nurse, is Petty Officer Blake on staff today?" Smitty asked, looking back at her.

"I'll send him in to see you if you'd like," she replied.

Smitty smiled, saying, "Thank you, Ma'am," then crossed the room to sit next to Jimbo's bed.

"Petty Officer Erwin Blake reporting as ordered."

It was the always playful Doc Blake standing at attention in the doorway.

"Have you Jarheads started any more fires lately?" he asked.

"No, but we might be fighting something worse very soon, Doc."

"Oh yes, that thing in Korea. I wish I could be going with you guys."

"Are you serious, Doc?"

"Cross my heart and hope to live. For me it would be the best of both worlds. I tried to get attached to a Marine unit when I was in the States, but the need at that time was on the big ships like the Midway. I'm probably in trouble with those folks now anyway, and besides Navy Corpsmen get to wear both uniforms when they're attached to Marine units. Sure, I'd go." Blake shot back.

"I wish I could arrange it for you, Doc, but I don't have that kind of pull. In the meantime I got something you can help me with. I'm sending a guy named Walters to take some pictures of my buddy Jimbo tomorrow, OK?"

"I've already got some pictures of him, and thank God they're not too bad."

"Not x-rays, Doc, I mean photographs of his head, his ribs, his bruises and, even more importantly, frontal shots where he doesn't have any injuries at all."

"I know, I was just kidding. Is there anything else I can do?" Blake asked.

"Yes, there is. What do you think of Captain Corwin?" Smitty asked.

"He's a great guy. Not a stuffed shirt like so many other officers who are full of themselves. He listens and he talks to me—not down to me like I was stupid. He has the respect of everyone in this hospital. You don't find many professional guys like him, and I personally, have learned a heck of a lot working for him."

"What else do you know about him?" Smitty asked.

"Well, he's forty two years old and his wife died about a year and a half ago," Blake answered.

"Where is the Captain right now?"

"He's in his office."

"Can you get me in to see him? It's about Jimbo."

"I'll see," Doc answered.

Smitty was so convinced of the justice of his mission that sitting in front of a high ranking Naval Officer was not as awkward as he had assumed that it would be.

"I know you are a very busy man, Sir, so I'll get right to the point. You must know by now that my friend, Private Terp, is in a lot of trouble and he's going up for a court martial next week. I'm trying as best I can to prepare his defense because I know for a fact that he's not guilty of any of the charges against him."

"Yes, but what does that have to do with me?"

"Well, Sir, he needs someone to represent him at his court martial and I was hoping that I could convince you to do that."

"Look at me, PFC Smith. I am a medical man, not a lawyer. I know nothing about military law. If I did, I might be convinced to help you."

"Yes, Sir, I understand, but I don't know much about the law either, and neither do most of the Marine Officers on this base. If I could, I would represent him myself, but a PFC in a court room full of officers wouldn't command much respect."

"I don't know, son, I'd have to think it over."

"Sir, could I come back to see you in a few days with all the facts? If, by then, I can't convince you that we have a good case I'll try to find someone else, but I've got to hurry because the court martial is next week. Would that be fair, Sir?"

"Your friend, Jimbo, is a very lucky man to have you on his side," Doctor Corwin responded with an affirmative nod.

~CHAPTER~

SIXTEEN

The morning of the court martial arrived with news that replacements were steadily arriving at Pearl Harbor. The Marines from both Camp Catlin and Pearl would be sent to Korea as soon as a transition could be accomplished. Jimbo was worried that he might not be going with them.

Smitty telephoned Nani to tell her the news. She was devastated.

"I knew this day was coming, and I knew I would dread it when it did. I lost my father in a war, and now I fear losing you."

"I'll come back to you, Nani, I promise," Smitty assured her.

"My mother knew you would be going, so she has been planning a going away party for you and CJ. Now, it looks like it will be this coming Saturday. You can invite all your friends. I hope you will all have time to come."

Nani sounded very troubled by the whole situation, but Smitty didn't feel that he could deal with her anguish at that moment.

"I have to go now, Nani. I have something very important to do before we ship out. I'll call you later."

The court martial began with little fanfare. Colonel Puller, who would preside over the hearing, expressed his surprise at seeing Captain Corwin representing the defense but greeted him cordially. The Captain took his place at the Defense Counsel table between Jimbo and Smitty.

As he struck his gavel on the table, the colonel announced that he hoped to complete the proceedings in a timely fashion since he had a war to prepare for.

The Sergeant-at-Arms read the formal charges. He asked Private

James Terp how he pleaded. Jimbo rose to his feet and emphatically stated, "Not guilty, Sir." The Sergeant-at-Arms asked that everyone be seated.

Major Quinlan who would be prosecuting the case called his only witness Sergeant First Class Lucian Urbino, United States Army.

"How long have you served in the army?" the major asked.

"Ten years," the sergeant boasted.

"And I see by your file that you have an unblemished record. Is that correct?" the major asked.

The sergeant sat up a little straighter and answered in a loud voice, "Yes, Sir."

Looking back at Walters, Smitty watched him squirm a little in his chair and shake his head negatively.

"How long have you served in the Hawaiian Armed Services Police?" the major asked the cocky soldier.

"Four years, Sir."

"Do you recognize the defendant?" the major asked, pointing at Jimbo.

"I do, Sir. He is Private James Terp, U.S.M.C."

The sergeant seemed quite poised and confident, sitting in the court room as if he had done this many times before.

"In your own words, sergeant, will you tell this court what happened on the evening of his arrest?"

"Yes, Sir," he responded. Then, like a seasoned witness, he recited his version of the incident.

"I was patrolling in Honolulu when I saw this Marine staggering along the street," he began as he pointed at Jimbo. "I asked him if he was drunk and he answered no, adding that I should go find someone else to hassle. I stepped out of my jeep and, as I approached him, he swung at me striking me, viciously, in the face. I staggered backwards, trying to regain my composure, then he struck again repeatedly with his fists. I immediately told him that he was under arrest, but it didn't stop there. He hit me again very hard on my cheek, just below my left eye. I was hit so hard I staggered backwards again. At that point, I took out my night stick and hit him across his chest. He seemed to be too drunk to feel it, so he came at me again. I struck him across his hands and arms repeatedly. He charged at me again and I hit him in the forehead, knocking him unconscious. I got him to his feet and put him in the back of the jeep, restraining him with handcuffs."

"What did you do then?" the major asked.

"Then I brought him here, to Pearl Harbor, and left him at the gate with their MPs."

"Is there anything you would like to add, sergeant?"

"No Sir, I believe that's all," the sergeant answered.

"That will be all for now," Major Quinlan announced.

Smitty leaned over to Captain Corwin and whispered in his ear.

The captain rose from his chair then, looking at Sergeant Urbino, he said, "I want to congratulate you, sergeant. It is rare to see a man with such a pristine record in the military service."

The sergeant pushed himself up further in his seat, sitting even taller than before. "However, I must ask you some questions about your recollection of the events that occurred that night. For instance, if I remember correctly, you said that Private Terp was drunk at the time you arrested him. Is that correct?"

"Yes, Sir, very drunk."

"I see," the captain responded scratching his chin, "and yet, when he was admitted to the hospital that night, the doctor on our staff found an unusually small trace of alcohol in his blood stream," the captain handed a copy of the report to Colonel Puller.

"You also testified that the defendant struck you in the face several times, yet I see no marks or signs of bruising anywhere on your face. It is my experience that bruises don't heal that completely in... let's see, less than a week. And further, you described a frontal assault from the defendant and yet, as you stated, and I quote from your testimony, 'I struck him across his hands and arms with my night stick.' The only injuries incurred by the defendant are from the rear, with none on his hands or arms. Even the bruising to his ribs is in the lower rear section of his back, as is shown by the photographs of the defendant that I submit in evidence to the court at this time. The court will also notice that there are no injuries or bruises shown anywhere on the front of his body—none—suggesting that all blows were struck from behind. More importantly, you indicated that you struck the defendant on his forehead, rendering him unconscious. Yet, when he was admitted to the hospital, there was no sign of trauma there. No bleeding, no abrasion, no lump, nothing. However, there were signs of blunt force trauma to the back of his head. You are not insinuating that this Marine turned his back to you before he attacked. Are you, Sergeant Urbino?"

Colonel Puller shifted his eyes toward the sergeant waiting for his response.

"No, Sir...I-I'm not... Sir," Sergeant Urbino stuttered as he squirmed in his seat. "I don't understand. I see so many situations like this—maybe I was thinking of a different incident."

"Yes, maybe you were, sergeant, but you seemed so confident when you wrote your report and when you described the incident here in this court room."

"I would like to call Corporal Andrew Tyne to the stand." the captain quickly stated.

"I have just a few questions for you, Corporal Tyne. It is my understanding from your report that you were with Private Terp that evening and that you left him only momentarily to go back into the bar to retrieve your cover and that when you came back he was gone. Is that correct, Corporal Tyne?"

Tyne nodded in affirmation, then responded, "Yes, Sir."

"Was he drunk when you left him?"

"Absolutely not, Sir. I've spent a lot of time with Jimbo, I mean Private Terp, Sir, and I know when he's drunk. We only had two beers each and we were going to head back to Pearl when I came back out of the bar."

"How long did it take you to retrieve your cap from the bar, Corporal?"

"Less than five minutes, Sir."

"And, when you came out, you saw him being driven away in the back of a jeep. Is that correct?"

"Yes, Sir," Tyne said.

"You don't think he got drunk in that five minutes that you were in the bar do you, Corporal?"

Chuckles were heard from every corner of the room until the sound of a gavel squelched the interruption.

"Five minutes doesn't seem long enough for an altercation such as the one Sergeant Urbino just described—does it, Corporal?"

"It seems to me that it took a lot longer than five minutes for him to tell it," Tyne answered.

"If the major has no questions for the corporal I would like to call the defendant, Private James Terp, to the stand."

Jimbo was no virgin in the court room himself. He had been tried for the same offense twice before. The captain wasted no time in presenting those facts to the court before the prosecutor did.

"I see by your file that you are no stranger to the court room, Private Terp. You have been charged on two former occasions and have been busted in rank on both of them. Isn't that correct?"

"Yes, Sir," Jimbo responded, casting his eyes down toward his shoes.

"And how did you plead to the charges on those two previous occasions, Private?"

"Guilty, Sir."

"And now you are pleading not guilty. Why is that?"

"Because those two other times I was guilty, Sir—guilty as hell. Excuse me, Sir. But, this time, I am not guilty. I don't mind being punished when I deserve it. I just don't like being falsely accused by anyone, Sir."

"I see, Private Terp, and I also see by your file that you served at Guadalcanal. Is that correct?"

"Yes, Sir."

Colonel Puller interrupted. "You were at the Canal, Private Terp?" he asked.

"Yes, Sir. I proudly served in your battalion, Sir," Jimbo replied.

"Is that where you got that Purple Heart ribbon that you're wearing on your chest?"

"Yes, Sir, it is," Jimbo responded.

"And the Bronze Star ribbon as well?" the colonel asked.

"Yes, Sir."

The colonel hesitated a moment, then replied, "I've heard enough. As I stated before, I've got another war to fight. This case is dismissed. Sergeant Urbino, I want to see you up front here right now," the colonel bellowed. "And Captain Corwin, if you can wait a few moments I'd like to speak to you when I get through with him."

The sergeant slowly approached the irate colonel.

"You, Sergeant, are a disgrace to the United States Army. I know your Commanding Officer and I'm going to suggest to him that he take one of those stripes away from you. I'd do worse than that, but I don't have time. Now you get your disgraceful self off my base. Sergeant-at-Arms, escort him to the main gate before I get really angry and do it myself."

The colonel turned to Captain Corwin.

"Captain Corwin, I know that you are a gifted medical man but I had no idea that you were a man of multiple talents. That was a masterful performance and, believe me, I have heard some talented lawyers' present cases before me in the past," Colonel Puller stated.

"I have to correct you, Sir. Here is the young man who deserves the credit," he said placing his hand on Smitty's shoulder. He prepared this entire case. He instructed me on what to say and when to say it. The pictures, which were so convincing, were his idea and he very tactfully coerced me into presenting this case on behalf of his friend and fellow Marine."

"And what is your name, son?" the colonel asked sternly.

"Private First Class Jay Smith, Sir."

"Well, Corporal, I can tell you that I never get over how loyal my Marines are to each other."

"I'm sorry, Sir, I don't mean to contradict you but I said private first class, Sir."

"Don't argue with me, son. If I say you're a corporal, then you're a corporal," Colonel Puller stated emphatically. "I will have First Sergeant

Cooper prepare the paperwork when I get back to my office. Now is there anything else I can do for you, Corporal Smith?"

"Actually there is, Sir. You see, Jimbo—I mean Private Terp, Sir—wants to serve with you again in Korea and…"

"With Captain Corwin's approval he will leave with us on Sunday afternoon for Japan." The colonel commanded brusquely.

He looked sternly at Smitty again. Is there anything else?'

"Well…yes, Sir…there is one more matter."

"Spit it out, Marine, I've got a busy day ahead of me."

"Well, Sir, there is a Corpsman named Erwin Blake who missed his ship and is temporarily attached to the hospital here at Pearl until his ship returns, but he'd like to go with us to Korea too. Is that possible, Sir?"

Smitty signaled to Blake to come forward.

The colonel looked him over very carefully then said, "This too is up to Captain Corwin. God knows I can always use Corpsman in my outfit. Are you sure you want to go, Petty Officer?"

"Yes, Sir, I sure do," Blake answered.

"Now Smith, are you done or do I have to work some more magic for you?" the colonel asked.

"I'm done, Sir, and thank you for everything."

The colonel flashed a rarely seen smile at Smitty before leaving the room.

Everyone was now free to show their jubilation at the results of the trial.

"I don't know if I'm happier about winning or about seeing Urbino lose," Jimbo said. "But we all have to hand it to you, Smitty. None of us—except you—expected that we could win."

"By the way, there will be a party on Saturday at Nani's house," Smitty said. "It'll be a combination victory and going away party. I want all of you to be there, especially you, Captain Corwin and you too, Blake."

The word came down the pipe that on Saturday there would be liberty for all hands that were shipping out to Kobe, Japan, which was the staging area for troops entering the Korean Peninsula. Stern warnings were issued that they were to return Sunday morning no later than 0300.

Smitty phoned Nani to tell her the good news about Jimbo's trial. He let her know that he had already invited all his friends except Billy, but that he would get in touch with him as well.

When Walters arrived at Nani's house Smitty went to the door to greet him.

"I want you to meet Nani's mother Lea," Smitty said.

Lea gasped. "I already know him," she said. "From the library—but I had no idea that he was one of your friends, Smitty."

Walters appeared to be a little embarrassed. He had no knowledge of the connection either.

"Yes, we have talked a lot about books and many other things. In fact, he tried to talk me into taking a Karate class with him, but I had to decline."

"Well, 'The Secret Life of Walter Mitty' is coming out at last," CJ said.

"I don't know how many of you know it, but PFC Walters is highly ranked in the field of Karate. In fact, he was actually taking the test to become a 'Black Belt' the evening of Nani's open house," Lea said. "But, seeing how he is reacting, I think I may have said too much."

Walters smiled and said, "It's OK, Ma'am, these guys would have found out eventually anyway."

He seemed to utter a sigh of relief when the doorbell rang, as if he had been saved, literally, by the bell—at least temporarily.

At the door was Blake, accompanied by Captain Corwin. Smitty had the honor of introducing his two newest friends to Lea.

"Lea, this is Edwin Blake, Petty Officer Third Class, United States Navy and his boss Captain Corwin who saved the day for all of us at Jimbo's court martial."

Captain Corwin held out his hand to Lea and said, "I'm Douglas Corwin and it is my pleasure to meet you, Lea. May I call you Lea?"

"Yes, of course you may, and thank you for helping these young men protect their friend."

Billy leaned over and whispered to Smitty, "Karate—and a Black Belt? I'll think twice before I piss Walters off again."

Smitty laughed then muttered, "Yeah, me too."

The young Marines, ever so gently, chided Walters about his Karate skills and teased Jimbo about his encounter with Urbino while Lea sat in the garden conversing with Captain Corwin whom she was now calling Douglas.

The doorbell rang again and in came Joi, Kee, and Mama Ahue.

"You didn't think you could have a party without me, did you?" Mama smiled.

"I have brought something very special with me. They are snail's tails and they are considered to be a Hawaiian delight. Try some," she urged, smiling again.

Everyone watched Mama Ahue uncover the huge platter that Kee had carried in. Then, they heard Mama rocking with laughter as she exposed the huge plate full of giant shrimp.

"Mama Ahue makes a joke, but you must try these with my special Mama Ahue sauce."

It didn't take long for the crowd to consume the entire plate full of shrimp.

"Don't they feed you Marines?" Mama laughed again as she sent Kee out to the car to get another platter.

Mama pulled Smitty aside and told him again how important it was for him to wear his cross all the time while he was in Korea.

"You must come back safe. Nani loves you," Mama pleaded.

"I know, and you must look after her for me while I am gone. If anything happens to me, you..."

"Shush, you must not talk like that. You must think positive, Smitty, and don't you worry. Mama Ahue will look after Nani, OK?"

The party broke up at 2100. All the Marines including the new one, Erwin Blake, decided to go into town to hoist a few brews to celebrate Jimbo's victory in court—and their last night in Hawaii.

Smitty thanked Lea, waved to Mama, kissed Nani, and asked them if they would come to the airport at 1300 the next day for a final goodbye. As he walked away, he thought he detected a tear in the corner of Nani's eye.

At the White Dolphin Saloon, they took turns buying drinks, toasting Corpsmen Blake, their new Marine. Then they toasted their idols Chesty Puller, General MacArthur, Captain Corwin, and even King Kamehameha. The ever mysterious Walters left before midnight, saying he had one more thing to do before leaving town.

"A Karate lesson, maybe?" CJ chided him.

"Something like that," Walters said smiling as he walked out the door.

After running out of people to drink to, they all left the bar at 0100, still sober but feeling no pain.

~CHAPTER~

SEVENTEEN

A warm sun crept over the horizon on another magnificent Hawaiian day as the Marines prepared themselves for a journey from which many might not return.

Everything had to be just right. It was what they had been trained to do in boot camp. All their gear was laid out on their bunks. Their rifles were checked to be sure they were unloaded, cleaned, and set on safety. On their bunks were their cartridge belts with first aid pouches, canteens, leggings, field jackets, helmets, and bayonets. Clips of ammunition, mess kits, and entrenching shovels would be issued to them in Japan. Their packs were filled with skivvies, socks, t-shirts, and other personal items. They checked and double checked to be certain that everything was right. An ass chewing was not something that any of them wanted, especially today. The chaos in the barracks was inevitable.

"Who took my belt?" and "Where the hell are my socks?" were just a few of the impatient cries that resounded throughout the room. Locker doors slammed and accusations flew until all of the Marines had resolved their issues.

With their packs at the foot of their bunks, ready to go, the Marines put on their dungarees, socks, and boondockers before heading to the mess hall for their last meal before leaving Hawaiian soil.

The conversation at breakfast was mostly confined to conditions in Korea, with occasional lapses into silence. Rumors were coming in from Camp Catlin that they would be flying directly into South Korea while others heard that the plan was to parachute the Marines directly into North

Korea. There were many stories floating around, probably started by the infamous 'Kings of Scuttlebutt.'

In actuality, the First Marine Brigade was presently sending additional troops into Pusan to shore up the American Army's hold on the perimeter defense along the Naktong River. The defensive lines were shifting back and forth on a daily basis, and only air superiority made the difference for the American and ROK troops. Despite the additional men being sent into combat, the Americans were barely holding on. More troops were desperately needed to strengthen their weakening grip on the fragile peninsula.

The young men returned to the Marine Barracks at Pearl Harbor for the last time. They grabbed their packs, slung their rifles over their shoulders and loaded onto the awaiting trucks that would transport them to Honolulu International Airport.

Nani, Lea, Lani, Joi, Kee, and Mama Ahue were there waiting for the Marines to arrive.

Smitty embraced Nani like there was no tomorrow. He rocked her back and forth and side to side. He kissed her until he was out of breath.

"All night I lay awake dreaming about you and us, Nani. Don't worry, I will come back. Mama Ahue says so and you know that 'Mama Ahue knows these things,'" Smitty said with a nervous smile, as tears rolled down Nani's cheeks.

"I love you so much, Smitty. You must come back."

She handed him a paper sack and said, "There is a newspaper article in here that will interest you and a gift from Lea. It's a book. You can read them on the plane."

The Marines were lining up in columns of two on the tarmac. Smitty hurried to join up with them. He puckered his lips once more and threw a kiss to Nani before they marched off to the waiting aircraft.

"Come on, CJ," Smitty said.

CJ was still locked in a tight embrace with Lani.

"I'll write to you," Smitty called out to Nani.

As the Marines marched route step across the airstrip the Marine Band from Pearl Harbor played the Marine Corps Hymn. The young Marines, who at first struggled under the weight of their heavy packs, were suddenly more erect, standing taller as they sang along.

> *From the Halls of Montezuma to the Shores of Tripoli;*
> *We fight our country's battles in the air, on land and sea;*
> *First to fight for right and freedom and to keep our honor clean;*
> *We are proud to claim the title of United States Marine.*

The passengers from flights just arriving and passengers who were preparing to depart stared in awe at the young Marines who appeared to be prepared for battle at a moment's notice. A few shouts from the crowd caught up to the Marines. "Semper Fi!" one civilian called out.

The Marines stowed their packs in the underbelly of the plane and got on board. They heard the groaning of the propellers as they stubbornly resisted, then the engines revved up and the plane taxied to the end of the runway.

Smitty remembered that he had picked up a letter from Carol that morning and, not having time to read it, had stuffed it into his dungaree jacket pocket.

Smitty got a window seat and CJ sat next to him. Billy and Walters were across the aisle. When everyone got comfortable, the usual kibitzing began among the excited Marines.

CJ and Smitty had heard it all before.

The engine noise grew louder as the sudden forward thrust forced them back against their seats. As the plane rose off the tarmac, Smitty stared at the scenery below. The Island of Oahu appeared to grow smaller and smaller in the distance.

"Hey, Smitty, what's this we hear about you making Corporal? Congratulations!" someone in the back of the plane shouted.

Smitty fumbled in his pocket to find the letter from Carol.

My Dearest Smitty,

Oh God, how I miss you. I am lying on my bed writing this letter and wishing you were here. I have not seen Ray in a long time. I believe that he has found someone else. Guys are like that but not you, Smitty. I always trusted you. I hope you won't be going off to that terrible country over there where they are at war. My sister's friend Donna lost her husband in that war in July. She got $10,000 dollars from his life insurance policy; imagine that, $10,000 dollars and she was only married to him for five months. I wish that we had gotten married before you left. I miss you so much.

Well I gotta go now. Donna is coming over in a few and we're going out to a party and dancing. I hope you still love me as much as I love you.

Love Carol

"Here you go, CJ, read this. It's from my old girl friend, Carol. Read it and eat your heart out."

CJ read the letter then looked back up at Smitty and said, "makes you glad you met Nani doesn't it?"

Smitty smiled, tilting his seat back as he listened to the chatter of the exuberant Marines all around him. Then he remembered the sack that Nani gave him before he left. He pulled out the newspaper. As he unfolded the crumpled pages the headline blared at him in bold letters:

ARREST MADE IN SLAYINGS

The Honolulu Police Department reported today that they have arrested a drifter named Gerald Needham for the slayings of two local boys last spring. He began to surface as a prime suspect when the body of his sometimes friend, another homeless man known only as Kona, was found murdered on Waikiki Beach. The MO from both of those crime scenes appeared to be eerily similar. When Kona was discovered the odor of gasoline was detected on clothing found lying on the beach near his body. This left the police to believe that he and Needham were undoubtedly linked to the fire at Camp Catlin as well, obviously in an effort to destroy evidence at the scene. The Honolulu Police investigation revealed that Mr. Needham had previously been investigated in New Jersey for threatening to murder his wife. Gerald Needham is presently being held without bail, charged with triple homicide and arson. An investigation into the arson may bring additional murder charges for the deaths of firefighters and military personnel who died in the blaze.

Smitty hurriedly read the article then passed the paper over to Billy.

"Holy crap, guys, they finally caught the guy who killed those kids," Billy said handing the paper to Walters.

Walters latched onto the newspaper like he had just won the Irish Sweepstakes.

"Well, I won't be seeing that paper again for a while," Smitty said to CJ.

"Yeah, knowing him he'll probably even read the want ads," CJ quipped.

Smitty settled back again in his seat and stared out the window at the seemingly endless ocean that spread out from horizon to horizon below the wings of the aircraft.

Jerry Needham, Smitty pondered, Kona—maybe—but not Jerry. He seemed to be such a likeable guy. Different, yeah, but to kill someone the way those boys were killed. That's hard to believe, but then it was equally hard to believe that anyone could do something that horrible. He was suddenly startled by the sound of the pilot announcing over the intercom that they should all lay back and relax because they had a long journey ahead of them before they would see land again.

Thanks a hell of a lot, Smitty thought. What did he think I was doing?

Smitty went back to staring out the window.

The beautiful blue Pacific Ocean he remembered from his voyage to Hawaii could be as unpredictable as a paranoid schizophrenic—at one moment calm and serene and in the next violent and punishing. He stared at the vastness of the ocean and pondered its depth, thinking about the stories he had read as a boy—stories about pirates, explorers, superstitions, monsters of the deep, castaways, and lost continents. He remembered being most fascinated by the harsh justice of the high seas which demanded that serious crimes be resolved by requiring the offender to walk the plank, plunging him into the ocean's eternal abyss.

After awhile, the excitement of this impending new adventure quietly wore thin. Smitty dozed off listening to the humming of the engines and began listening to his own quiet voices. The ones inside his head, constantly questioning, "Are you sure you're ready for this?"

When he woke again, he found the newspaper lying on his lap and another story, a much smaller article, caught his eye. It seemed almost lost in a sea of black and white embedded on a page relegated to display ads, city business, and police reports. It read:

SOLDIER ATTACKED ON HOTEL STREET

Last night a member of the Hawaiian Armed Services Police was found on Hotel Street lying in the doorway of a brothel. He was identified as Sergeant Lucian Urbino. He was face down on the pavement suffering from a fractured right hand, a cracked rib, and a broken nose. It appeared that he had been severely beaten with his own night stick. The stick was broken into two pieces which were found lying next to his crumpled body. The only evidence the police have in identifying his attacker is the impression of an eagle, globe, and anchor deeply imprinted on his left cheek. Anyone who witnessed or has any information about this assault is urged to contact the Honolulu Police.

Smitty handed the paper back to Walters.

"I suppose you read this article."

"Yes I did," Walters replied, showing no emotion at all.

It was obvious to Smitty that Walters didn't want to discuss it.

"They'll probably never catch that guy. He's probably hundreds of miles away from Honolulu by now—you think?" Smitty asked Walters, knowing that he wouldn't get an answer.

Walters looked at Smitty and both smiled an all knowing smile together.

"Damnedest guy I ever met," Smitty muttered to himself.

He remembered Nani saying that Lea had put a book in the sack for him to read. He pulled it out and shook his head, smiling. The title of the book was <u>Animal Farm</u>.

If Lea says it's good it must be good, Smitty thought, and this is going to be a long journey. He began to read.

When he finished reading the book, he laid back and dozed off again.

Smitty awoke to the voice of the pilot on the intercom.

"Gentlemen, we have just completed the first leg of our journey. We have traveled 2,300 miles, and now we are about to land on Wake Island to refuel before continuing our flight into Kobe, Japan. We will be remaining on the ground for about two hours while we check out the aircraft before taking off again. You will have time to stretch your legs a little and have a cup of coffee. It's a huge island, so don't get lost or we'll have to leave without you," he said facetiously, then chuckled.

The Marines all strained to look out the windows of the aircraft.

"He's full of it. There's nothing down there but water," someone said.

The plane was descending gradually when, suddenly, a Marine spotted a dot on the distant horizon.

"How the hell are they going to land this big plane on that postage stamp?" Smitty said to CJ.

Wake Island was a well documented episode in Marine Corps lore and was one of many battles studied by Marine Recruits in boot camp.

The Japanese attacked the American installation on the tiny atoll on the same day that Pearl Harbor was bombed. The American contingent consisted of just 450 Marines, 70 sailors, and 1,200 civilian construction workers who held the island for two weeks against air, land, and sea assaults. They fought doggedly with rifles, machine guns, shovels, twelve fighter planes, and six shore batteries in a futile cause. The Americans repelled repeated attacks, sinking five enemy ships and damaging eight others. During subsequent bombing raids they shot down twenty Japanese aircraft and damaged many more.

When asked in a radio communiqué, "What do you need most?" the heroic Marines facetiously replied, "Send us more Japs."

Hopelessly surrounded and with no means of being reinforced, they fought on until ordered to surrender by a Naval Commander.

Landing on Wake still appeared to be an impossible task but, once on the ground, everyone expressed both relief and exhilaration about being allowed to set foot on such historic ground. Like most Marines, they enjoyed the opportunity to stand up straight again and stretch their legs on terra firma.

"I saw you reading one of my favorite authors on the plane," Walters said to Smitty.

"You mean <u>Animal Farm</u>? Smitty asked.

"Yes," Walters replied, "did you like it?"

"Very much."

"Then I think you'll like this one. It's Orwell's latest and it's called <u>1984</u>. I just finished reading it myself," Walters said, handing the book to Smitty.

When the Marines re-boarded the plane Smitty sat down next to Billy.

"Relax gentlemen, we still have a long way to go," the voice on the intercom reminded them.

"Well, what do you think?" Smitty queried Billy.

"About what?"

"About the arrest of Gerald Needham for killing those kids. You remember him, don't you?—the guy we met at the Kahuna Bar in Honolulu. He was with that Kona character. They say that they both set the fire at Camp Catlin, and that Jerry eventually killed Kona too—probably to keep his mouth shut."

"Oh, yeah, I thought you were talking about going to Korea. Yeah, I remember them, and we bought those bar room bums beer that night. I feel relieved that they got him, but they sure didn't look like guys who would do something like that—did they, Smitty?"

"I don't know. What's a murderer supposed to look like, Billy? Maybe they were just drunk when they did it?"

"Well, anyway, I'm sure glad it's over," Billy said.

"It's not really over yet, Billy. There will be a trial, and I'm sure Nani will write to me and let me know how that goes. I'll keep you informed."

As Smitty settled back in his seat again he glanced over at Walters who was writing in a book on his lap.

"Decided to write your own book, Walters?" Smitty asked.

"Not really, just keeping a diary. I thought I might enjoy looking back at all of this someday."

116

"By the way, Walters, you never did tell me how you got across that ravine back in Hawaii," Smitty asked casually.

"Oh yeah, well it was really much simpler than anyone thought. While everyone was patiently listening to the ravings of the two company clowns and their bridge idea I slipped off in the opposite direction, heading north. I began to hear the ocean slapping against the shore below. The cool breeze that followed was quite refreshing. I looked to the west again and there was a gradual slope that went further up and back toward the south. I followed it and soon I could hear Sergeant Allen calling to you guys to hurry. I looked over the side and there you were getting ready to follow him west. The rest, of course, is history."

Smitty smiled, shaking his head. Only Walters would ever guess that sometimes you have to back up a little and size up the situation before you could get going forward again. Then, with a nod, he opened the book Walters had given him and began to read.

As the wheels touched down at the airport near Kobe, Japan the Marines uttered a sigh of relief. It had been a very long and arduous journey that would become longer and even more arduous before it would end.

~CHAPTER~

EIGHTEEN

"Hey Joe, you wanna meet my sister? She verry pritty. She make you verry happy, Joe. Come on, Joe. My sister show you really good time. Only fi dollah, Joe," the Japanese boy said as he tugged insistently on Smitty's sleeve.

All up and down the street it was the same—young Japanese boys plying their wares to any GI willing to part with a few bucks.

CJ, Billy, Doc, and Smitty, however, were dedicated sight-seers on the streets of Kobe that evening, just looking for a good place to eat.

"There's a restaurant dead ahead, let's check it out."

As they attempted to enter the restaurant, an elderly Japanese lady kept pointing to their feet.

"I think she wants us to take our shoes off," Smitty said.

Once inside, they were escorted very ceremoniously into an ornately designed private room filled with Japanese art and symbols. A younger Japanese girl bowed to each of them as they entered. She invited them to sit cross legged on pillows around a table that was just twelve inches above the bamboo matted floor.

"You like some Sake, maybe?" the shy almond-eyed Asian girl asked very obsequiously.

"What is Sake?" Billy asked.

"Rice wine, verrry good," she smiled a tempting reply.

"OK," bring us each a bottle," CJ said.

She laughed. "No, no, first you try one grass," she said, "if you like, I bring more."

Billy scratched his head. "Did I hear her right? Did she say grass?"

118

She brought four small wine glasses and filled each of them half full.

"You like?" she begged courteously, smiling and bowing from the waist as they sipped the wine.

Billy acknowledged affirmatively. "This stuff is good."

"You order food now?"

"What do you suggest?" Blake inquired.

"We have very good Sukiyaki. You want to try?"

"What is it?" Blake asked, "I don't eat anything if I don't know what it is. My mother raised me that way."

"Yeah, well I'll bet your mother never told you about SOS and I'll bet you ate that crap more than once since you joined the military," Smitty laughed.

"OK, OK, bring it on. One thing is for sure, it can't be any worse than anything we've had before," Doc said.

Once they all got a taste they ordered more and ate and drank until they were stuffed.

"What's up for tomorrow?" Blake asked Smitty.

"Tomorrow we turn you into a real Marine, Doc. The powers tell me that they plan to put us through some very rigorous physical training; lots of rope climbing, running, and pushups in the morning. In the afternoon, we're going on a five mile forced march."

"I can handle five miles easily enough," Blake replied. "I used to walk five miles to school every day," he said laughing.

"Yeah, but this will be five miles there then turn around and five miles back, and all of that while wearing a full pack and field gear—you'll see," Smitty winked slyly at CJ.

The next evening, Marines began forming up from everywhere: some from stations in Guam, some from the Philippines, and Okinawa – all joining up with others coming in from Camp Pendleton in California and, of course, from Hawaii. They were to be part of the reinforced First Marine Division. Most of the Marines from Hawaii were assigned to Fox Company.

Unlike World War II, when Negro Marines were confined to units with other Negroes, President Truman ordered that they be integrated into previously all white Companies.

PFC John Wayne Eckles was one of those Negroes and he was immediately assigned to First Platoon in Corporal Tyne's First Squad. There was nothing about him you couldn't like. He was a typical 'Gung Ho' Marine from a dedicated Marine Corps family; his dad had been in the Marines before him. John Wayne Eckles grew up in Washington, DC and, although his mother had encouraged him to go to college, he decided to follow in the footsteps of his beloved father. John always enjoyed the stories that his dad told him about the Corps and decided that college could wait until he was older, when he would know more about what he wanted from life.

PFC Eckles loved telling his favorite boot camp stories to other Marines.

"You know how in boot camp," he began slowly, "if you wanted to talk to the Drill Instructor privately you were supposed to go to his room and knock on the door three times and not enter until he ordered you to," Eckles hesitated until he was convinced that everyone was listening. "Well, one day I did that. I stood outside his door and rapped sharply three times with my knuckles. From inside, I heard a firm gruff voice sing out, 'I can't hear youuu,' so I rapped on his door three more times—only much harder. From inside I heard him bellow, 'I still can't hear youuu,' so I made a big fist and slugged that door so hard it rattled on its hinges. Then, guess what? From inside I heard him scream again, 'I stillll cann't hear youuu.'" Eckles paused for a moment.

"By then I was totally frustrated, so I took a deep breath while I tried to run my fingers through my black wavy hair, forgetting that, just a few weeks before, it had been reduced to bristles. That was when I foolishly yelled back at him, 'then how the hell do you know I'm out here?' I remember thinking later that maybe I would've been better off if I'd taken two deep breathes instead of one before I opened my big mouth." Eckles hesitated.

"It didn't take long to realize that I was in deep trouble, so I ran down the hall back into the squad room where I tried to get lost among 69 other recruits, but it didn't take him long either. He came stomping across that deck and I swear I saw fire belching out of his nose. Every recruit was on his feet standing at attention as he stormed past each would-be-Marine, glaring in evil delight as he went. Then, very slowly, enunciating every word, the DI said, 'which-one-of-you-sorry-ass-skin-heads-was-just-down-the-hall-pounding-on-my-precious-door?' My stomach jumped up inside my throat, trying desperately to block my words—but to no avail. My big feet stepped forward automatically, and my body followed reluctantly behind, standing rigidly at attention. 'It was me, S-S-Sir,' I confessed in a trembling voice, respecting the Marine Corps Code of Honor. My conscience had just admitted something that my mouth would have preferred to deny." Eckles stood for a moment, shaking his head as if he were reliving the whole ordeal.

"For three days after that my life wasn't worth living. I scrubbed pots and pans in the galley during the day until my hands looked like shriveled prunes. I ran through what seemed like endless miles of clinging sand in my boondockers and full field pack, carrying my rifle at port arms for agonizing hours every evening. I did pushups until my shoulders ached worse than my tired feet. I suffered insults that would have made my poor mother cry. But you know what? I made PFC out of boot camp anyway. I think that wonderful bastard got to like me."

PFC Antonio Flores joined Fox Company from Guam. Flores hailed originally from El Paso, Texas. His family was very poor and he joined the Corps because he couldn't find a decent job at home. Despite the size of his meager paycheck, he always managed to send a little money to his mother. He constantly pruned his small, thin moustache like he was going to the high school prom instead of off to war.

Smitty's four man fire team in the First Squad was comprised of himself, CJ, Jimbo, and Walters.

Billy Hoyt's fire team was made up of Flores, Tommy Graham, who Billy knew from Camp Catlin, and Brad Butler who also came in from Guam.

Another corporal from Camp Pendleton named Gordon Murphy headed the third Fire Team. Wilson, Thomas, and Eckles rounded out his foursome.

The Platoon Sergeant was James J. Collins, who also came in from Camp Pendleton. The son of a Merchant Marine, Gunnery Sergeant Collins was raised in San Diego, California. He was very harsh and physically tough enough to back up everything he said. He had been awarded a Purple Heart at Iwo Jima.

The radio man was Corporal Ryan Karlstrom. Ryan was a big, strong Swede from Minnesota. He needed to be strong to walk and run carrying the bulky radio that would be strapped to his shoulders.

Petty Officer Third Class Erwin 'Doc' Blake would be the Medical Corpsman assigned to First Platoon.

To fill out the remainder of the roster, First Lieutenant Carl Peterson was assigned to the group as Platoon Leader. Carl was a tall southern boy from Tallahassee, Florida. He was probably the same age as Corporal Tyne but he appeared to be younger, with his handsome baby face. He was a battle hardened veteran of World War II, who had been awarded two Silver Stars and a Purple Heart during the Pacific Campaign.

It didn't take long for scuttlebutt to start wending its way through the ranks but one thing was becoming perfectly clear to everyone; with the large gathering of troops being assembled, something really big was in the wind.

Lieutenant Peterson wasted no time in getting to know the men under his command. He met with them at frequent intervals throughout the day referring to them by name and rank. He studied them and their actions until they felt like his eyes were piercing holes through them. He learned to recognize each of them from behind as well as from the front.

"We'll be moving out in the morning and loading aboard a troop transport heading directly to Korea," he told them.

"Pusan?" one man inquired.

"I can't tell you where right now, but we will all know by this evening," the Platoon Leader replied.

"Is it going to be a surprise?" another Marine asked.

"For the North Koreans it will be," Peterson replied, "we hope," he hastily added.

The ship was still being made ready to set sail when the Marines arrived at the pier. Sailors were scurrying around, handling lines, and pushing the brow into place so the Marines could go aboard. It wasn't the newest ship in the Navy, in fact it looked like it had been scraped and re-painted a thousand times before, but it appeared to be quite sturdy and capable of carrying the Marines the short distance between Kobe, Japan and the Korean Peninsula.

Every Marine snapped a hasty salute in the direction of the National Ensign flying on the aft deck before going aboard.

Below deck, they found themselves in very cramped quarters offering them a choice of canvass covered racks similar to a hammock but no bigger than a stretcher. The racks were stacked five high from the deck to the overhead. The canvass was stretched on steel frames attached to vertical poles with chains extending from the bulkheads to support them on each end. If you chose the very top rack you were exposed to heat from the pipes carrying hot water and steam throughout the length of the overhead compartment. If you chose the bottom rack, which was only ten inches from the deck below, you risked getting splattered with vomit if someone got sea sick above. The racks between the top and bottom were so close to each other that you couldn't roll over without batting the guy above you in the ass. To get to the top bunk you had to climb stepping on the frame of every rack below. There were about 100 bunks in each stifling compartment.

"Just like home," one Marine quipped.

"Yeah, Marine Corps style, first class accommodations. I'd like to meet the sadistic bastard who designed this honeymoon suite," another Marine grumbled.

Each Marine selected his own rack then hurried back to the ladders which would take him topside to get a breath of fresh air.

Lieutenant Peterson addressed his platoon on the aft deck.

"If any of you think it's uncomfortable on this ship just wait 'til you get ashore. The word I've received is that our guys at the southern end of this peninsula are getting their tails kicked by superior numbers and superior weapons. When we go ashore, we'll be taking more modern weapons with us than the ones that have been available to our fellow Marines and soldiers at Pusan. They've been waiting anxiously for help, and we'll be like the Cavalry coming to their rescue. This evening Captain Colson, our Company Commander, will be giving you the whole scoop about where we're going and what to expect when we get there. In the meantime, relax, get ready for some good ole Navy SOS for lunch, enjoy the ride, and pray for good weather for tomorrow."

"I knew I should've gotten a carry out at that Japanese Restaurant," CJ mumbled to Smitty.

It was a humid September day and it was hard to believe that, just a few nautical miles away, men were fighting a desperate battle just to hold their ground and stay alive.

"We're here complaining about sleeping quarters and hot chow and those guys are living off the land and eating C-rations in 110 degree heat. We ought to be ashamed of ourselves," Smitty said.

"OK, OK, but let's save the doom and gloom for tomorrow. I want to savor this moment while I still can," CJ said.

Lieutenant Peterson assembled First Platoon on deck again. They were soon joined by the Second and Third Platoons plus mortar, medical, and machine gun sections.

"Marines, I want you to meet Captain Colson. He is the Commander of Fox Company," the lieutenant told them.

Captain John Colson stood six feet two inches tall and carried himself like a prize fighter just entering the ring. The Captain stood silently for several moments while he slowly scanned the young men who stood before him. The Marines listened courteously as he began to speak.

"Gentleman, take seats on the deck and make yourselves as comfortable as possible. Tomorrow you will be embarking on an invasion into South Korea that will take you behind enemy lines. We are going to be making an amphibious landing into a seaport town along the west coast of Korea called Inchon. As you know, during World War II Marines made dangerous and difficult landings on islands all over the Pacific. This invasion is already seen by most military strategists as virtually impossible. The enemy believes that it's impossible too, but that is precisely why we are going to do it."

The Marines nervously looked around at each other as the captain continued.

"General MacArthur knows three things: first, our troops at Pusan are helplessly defending positions that are virtually indefensible. Good American soldiers are being slaughtered there needlessly. I personally know that because I and my staff were recently pulled out of Pusan and we are here now to join in this new assault on a determined and overconfident enemy. You men will be making this invasion side by side with seasoned warriors, so listen to them and hopefully you will live long enough to complete this mission. Secondly, MacArthur knows from his experiences in the Pacific Campaigns that the Marines are the only combat unit in the world that can do the improbable. Amphibious operations are what we are trained to do best. And thirdly, General MacArthur does not believe that the enemy is expecting us to land there because they know for certain it can't be done. What we are hoping is that their positions will be minimally fortified. And we, of course, hope that 'Mac' is right." The captain paused for a moment to take a sip from his canteen.

"Here are the problems. There is an island called Wolmi-do that commands the Inchon harbor. It will need to be neutralized before we can go ashore. There is no beach to land on when we arrive. There is a high seawall, so we will be forced to climb up makeshift ladders, one at a time, to get ashore. It will be risky, but it is imperative that we land quickly and establish a beach head so that the rest of our Marines can come ashore. If the enemy meets us with even a small contingent of trained troops they could stall our invasion hopelessly. The bad news is that once we get ashore, there will be no way to refortify our positions or evacuate, if necessary. We have only three hours to make our landing before the tide goes back out again. Once we get there we are stuck there. As we get closer to our landing site, you will be hearing our naval gunfire softening up the beach where we will be landing sometime tomorrow. Always remember what the Germans called us during World War I when we kept pursuing them no matter how much shit they threw at us. For those who don't remember it was 'Teufel Hunden' which translated into English as 'Devil Dogs'. Always remember that. We are 'Devil Dogs'.

Now try to get a good night's sleep. It might be a long time before you get that chance again for quite a while. Are there any questions?"

"Is there any good news, Sir?" a Marine shouted out.

"Yes, we are 'Devil Dogs'," was the reply, "now is there anything else?"

"Yes, Sir, can we eat now?"

It was a typical Marine question that received no response.

Smitty and Walters sat together at chow.

"I'm glad I got on your team. I'd go nuts if I had to follow that slow ass Billy Hoyt," Walters told Smitty.

"Well, to be honest, Walters, there aren't many guys in this outfit who can keep up with you."

"This war or conflict or whatever euphemism they're using now is a lot worse than I thought," Walters said, changing the subject.

"Maybe you can tell me, Walters, cuz I wonder how we keep getting into messes like this. Seems like we just finish a war and we're back in another one. What gives?" Smitty asked.

"A lot of people wonder the same thing, Smitty. Dictators, tyrants and despots seem to crop up in the world like weeds. It doesn't seem to matter what the war protestors and conscientious objectors think. War, in an imperfect world, is inevitable. You can't wish war away by complaining or carrying signs any more than you can successfully ban murders, earthquakes, or house fires. People who want to disband our armies thinking that that will end war are also going to have to disband firefighters because they don't like fires or disband policemen because they hate crime. It's all part of the same foolish philosophy. Like it or not, Smitty, history has proven that war is an expensive commodity if you want to preserve your freedom, and because there are crackpots who will always want to deprive you of that freedom, war is here to stay."

PART TWO

HELL

~CHAPTER~

NINETEEN

The Marines didn't get much sleep confined to their stuffy quarters below deck. To make matters worse, what little they did get was constantly interrupted by the intensifying sounds of naval gunfire as their ship drew closer and closer to the coastal waters of Inchon.

By dawn's hazy light, the ship's company was treated to a live display of fireworks more spectacular than any Fourth of July celebration back home.

"If I had known it was going to be this exciting I would have sold tickets and made some bucks," a sailor was heard to exclaim between barrages.

The Marines manned the rails and watched as troop carriers loaded an advance party into landing craft and sent them off toward the tiny island of Wolmi-do. The remaining Marines waited nervously listening to the distant sounds of heavy machine gun fire as their comrades went ashore to secure the island.

"When do you think we'll be going in, Lieutenant?" Billy Hoyt asked.

"Don't rush it, Corporal. Whenever we go, it'll be soon enough."

"I believe you, Sir, and believe me when I say, I'm in no hurry."

The bombardment of Wolmi-do let up, but the big guns continued to punish the distant shores of the harbor at Inchon. The lieutenant confirmed some scuttlebutt that the battleship Missouri was over on the east side of the South Korean peninsula. It had been deliberately dispatched there by the Navy to divert the attention of the North Korean People's Army. MacArthur's plan was to confuse the enemy and make them believe that the Marines would be invading at a more plausible landing site.

The mood of the Marines shifted constantly the remainder of the morning from anxious, to excited, to bravado—all intended to disguise their well hidden fear of the yet unknown. Most of them had never witnessed death up close and personal before and those who hadn't, worried about how they would deal with it when the time came.

Smitty worried too. His main concern was with how he would perform when he came face to face with an enemy determined to destroy him. He had learned about the principle of 'fight or flight' in a psychology class in high school, but never experienced a situation where his true mettle was tested. The thought of failing his fellow Marines pained him now like a throbbing toothache. It was a little like his first day in kindergarten, he thought, when his father dropped him off at school, assuring him that everything would be OK - and yet, at this all important moment in his life, he just couldn't seem to shake that nagging doubt.

He sought out Jimbo who had been calmly standing at the rail observing the action.

"Got any good advice for a freshman?"

"Yeah, keep your head down, Smitty, stay off the ridge line, stay close to me and forget all that tactical crap they taught you in boot camp. When the shit hits the fan on that beach, the enemy will have the upper hand, and all the rules will go out the window. There'll be so much happening you won't be able to sort out the real from the unbelievable. Just rust me, and stay close. Things will level off after we get firmly established on the beach."

"You should be leading this fire team—not me," Smitty said.

"You just stick with Jimbo and by the time this day is over you'll be an old pro—or you'll be dead," Jimbo added with a chuckle.

"Thanks a lot. I feel a hell of a lot better already," Smitty replied smugly.

Smitty was still questioning himself about the killing part. Everything he had ever been taught focused around four simple words, 'Thou shalt not kill'. He had given those words a lot of thought even before he joined the Marines, but World War II was over and he never suspected that he would ever be placed in a situation where he would have to kill anyone. Now he was going to be forced to make that decision.

When the time came, would he be able to do it? How would he respond? Those thoughts consumed him now and caused him great trepidation. Would he kill? Would he have a choice? And - could he pull that trigger knowing that there was a human being on the other end of the barrel - not a paper target but a human being? As hard as he tried to stifle them, those morbid thoughts continued to linger over and over in his subconscious.

He wanted to ask Jimbo about it again, but felt that he had sloughed that subject off once before in Hawaii. So, he kept his fears quietly hidden within. Maybe later, he told himself, maybe later, but he knew time was rapidly running out and "later" would be here all too soon.

Smitty watched in awe as small boats headed toward the ship.

"What are those boats called?" he asked Walters, knowing that if anyone would know it would be him.

"They're LCVPs, which means Landing Craft, Vehicle Personnel – better known as a Higgins boat. I can arrange a ride in one of them for you, if you'd like," Walters chuckled. "You should feel right at home in there. The engines were made at General Motors in your hometown, Smitty. But you knew that, didn't you?"

"Sure, I knew that." But Smitty really didn't and he figured that Walters, sly fox that he was, probably knew that too.

The LCVPs pulled alongside the ship. Some piloted by sailors who, just months before, had been driving fork lift trucks. The smaller landing crafts fought the swift current and the steady winds as they tried to hold their positions alongside the hull of the sturdier vessel.

"Be careful climbing down those cargo nets, men, and don't try to drop into the boat prematurely," Lieutenant Peterson cautioned, watching as the boats rocked away from the ship then came slamming back against its hull. "One false step and you'll drop between the boat and the ship, and we won't see you again."

That's encouraging, Smitty thought.

Smitty reached inside his dungaree jacket and fondled the cross that hung from his neck, just to reassure himself that it was still there. The words of Mama Ahue echoed inside the labyrinths of his mind, "You must promise me that you will wear this at all times so that God's Grace and Mama Ahue will be with you wherever you go." Then, without another thought, Smitty went over the ships rail as his reluctant legs led him cautiously down the cargo net and into the waiting LCVP.

The Marines were wearing full backpacks and carrying weapons and cartridge belts filled with ammunition. The temperatures were already rising, and the heat of the day coupled with the nervousness they felt caused ringlets of sweat to roll down their faces.

It had become a daunting task just getting all of the men loaded into the uncooperative boats that pitched to and fro with every wave. Once inside the open boats, men jammed together to make more room for others. Curses resounded within the tight enclosure.

"Just like the subway in New York," Jimbo quipped.

They looked up, but could barely see anything but a hazy blue sky above the sides of the small craft. As it pulled away from the ship, the engines revved louder and the noxious odor of diesel fumes defied their sense of smell.

The boat began to pitch from side to side as it circled the approach area, waiting for the remainder of the first wave of boats to align in formation. Then they felt a sudden nauseating forward thrust as the LCVP rushed rapidly toward the sea wall, zigging and zagging to avoid enemy fire coming from the beach.

"I think I'm gonna' puke," Billy Hoyt confessed aloud.

"You do and I'm gonna' toss your sorry ass over the side," Walters warned.

In the movies, the front gate of the LCVP would drop down and the Marines would come scrambling out, rushing onto the shore with John Wayne pumping his rifle up and down, leading the way - but this was not a movie. This landing would be very different from any they had ever seen in documentaries or movies. For one thing, there really was no beach, per se, though that's what it was called. And for another they were actually in the scene and not in a cozy theatre seat with a box of popcorn in their lap.

The landing craft eventually slowed before violently butting heads with the sea wall as the Marines scrambled up six foot scaling ladders, crudely fashioned from wooden storage pallets.

The gunfire that greeted them was brutal. The enemy clearly understood that once the Marines established themselves on the beach, they, and not the Marines, would be in trouble. So they concentrated heavy fire on the stationary boats. When the Marine at the top witnessed a wounded man tumble back into the boat the men below him had to push him up the ladder and force him over the top.

On the beach it was just as Jimbo had described—utter chaos. Officers and sergeants barked out orders to keep moving forward amidst cries from the wounded. Exploding grenades and the discordant chatter of automatic weapons continued to invade their already violated ear drums.

Stay close to Jimbo, a little voice kept urging inside Smitty's head. Yeah, right and you'll wind up a seasoned combat veteran Smitty argued— or maybe dead, another little voice that sounded a lot like Jimbo's argued back.

"Shift right. We're going to try to flank them," Lieutenant Peterson called out.

"I see the town just ahead. Watch out for sniper fire," Sergeant Collins commanded, as bullets stirred the red clay colored dust ahead of them.

Smitty watched as shells began to rain in on enemy positions. He looked back to see a mortar section calling out coordinates. The Marines were steadily moving forward toward the seaport town of Inchon and had already established a solid foothold on the beach. They saw enemy combatants with their hands raised above their heads, but they had no time to screw around with prisoners. It was all happening so fast that even the combat seasoned veterans hardly had time to think. Wounded were being attended to by medical corpsmen back near the beach.

Smitty caught a brief glimpse of the LCVPs heading back out of the harbor to avoid being stranded on the mud flats that formed as the tide pulled away from the shore. There would be no turning back now.

"First Squad, form up over here," Corporal Tyne was shouting with his Texan twang, "but stay down we're still taking sniper fire."

"Are we all here?" Tyne asked.

"We will be soon. I can see Hoyt's fire team dragging themselves up from the rear," Walters grunted sarcastically.

"You guys better hurry or you're gonna' miss the war," Tyne shouted.

"Wouldn't that be a shame," Corporal Hoyt echoed back.

"Anyone missing?" Smitty inquired.

"No, thank God we all made it this far."

"No thanks to those lousy North Koreans. Either we're lucky or they're just lousy shots. Either way I ain't complainin'," Billy stammered.

"Maybe you were just out of their range," Walters said echoing more sarcasm.

Suddenly, a new barrage of sniper fire greeted the Marines.

"That's crap," Billy blurted out, "look at my helmet."

Sure enough there was a brand new crease on the side of Billy's helmet from a round that hadn't penetrated the steel.

"Well at least some of this Government Issue they gave us works," Flores said in an effort to insert some humor into a very serious situation.

"Can it, you guys, we still got a war to fight. A lot of that fire is coming from that building up ahead. I believe they've got some automatic weapons there and we've got to knock 'em out before they open up on those Marines on our left flank," Tyne ordered. "Smitty and Murphy, take your fire teams around to their right. Hoyt take your guys around to the left, and the rest of us will try to draw fire from here."

On the edge of town, Smitty saw the building in question. It was ideally situated, giving a clear line of fire in every direction facing the beach. Little spurts of gunfire spit from the windows every now and then in an attempt to disguise the fully automatic power of the weapons inside.

"This is a clever trap designed to lure us in, then open fire on us,"

Smitty said. "CJ, I want you to go back and point out this building to our Mortar Section and have 'em drop a few shells into that spider's nest."

Smitty, Jimbo, and Walters watched as CJ stealthily worked his way back toward the beach while Gordon Murphy's fire team slid into positions on their flank.

"Look!" Smitty shouted, "I can see one of them in the window pointing his machine gun in our direction." As Smitty stood up to assess the situation, rapid fire spurted from the automatic weapon belching out a trail of tiny puffs of dust leading to their positions. Smitty dove into a prone position just as an ear piercing scream rang out from his left flank. He watched Corporal Murphy's body as it seemed to rise up then fall to the rhythm of the chattering machine gun. Murphy rolled over on his back, blood gushing from his head and torso. Smitty didn't need a corpsman to tell him that Gordon Murphy was dead.

His .30 caliber carbine trembled in his hands as he leveled his sights at the figure in the window frame above. The moment of decision had arrived all too soon. His mind swarmed with thoughts of right and wrong. His finger wrapped around the trigger, but the pressure wasn't there. A burst of gun fire came from the window, striking the ground in front of his fire team. Smitty rose to his feet again. Now the decision was made. His eyes closed momentarily as his rifle recoiled five times, the butt cutting sharply into his shoulder but the real pain was not in his body - it was in his sub-conscious mind. Smitty suddenly slammed forward, face down on the ground, with bullets buzzing all around him like a swarm of pist-off bumble bees. Jimbo had taken him down with a tackle that would have made his football coach proud.

"What was the first thing I advised you to do when we were aboard ship?" Jimbo asked.

Smitty answered a little groggily. "Keep my head down? Was that it?"

"Yeah, rule number one—keep your head down," Jimbo said as the mortar rounds came screaming overhead, crashing onto the building ahead obliterating it.

"Thanks, Jimbo. It's like I said before, you should be in charge here."

"Don't worry about it, kid, you killed him—but you sure scared the hell out of me doin' it. What took you so long?"

"I guess I spent too much time thinking, Jimbo."

"But you did good. You saved a lot of Marines lives, Smitty," Jimbo reassured him.

"Yeah, I know, I'm becoming a pro—and I'm still alive, thanks to you."

The words, *You killed him,* reverberated inside Smitty's head as he stared at Murphy's lifeless body lying on the ground in front of him. Silent tears welled up and rolled down his cheeks. It was over now. And thanks to Corporal Murphy, the ultimate decision was easier than he thought it would be. As Jimbo said, he had saved some of his other buddies' lives. It was his first kill and he was certain now it wasn't going to be his last.

However it would be a long time before he wiped the last stray tear from the corners of his clouded eyes.

~Chapter~

TWENTY

A light rain had begun as the Marines made their way, house by house and street by street, through the city of Inchon. Small pockets of resistance were still being encountered, but the flare-ups were quickly disposed of by the cautious Marines. The enemy, what was left of them, was steadily high-tailing it out of Inchon heading toward the South Korean capital of Seoul, where they could find support from the larger concentration of NKPA assembled there.

By noon the Marines had completely taken Inchon and had accomplished all of the major objectives of their first day of fighting. Marine casualties were far below what had been anticipated. Nevertheless, there were still too many for the Marines to accept.

The job of mopping up in Inchon was left to a South Korean ROK Regiment, as the Marines swept closer to Kimpo Airfield and from there on toward the Han River. However they soon discovered that the bridges over the Han had been blown up by the fleeing NKPA, so they crossed the river on LVTs that were originally developed for use on land or water. The LVTs had tank-like tractor treads and could carry about 20 fully equipped Marines at one time. The going became very slow for a while and the Marines who had landed in the second wave at Inchon were catching up to Fox Company, as were elements of the Seventh Army Division.

After crossing the Han, the action began to increase as scattered units of the North Korean Peoples Army attempted more delaying actions against the pursuing Marines.

Fox Company, now located to the south of Seoul, was taking the brunt of the trapped enemy's hopeless attempt to free itself from inevitable extinction.

Tyne's First Squad was halted by a machine gun nest to their left. Corporal Tyne was discussing his plan to knock it out when they saw an American Soldier crawling slowly across the ground. He appeared to be working his way toward the bunker. Suddenly, he rose up and lobbed two grenades in the direction of the enemy. One very neatly entered an open slot from which an enemy gun protruded. They could hear the screams from the North Koreans inside as it imploded. The American soldier immediately collapsed backward to the ground.

"Come on Marines," Corporal Tyne shouted, "let's finish them off."

They reached the summit of a small rise pouring point blank fire into the impotent enemy bunker. Doc Blake ran to attend to the wounded soldier. Eckles stepped over the body of a dead North Korean lying on the ground and pumped two quick shots into the backs of two North Koreans who were fleeing to the east.

"That's two Commies that we won't have to deal with later," Eckles exclaimed.

When First Squad came back down off the ridge they watched as Blake bandaged the young soldier's right arm and shoulder.

"You're gonna' be OK now, kid. You got a million dollar wound, so now you'll have a Purple Heart and a ticket out of this place," Blake smiled at him.

With blood spattered on his face it was difficult to interpret the young man's reaction to Doc's words.

"What's your name, soldier?" Smitty asked, as his comrades came running up to join him."

An army lieutenant answered for him. "He's Private Woodrow Philip Jackson," he said.

"The third?" Smitty exclaimed exuberantly.

"How did you know that?" the wounded soldier asked.

"Hey guys, this is our old buddy from Hotel Street. How you doin', kid?"

"I don't know. I've never been wounded before. Have you?" Jackson asked hesitantly.

"Oh yes, we Marines are under strict orders to get wounded at least once a day just to show how tough we are," Walters chuckled.

The young soldier smiled. "Do you think that HASP guy is going to get me when I get back?" he asked, recognizing Smitty and Walters.

"I don't think that HASP guy is going to get anybody for a long time to come," Smitty told him assuredly while smiling at Walters.

"I just gave you a shot for pain, so you're going to feel drowsy in a little while, Jackson," Doc told him.

Looking at his lieutenant the private said, "I guess you're going to have to replace me aren't you, Sir?"

"They don't have anyone in the whole United States Army who can replace you, Private Jackson, so don't worry about it," Jimbo said.

"He's right, Private Jackson, and what's more I'm putting your name up for a Bronze Star," his lieutenant said, as he scrawled Jackson's name in his notebook.

As his fellow soldiers carried him back toward the beach, Walters called out to him, shouting, "And when we get back don't forget you still owe us five bucks."

As evening approached the 100 degree heat of the day escaped into the atmosphere, and the sprinkles of rain that had begun to fall again felt pleasantly cool. The humid temperatures continued to drop until the Marines were forced to put on their field jackets and ponchos. Lieutenant Peterson finally gave the order that they had all been waiting for.

"We'll stop to eat chow here," he ordered. "And if you think today was bad, wait and see what the North Koreans have in store for us tomorrow," the lieutenant quickly added, then paused for a moment.

"Captain Colson has us on point tomorrow morning, so we will be leading the other companies toward Seoul in an all out offensive. This enemy feels like cornered rats right now, so expect the worst from them and give them your best. Tonight, we will assume a defensive posture so stay alert. Dig four-man foxholes and try to get some sleep. You will be on fifty per cent watch, which means that half of you will be awake at all times during the night. Is that understood?"

Walters and Smitty decided to take the first watch while Jimbo and CJ napped.

"From what I've seen of this place, it ain't worth fighting over. What are we doing here?" Smitty casually asked Walters.

"Principles, people's rights, and peace in the world are why we're here. Possessions, power, and pride are the reasons the North Koreans are here. And geography plays a major role in all of it," Walters answered very profoundly.

"I don't understand what you mean by geography?" Smitty queried.

"Well, Korea juts out into the Pacific Ocean very close to Japan and, tactically speaking, it would be an advantage to any Communist regime as a strategic jumping off point for any future wars with democratic nations."

"I see," said Smitty.

He really didn't, but he didn't want to say so. And, besides, what

Walters said made far more sense than fighting over an underdeveloped country whose rice patties smelled like outhouses.

There was still some light left in the evening sky as the moon played hide and seek with the swollen clouds. The rain had let up, but Walters and Smitty didn't want to get too comfortable or they too might fall asleep. They continued to whisper softly so they wouldn't keep Jimbo and CJ awake.

"I've always admired your ring, Walters, especially now that I know a little more about it. It must be very important to you," Smitty said smiling.

"I believe you know that this was a gift from my father, Smitty. He meant a lot to me. We were very close. It is the only thing I have to remember him by since he was killed. My father was more than just a great man. He was my coach, my teacher, and my mentor."

"You say he was killed. What happened?" Smitty asked, taking advantage of the opportunity to learn more about his elusive friend's background.

"I don't like to talk about it, but maybe if you read this you will understand," Walters said.

Walters pulled a crumpled, aging copy of a newspaper clipping from his wallet and handed it to Smitty who strained his tired eyes to read the words in the waning evening light.

A tragedy struck Eagle County just before midnight last night. John Walters, celebrated coach of the victorious Custer Devil Dogs, who won the State Championship last year, died at Eagle County General Hospital early this morning from gunshot wounds. He left his home late last night to go to the Night Owl convenience store and never returned home again. The police report indicated that upon entering, he discovered that the store was completely unattended. He went to the dairy section where he heard a muffled sound that drew his attention and he saw Laura Peters, the night clerk, lying on the floor with her hands bound behind her back.

Her eyes signaled to him that there was still danger lurking in the store. Then, a man came rushing out of the back room with a gun in his hand and John Walters pounced on him, knocking him to the floor. The man staggered to his feet and fired two shots into Coach Walters, one striking him in the left shoulder, the other in his lower rib cage. Then, the man turned and pointed his pistol at Miss Peters, but before he could fire,

John Walters, who the assailant must have thought was dead, jumped on his back, disarming him. The two men struggled for possession of the weapon and the coach won. Just then, another man, Earl Hines, the store manager, came out of the back room as if he were being pushed from behind. The second assailant, who followed behind him, fired a shot at John Walters striking him in the groin. John Walters raised the weapon and killed him instantly with a shot to the center of his chest. The first assailant then jumped on Walters and, in the struggle, more shots were fired and both men were found lying on the floor, dying, when police arrived.

When interviewed, Earl Hines said that were it not for John Walters the intruders would certainly have killed them both, referring to Miss Peters and himself. He and Miss Peters gave the report to the police, but she was too frightened and was unable to comment to this reporter. An ambulance rushed John Walters to the hospital where he spent several hours in an unstable condition before the doctors pronounced him dead at 6:07 this morning.

John Walters was a wonderful teacher, a great community leader, and the husband of Jessie Walters. He leaves behind two sons, PFC George Walters USMC and a younger son, 15 year old Winston Walters. John Walters, a Marine during WWII, lived and died like a hero. This sudden and tragic end to a gentle and noble man numbed all who had the pleasure of living in the same world with him. This community will sorely miss him.

"That happened while I was stationed at Quantico. I went home on leave for the funeral and was transferred to Hawaii shortly after that."

Smitty very slowly handed the newspaper clipping back to Walters.

"Tell me something, Walters, do you believe in God?" Smitty asked very casually.

Walters smiled back at him through the darkness of the night.

"That's a strange question to be asking me especially now. Why do you ask?"

"I don't know I guess I've been wondering more about it - you know with all we've been going through and all that we've seen and done."

"Still thinking about killing that North Korean sniper is that it?"

"Yeah, that and all this mess were in and whatever else lies ahead. I just wonder what God would think about all this crap."

"So you're asking if I believe in God." Does that mean that you do or that you don't, Smitty?"

"I guess I just don't know for sure and I just wondered what you thought."

"Well Smitty I think the important question isn't whether I believe in God but whether God believes in me."

Smitty leaned back and stared at the starry sky above. The ever elusive and mysterious Walters hadn't let him down and now Smitty puzzled more over the response Walters thru back at him than the question he had originally asked.

The always hungry Marines crouched in their foxholes and nibbled on crackers from their ration boxes. Overhead, a yellow crescent moon against a sky of scattered clouds peeked out at Smitty looking occasionally like a wedge of lemon on a plate filled with his favorite southern fried catfish. It was just a fantasy, but it reminded him for a moment of real food and especially of being home.

It was relatively quiet the remainder of that night and, despite the intermittent rain showers, a few of the young Marines did manage to get a little sleep.

~CHAPTER~

TWENTY ONE

The rain showers were slowing to a halt as daylight peeked over the horizon revealing a desolate countryside. First Squad scrambled to its feet, wet and hungry. They repacked their ponchos and blankets, lit a fire, and heated some C-rations. Hogging down a hurried breakfast, they reassessed the ragged terrain that lay ahead.

In the distance, they saw the movement of scattered concentrations of troops they knew were not their own. Less than a quarter of a mile to the front they saw a cluster of Russian-made T-34 tanks. Karlstrom immediately radioed back to headquarters, requesting air support to meet the threat that hindered their advance. Soon, two Corsairs swooped down. One dropped napalm on the lead tank. The Marines on the ground watched the jellied gasoline encompass the tank with flames. The other Corsair strafed the NKPA troops straggling behind them. The planes successfully knocked out three of the enemy tanks, while American tanks moved up to destroy the rest. The Marines cheered, seeing the fire power of their weapons arsenal working so effectively.

Fox Company advanced forward but ran into so much heavy resistance that they had to radio back to get support from Dog Company. With their assistance, Fox was able to stave off enemy forces determined to penetrate their lines.

From their vantage point, the Marines noticed that the local terrain was much flatter than it was to the north, where mountainous peaks could be seen in the distance. The flatter land and warmer climate was probably the reason South Korea was better adapted to an agrarian society. The other thing they noticed were the pungent fumes that crept into their

142

nostrils from the human excrement used to fertilize the rice patties along the countryside.

"Damned if I'm ever gonna' eat rice again," Wilson mumbled, trying to hold his breath.

As the Marines moved closer to Seoul, they could hear the constant whine of American artillery shells screaming overhead before exploding in the distance. Seoul was now under constant and relentless siege.

Fox Company started taking in small arms fire from a hill ahead of them. Karlstrom radioed Dog Company asking them to circle around the enemy stronghold to the right while Fox made their way around the left side of the hill. On the other side, the men of Fox Company halted and watched as enemy soldiers, male and female, stripped and changed into civilian clothes that had been concealed in their packs. They were hoping to mingle in with the civilian population and escape back to the north unscathed. Dog Company flushed out the remaining snipers on the hill, while Fox rounded up prisoners.

Karlstrom radioed headquarters asking them to send ROK troops to take the prisoners off their hands. Before they arrived, the Marines picked up more soldiers straggling along the roads. By now the weary enemy soldiers who had been so cocksure and confident just a few weeks before were tired, hungry, and more than willing to surrender. The ROK soldiers beat and brutalized the NKPA prisoners while interrogating them for information regarding their remaining troop strengths.

"God, these people are savages. Are you sure we're fighting on the right side?" Smitty asked Walters.

A ROK officer overheard the question and politely interrupted them, speaking in fluent English.

"I am an interpreter and I can understand your consternation," he said.

"Consternation? Hell, you speak better English than I do. Where are you from?" Smitty asked.

"Allow me to introduce myself," the lieutenant said, trying to be very precise with his pronunciations. "I am Lieutenant Kim Dong Po. I was born in Seoul and attended the university there. I have studied English since I was a young boy. I learned a lot of slang from American GIs when I was a member of the Seoul Police Department. The NKPA attacked our city and slaughtered my people indiscriminately—not caring whether they were young or old, male or female. I joined the ROK Army to help stop the atrocities."

Smitty kept glancing over at Walters, who seemed to be a little perplexed, as the lieutenant spoke. The lieutenant continued. "I can understand why my people are so vindictive and I also understand why you don't understand—but, in time, you will."

"I'm delighted to meet you, Kim. My friends call me Smitty. I guess the thing I don't understand is how the North could treat you so unjustly in the first place. You guys are brothers and cousins whose only crime is living on opposite sides of a controversial line dividing North and South," Smitty responded.

"While I was at the university I studied your American history and I thought the same as you when I read about your Civil War, Smitty."

As the ROK soldiers marched the prisoners back toward Inchon, Smitty removed his helmet and scratched his head. "I guess he told me," he said to Walters. "This guy sounded like the Korean version of you. Did you hear him with his fifty dollar words—consternation—indiscriminately—atrocities—vindictive? Hell, I think this guy's got a PhD. For a minute there I thought I'd need an interpreter to understand the interpreter."

Walters just smiled and shook his head. "Maybe you just need to read more books, Smitty."

The Marines could tell by the ever-increasing din of the big shells landing in front of them that they were on the doorstep of Seoul. The temperature, by noon, had soared into the 100 degree range. Only the occasional skirmishes with die hard North Koreans kept them from thinking about their miseries and bodily needs.

The Marines stopped at a well next to a farm house to fill their canteens. It was the first time they had stopped moving since dawn.

"Company Headquarters tells me that we are going to be running into heavy resistance soon, so be prepared to reload often," Lieutenant Peterson advised.

"What does he mean 'heavy resistance soon'? What the hell does he think we been doing all day, playin' games?" Billy muttered sarcastically.

A truck from the rear pulled up alongside them and the driver advised that each Marine take extra bandoliers of ammunition from inside the truck.

Gunfire suddenly erupted again and the Marines took cover as the truck turned and sped back toward Inchon. A few hundred feet away, it burst into flames and exploded.

"Damn, these guys are gettin' serious," someone commented, as the Marines returned fire.

Their forward progress could now be measured in feet and occasional yards instead of miles, as they slugged their way forward at a snail's pace. Both Dog and Fox Companies were reporting numerous casualties, and

Doc Blake soon discovered that he had a full time job tending to the wounded.

By evening, the Marines were exhausted not only from the battle but the blistering heat as well. Things calmed down as they set themselves up in defensive positions again. Karlstrom reported that losses from both companies were quite heavy. A sergeant from Second Platoon of Fox Company and several other Marines had been evacuated, as was Brad Butler of Billy Hoyt's fire team. Jimbo received a flesh wound on the calf of his left leg, but he refused treatment.

"I've gotta' stay here and look after you, Smitty," he insisted. But Doc Blake was even more insistent as he applied a dressing to his wound.

"Lieutenant Peterson was telling me that President Truman has re-labeled this mess a 'Police Action,'" Walters said. "I guess he's still knocking himself out trying to convince the American public that this isn't a war. Politicians are strange animals," Walters added.

"Well, if this is a 'Police Action' then I want policeman's pay," Thomas declared.

By now the Marines were closing in on the outskirts of Seoul under intermittent sniper fire. Suddenly an enemy mortar shell landed close by and they heard a familiar voice cry out, "Corpsman, Corpsman, I've been hit." It sounded like Wilson. Smitty and Doc Blake advanced cautiously and found Wilson lying on his face.

"I think I've been hit bad, really bad," he moaned to Doc.

"Where?" Doc asked.

"I got it in my hip," he said groaning. "I can feel the blood running down my leg. You gotta get me outta here."

Smitty and Doc Blake carefully rolled him over onto his side. Doc examined him carefully. "Yeah, it's bad," Blake said. "Worst I've ever seen. I think I'm going to have to amputate his leg, Smitty. Give me your bayonet and hold him steady."

"Oh God no, don't cut off my leg," Wilson pleaded.

"Get up you shithead," Smitty ordered. "You're not wounded. The impact of the mortar shell must have thrown you on your face and a piece of shrapnel tore a hole in your canteen. That's just warm water running down your pant leg."

PFC Wilson reached down and rubbed the wet area then looked at his hand.

"You're damned lucky it didn't hit you in the ass or you'd have severe brain damage," Smitty exclaimed.

"You guys won't tell anybody about this will you?" Wilson pleaded shamefully as he struggled to his feet.

"We'll see. That depends on you," Blake answered, winking at Smitty.

Darkness was rapidly capturing the light of day, and Lieutenant Peterson decided that this was as good a place as any to settle in and rest before their assault on Seoul early the next morning. Smitty and Jimbo cut a foxhole out of the rich and fertile soil on the outskirts of the big city. Since the fighting had let up considerably, the lieutenant ordered everyone to be on fifty percent watch for the rest of the night. The break in the action was welcomed by everyone and sleep was a luxury that was long overdue. Smitty insisted again on taking the first watch.

Temperatures were dropping, cooling his body from the extreme daytime heat. In the distance he could see and hear heavy artillery barrages as they slammed into the South Korean capital of Seoul, softening the enemy defenses. A chilling rain helped to give the illusion of a sudden thunderstorm as flashes in the sky from the exploding phosphorous shells illuminated the clouds overhead. It reminded him of the heavy bombardment at Inchon days before.

Overhead, the eerie whistling of rockets with death as their passenger performed their contradictory mission of taking lives while saving many more at the same time.

Jimbo lay sleeping soundly beside him, his poncho wrapped tightly around his head and shoulders to shelter him from the rain. Smitty watched over him with great pride knowing that Jimbo trusted him with his life.

In the morning, Fox Company circled around to the north side of Seoul. Their assignment was to cut off fleeing enemy soldiers and try to find American prisoners who were captured earlier in the invasion. A South Korean prison on the outskirts of Seoul was their new objective. They knew it was located somewhere dead ahead of them, but it was still slow going as they cleared out nests of recalcitrant North Koreans along the way.

Fox Company completely surrounded the prison to prevent the escape of anyone who might still be inside. Entering the building, First Squad felt danger lurking behind every door. They heard moaning coming from a jail cell and discovered an emaciated man who looked like he hadn't eaten in many weeks. It was an American Soldier who had been captured in the south, near Pusan, and had been abandoned by the fleeing enemy. By some miracle he was still alive and able to speak.

"They've all gone," he said weakly, staring with lifeless eyes. It was as if his gaze was fixed on a distant point, many miles away. "Look in the court yard," he whispered, as Doc Blake attempted to help him, not knowing where to begin.

"The tyrants murdered them just before you got here. They must have thought I was dead."

In the courtyard, the other Marines had already found what the confused soldier had been alluding to. Death was everywhere. South Korean civilians mixed in with American soldiers, minus their weapons and boots, were stacked like cords of firewood—so many that the Marines could not count. The stench was nauseating. The sight was unforgettable. It was just as the South Korean interpreter had tried to describe. Actually seeing it was far more horrific than the ROK lieutenant could ever have articulated. Many Marines, who were already traveling on nearly empty stomachs, threw up at the sight. This scene justified the animosity and pure hatred that the South Koreans felt toward their former countrymen.

"I'll never question these people's sense of justice again," Smitty announced, stepping away from the building into fresher air.

~CHAPTER~

TWENTY TWO

With the Marines and Army mopping up in Seoul, to the jubilant cheers of its citizenry, and with the NKPA on the run, the need for further combat dwindled. All of the captured North Korean soldiers had been turned over to the ROK army for internment in prisoner of war camps. Unfortunately, about 30,000 of the original 70,000 enemy forces had escaped back into North Korea.

That evening, the Marines were treated to hot chow catered by the United States Government. As bad as it was, it tasted like an epicurean delight compared to the vacuum packed, tasteless government issued C-rations they had been eating for the past several weeks.

Afterward the Marines began retracing their steps back to Inchon where ships were waiting to take them to a yet unknown destination somewhere in Korea.

Along the route, they met up with a group of young Marines who looked like their dungarees were still fresh out of the box. They obviously hadn't seen a day of combat and were there as replacements for other men who had been killed or wounded in battle.

Wilson and Thomas greeted them as they arrived. Sitting them down along the roadside, Wilson began: "The President of South Korea and the President of the United States are at Inchon waiting for us. We are all going to be decorated with a new specially designed medal for bravery. Then they plan to fly us to an exotic island for two weeks of fun and relaxation with lots of cold beer and hot dancing girls in skimpy costumes. After that, we'll be flown back to the states on luxury air liners with first class accommodations. When we get there, a ticker tape parade will stretch from San Francisco to LA, all in our honor."

"Really?" an astonished young Marine, who reminded Smitty of their Army buddy, Private Jackson, responded.

Doc Blake shook his index finger at Wilson and gave him a warning gaze. "Don't forget that hole in your canteen, Wilson. Doc reminded him. That shut him up immediately.

Smitty and Walters just shook their heads and walked away. "Those 'Kings of Scuttlebutt' never quit, do they? When they get back home they're probably going to run for public office and wind up in Washington, DC," Walters said with a wry grin.

Their humor, though often unusual and out of place, was actually good medicine for the morale of the battle weary Marines.

Along the roadside, as they made their way back to Inchon, the occasional corpse of a North Korean soldier or the remains of a burned out T-34 tank would appear as a reminder of some of the costly tolls of war. The most gratifying sights of all, however, were the South Korean civilians who greeted them all along the way waving South Korean and American flags. Women and children came out of hiding to hug the blushing Marines.

Others who had fled the communists earlier now felt that it was safe to go back home again. They clogged the roads, leading their ox carts loaded with personal possessions, as they headed back toward Seoul.

"These people have learned the true value of freedom first hand," Walters said, as he and other Marines gave the children candy and gum from their C-ration packages.

The docks at Inchon were swelling with wounded and dead Marines who would be the first to deploy on ships back to Japan. The more seriously wounded had already been flown out from Kimpo Airfield.

Back on board the troop transports, the Marines eagerly flocked to the comfort of the bunks that they had previously found so unbearable. They stood in long lines to get into lukewarm showers that felt much more soothing than the intermittent rain showers they had become accustomed to in Korea. When they got further out to sea they took deep breathes to flush their sinuses, ridding them of the pungent stench of death and the foul clinging smell of rice patties.

Lieutenant Peterson informed them that they were being transported to the east side of the peninsula to make another invasion. This time they would be landing in North Korea at a place called Wonsan. The objective was to cut off and destroy the remaining 30,000 NKPA before they could re-group and re-arm.

It didn't take long for the shipboard boredom to set in again, and the restless Marines began to seek out something to do besides the usual card games that were ever present below deck.

A company of ROK troops on board provided some welcomed entertainment. On the upper decks, they competed in a form of Indian Arm wrestling. Two contestants clasped their right hand in the right hand of their opponent as if shaking hands. Then they extended the outer side of their right foot so that it was parallel and touching the outer side of the right foot of their adversary. From a crouched position with their right foot firmly planted, they would twist and pull, trying to knock the other person off balance. The ultimate goal was to get the opponent to move his planted right foot. These contests could be as short as one minute or go on for five minutes, depending on the skill of the contenders. Once the opponent was forced to move his right foot, in an effort to maintain his balance, the test of skills ended.

After a while the ROKs enticed the Marines to join in, challenging them to compete. Smitty watched as the shorter in stature and craftier South Koreans maneuvered until they could slam their right wrist behind the knee of the taller Marines, forcing their knee to buckle throwing them off balance. Smitty studied the technique as the South Koreans continued to take advantage using their lower center of gravity. They gloated at being able to outsmart their larger opponents.

Then, Smitty had a startling revelation. If he forced the Koreans into a more upright stance he could take away their advantage. Smitty challenged the South Korean champion to a duel.

On the word 'Go' Smitty quickly stood upright from a squat position, turning his wrist he pulled his Korean opponent's shorter arm toward him then over his right shoulder, as he stepped back with his left foot, to the full extent of his longer arm. The shorter Korean immediately lost his balance and hastily fell forward, stumbling across the deck, almost going overboard.

After that, the Koreans lost incentive and discontinued the games for the rest of the voyage - and boredom settled back in again.

Smitty retired to his favorite place—the furthest point back on the stern of the ship. It was quieter there, like the roof on the brig at Marine Barracks in Pearl Harbor. He looked for solace, hoping it would help rid his mind of the boredom and confinement of shipboard living. He sat on the deck and leaned his back against the aft deck superstructure. He watched the wake as it swirled forming frothy white waves that left a lengthy trail behind the ship then closed his eyes. He dozed off for a while thinking of Nani, but could find no lasting solace there. The haunting faces of the young boys in the old munitions barn at Camp Catlin, the atrocities to innocent Korean civilians, the dead American soldiers in the courtyard at Seoul, and his fellow Marines who were killed in action kept intruding his mind's eye.

The sheer injustice of it all haunted his memories. He heard a sound and awoke to the sight of Eckles standing by the rail.

"Sorry if I startled you, Smitty, but I was hoping I'd find you somewhere on this ship. I wanted to ask if you knew much about guns," Eckles said as he withdrew a hand gun from under his dungaree jacket. "Remember when we knocked out the machine gun nest on the way to Seoul?"

"Yeah, I remember," Smitty answered.

"Well, I pulled out this gun and tried to shoot one of those fleeing North Koreans, but all this damn thing did was go click. I knew it was loaded. I checked it again later after I shot them both with my M1. That scared the hell out of me, thinking I might have relied on it in a really tight situation."

Smitty took the gun from Eckles and examined it. "It's a beauty. Where did you get it?"

"I bought it at a pawn shop before I left for Korea. My dad said I ought to carry a hand gun because it might come in handy in a foxhole—maybe even save my life."

After looking it over very carefully Smitty said, "It's a shame. Didn't you test it? This gun will never fire the way it is. It has a faulty firing pin mechanism."

"Yeah, you're right, Smitty, I should have tested it, but I guess I just assumed it would work," Eckles said.

Smitty confirmed that it was loaded then he raised the gun up pointing it over the stern of the ship and squeezed the trigger twice, but all it did was go click, click.

"You had best hang onto it and try to get it fixed when we get back home. I think it's worth keeping, but in that condition it could never save anybody's life except the guy you were pointing it at," Smitty said.

"Thanks, Smitty," Eckles said and stuffed the gun back inside his jacket.

The word soon spread aboard ship that they would be out to sea longer than expected. The message could not have come from either Thomas or Wilson because it was true. Mines in the Sea of Japan left over from World War II blocked their path to Wonsan Harbor—a fact that had been overlooked by MacArthur's Intelligence Command. Mine sweepers had to be brought in to clear the way before the Marines could land. The transport ships were forced to see-saw up and down the coast behind the mine sweepers until they cleared and detonated the mines in their path. It took them several valuable game changing days in what was being jokingly referred to by the Navy and Marines as "Operation Yoyo".

CJ, Walters, Billy, Tyne, and Jimbo joined Smitty and Eckles on the back deck to make sure they had heard about the extended delay in reaching Wonsan.

"Why do we do it? Billy queried suddenly.

Everyone stared at Billy with bewildered looks on their faces.

"Why do we do what? CJ responded.

"Oh, I don't know, I guess I was just thinking out loud," Billy said. "But I always wondered why we keep putting ourselves in harm's way for people who can't get their shit together for themselves."

"There's a lot of evil in this world Billy and it won't just go away by itself. Left alone it'll just get worse and eventually wind up in our back yard," CJ said.

"Yeah, but why us?"

"Were you drafted, Billy?" Walters asked.

"No, not really," Billy answered.

"Neither were we. Jimbo and Tyne both reenlisted. Somebody in this world has to do something besides close their eyes and complain about injustices and I guess we're it," Walters said looking up from the diary he was writing in.

A Canadian ship caught up to their transport and pulled alongside. A voice from the ship announced over their public address system that they were carrying mail and wanted to shoot a line across so they could convey the mail bags to them via a cargo trolley. As they pulled away to head back south the Canadians called out, "Good luck to you Yanks ashore!" while the Marines waved back in gratitude for precious words from home.

At mail call Smitty got two letters, both were from Nani. As he hurried away to open them he heard CJ's name being called. When he arrived on the afterdeck he sat down with his back against the bulkhead. Smitty checked the postage on his letters and hurriedly opened the one that had the earliest postmark.

My Dearest Smitty,

I pray that you are reading my letter and that you are safe from harm. The newspapers say that the First Marine Division has successfully landed at a place called Inchon. I can only assume you are with them. Lea and Lani think about you and CJ everyday and pray for your safe return.

I started my classes at the University a few weeks ago, and I am just now adjusting to college life. Kee keeps talking about joining the Marines and we expect something will happen any day now.

The trial of Mr. Needham is due to start soon and everyone expects that he will be found guilty. I remember seeing him hanging out around our school occasionally but thought nothing of it. He appeared to be very pleasant, though down on his luck. Hardly the type who would do such a terrible thing, but how can anyone be sure?

I will write again soon.
All my love,

Nani

Smitty hurriedly opened the second letter. Enclosed with the letter was a stick of gum. He popped it into his mouth and read:

My Dearest Smitty,

Just a short note to keep you up on what is happening here. The newspapers are applauding the successes at Inchon and Seoul. Mama Ahue keeps telling me not to worry and that you are still safe. Then she adds, "Mama Ahue knows these things." She is a wonderful person and she keeps telling me that she loves us both very much.

I just heard on the radio that General MacArthur has made a decision to pursue the North Korean People's Army back into North Korea, and he is predicting that the conflict there will be over by Christmas. All of us here are certainly hoping that is true. Please write to me when you can.

Love, always and forever,
Nani

The sweet taste of the chewing gum brought back visions of the first day he had met Nani. Smitty leaned back and felt the fresh autumn breeze flow across his face. He closed his eyes and allowed his thoughts to return to that sandy beach at Waikiki. It was then that he realized that he missed Nani far more than he would ever have imagined. A war that he had felt eager to participate in had succeeded in separating him from the people that he truly loved. Soon he drifted asleep to the sounds of the quiet waves swirling behind the ship.

~CHAPTER~

TWENTY THREE

By the time the ship reached Wonsan Harbor, the NKPA had already funneled their way back into the mountains of North Korea. It appeared that General MacArthur's second strategic invasion had been foiled. Military intelligence should have foreseen the presence of mines in the Sea of Japan left there since WWII.

As the Marines came peacefully ashore, instead of encountering an awaiting enemy force, they were greeted by Army troops who had traveled over land and arrived ahead of them. To their further embarrassment, the USO and the comedian Bob Hope were there as well. Bob delighted in taunting them with his satirical humor, jokingly flaunting his ability to land ahead of the Marines. It appeared to be funnier to belittle the Marines for the SNAFU than it was to blame the so-called 'Intelligence Department' who sent them into that mess in the first place. However, the Marines took no offense to Bob who was just doing his job entertaining the GIs, however the Army troops were truly amused.

The Marines didn't have time to stay for the entirety of Bob's show. Their job wasn't over yet. Now they would be pursuing the enemy to the north instead of intercepting them coming up from the south. They quickly loaded onto the open flat cars of coal burning freight trains that could easily be mistaken for relics of America's old west.

The train chugged up the rugged coastline toward the seaport town of Hamhung. As they moved along the rails, the Marines were savagely showered by cinders, smoke, and ash spewing back into their eyes and nostrils, occasionally burning their skin, making an otherwise unpleasant journey unbearable.

"Traveling Marine Corps style again," a Marine grumbled.

Eighth Army, still at Seoul, received new orders as well. They were advancing north on trucks along the west side of the peninsula toward Pyongyang, the capital of North Korea.

When the Marines eventually arrived at Hamhung, looking more like coal miners than warriors, there was a lot of complaining about the waste of time it had taken to shower before leaving the ship.

"I would swear that I'm at least two shades darker than when we left Wonsan, wouldn't you agree, Smitty?" Eckles taunted facetiously.

"I think we all are," Smitty answered with a chuckle.

"Don't think you're kidding me, Smitty. I believe you're beginning to like your new look, but you'll never catch up to me no matter how hard you try," Eckles quipped.

Smitty laughed looking at CJ and Walters whose faces looked as black as they had after the fire at Camp Catlin.

"Looks like we're all equal now, eh Eckles?" Walters said joining in the laughter.

Upon their arrival at Hamhung the Marines were greeted with another grizzly sight. South Korean dissidents and American soldiers who had been captured back in July and August were found inside of caves. The North Koreans had ordered that the caves be sealed shut by bulldozers when they heard that the Americans were advancing close behind them. All of the hundreds of innocents were suffocated. It was a clear violation of the 1949 Geneva Convention that provided safeguards for the wounded prisoners of war and civilians in war zones. The North Korean soldiers were quickly earning the reputation of being ruthless murderers. Smitty decided that day that he would prefer to be killed than ever be taken prisoner.

The Marine's last day of non-combat was a visit to the apple rich orchards near Hamhung, where they gorged themselves with firm, sweet Korean apples, then stored some of them in their field packs for later.

The Marines loaded onto trucks that would carry them closer to the Yalu River separating North Korea from Communist China, but even that luxury was short lived as the Marines were ordered to dismount from the trucks and continue the rest of the way on foot. The Marines stopped in an open area where truck loads of cake were dropped off to honor the birthday of the United States Marine Corps. It was November 10th.

After a brief rest and a short celebration Fox Company moved out again, very cautiously, along a narrow mountain pass that had a steep ridge rising on their right flank and a gradual slope that tapered down into a barren valley to their left. Occasional fire fights were heard toward the head of the column, but nothing of a serious nature until they neared the small town of Hagaru. They halted there, mainly to size up the situation and knock out some pockets of resistance before proceeding any farther north. First Squad took advantage of the opportunity to rest their backs against the side of the down slope to their right. Smitty closed his eyes and allowed thoughts of home to consume the reality of the moment. He heard gunfire in the near distance but closed his mind to the danger. He would deal with that later, he thought.

"First Squad on your feet," Smitty heard a familiar voice cry out. "We're going up this ridge. Seems that the enemy has surrounded one of our flank guards and is in the process of wiping them out."

Smitty responded automatically. With his rifle at port arms he ascended the steep slope, stumbling occasionally on the loose gravel and rocks. A swarm of death-laden steel jacketed "killer bees" suddenly buzzed above their heads, signaling that a welcoming party lay in wait to greet them. Smitty made it to the crest first and began rapidly returning fire so the rest of the squad could reach the peak.

The squad spread out and advanced along the ridge toward the enemy, being cautious not to fire on their own Marines who were in a desperate situation further north along the precipice. The sounds of exploding rifle fire became louder as First Squad moved stealthily ahead. Smitty moved around a large boulder to his right and saw the backs of the enemy soldiers as they fired relentlessly into the ranks of the overwhelmed Marine flank guard. He concealed himself behind the boulder and began picking off one soldier at a time, while the rest of his squad advanced along the ridge doing the same. Smitty called out to the trapped Marines, letting them know that they were there. The enemy soldiers began scattering out across the plateau to the east.

The firing ceased as First Squad joined ranks with the exhausted Marines.

"Where the hell've you guys been?" a surly Marine sergeant with what appeared to be a blanket of blood across the front of his uniform asked with a growl.

It was evident that these guys had been fighting a hopeless battle for some time.

"Did you ever think of surrendering?" Smitty asked facetiously, knowing the answer.

The sergeant gave Smitty a fierce glance then, feeling safe again, he closed his eyes.

First Squad began gathering up the wounded and carrying them down the hill.

Smitty stood the surly sergeant up onto his feet, then turning his back to him, placed the bloody sergeant's arms up over his own shoulders. He wrapped the sergeant's arms around his neck and across his chest, fitting them tightly under his chin.

"Hang on Sarge' this is gonna' be a bumpy ride," Smitty warned.

Smitty bent forward, and with the wounded man strapped tightly to his back, started down the steep incline. They fell several times before reaching the Marines on the main road below, but each time Smitty unhesitatingly started again.

"Leave me here!" the sergeant bellowed.

"Can't leave a brave son-of-a-bitch like you behind Sarge," Smitty bellowed back. When they reached the main road again Smitty went back up to help more wounded.

"Here's another one," Smitty said, glancing over at Blake as he bandaged one of the wounded. "How's the sergeant doing?" he asked.

There was no response from Blake as he shook his head from side to side.

Smitty went back with his head down and rejoined his squad.

Skirmishes with the enemy along the narrow road ahead began to yield unusual results. A group of prisoners were rounded up, and all were wearing new and different battle gear that they had not seen before on the North Koreans. These uniforms were tan in color with a quilted pattern, and their shoes were made from a canvas material like gym shoes. They wore peaked caps with ear flaps that tied under their chins. The language they spoke was quite different, and the interpreters quickly ascertained that these troops were Chinese - not Korean. That information was forwarded to headquarters in Japan, but MacArthur's advisors dismissed this nuance as irrelevant.

Confidence was so high at the American headquarters in Japan that plane loads of fresh turkey with stuffing, mashed potatoes, yams, cranberry sauce, and pumpkin pies were shipped into the war zone for Thanksgiving Day. Rumors, supposedly coming from headquarters, were that the war would be over by Christmas.

All of the grateful Marines reminisced about home as they savored the best meal they had eaten in what seemed to be forever. While eating, they decided to exchange home addresses and telephone numbers.

"Just in case we don't survive this mess, some of us can visit the others families and tell them what went on here. If we all get back safe we can get together somewhere and celebrate," CJ said confidently.

"One thing we know is that when we get back there ain't gonna' be no one who understands what went on here anyway—even if we tell 'em," Flores said.

What the young Americans didn't know was that hidden in the hills above them was a heavy concentration of a brand new enemy—120,000 of them—ten times their own numbers. They were members of the Red Chinese People's Volunteer Army. The PVA, as they were called, had entered into Korea across the Yalu River at night—right under the noses of MacArthur's Intelligence staff in Japan.

What was even worse was that the temperatures had already dropped to 10 degrees below zero. It was the earliest and coldest weather in over a decade in that region. Headquarters had anticipated winter but not this arctic blast and certainly not this early. The Marines were hurriedly issued hooded parkas, leather gloves with wool liners, insulated boots, and an extra pair of heavy socks.

As the narrow road suddenly widened the valley surrounding the town of Yudam-ni opened even wider exposing menacing saw-tooth mountain peaks resembling the gaping jaws of a giant beast.

They had arrived at a place called the Chosin Reservoir. It was an ill-boding site for the Marines who never suspected that such a vast and desolate area had been awaiting them. As far as the eye could see there was no sight of anything alive or green – just a wasteland deprived of any life forms - no trees, no birds, no grass, no shrubs, not even a bush.

"I hate to tell you guys, but this place gives me the creeps." Eckles exclaimed as he kept looking over his shoulders to the left and right at the mountain peaks surrounding them. "It looks to me like these Chinese Reds are sucking us into a trap. Those jagged peaks remind me of snarlin' teeth. I can't help but feel like we might be walking right into the jaws of an angry dragon," Eckles exclaimed.

"Oh chud up, Eckles," Flores shouted. "You been reading too many comic books and you're givin' me the creeps with your snarlin' teeth and angry dragon bull chit."

Fox Company continued advancing further north to the far side of Yudam-ni near the now frozen reservoir before turning west, hopefully to link up with the Eighth Army troops coming up from Pyongyang. The remainder of the First Marine Division stayed in the valley near Yudam-ni, cautiously awaiting the results of the probe to the west.

Snow had begun to fall, only lightly at first, but with the wind gusts factored into the equation even their heavy parkas could not prevail against the mind numbing cold that stalked them.

Rounding a bend in the mountain road ahead, the Marines were suddenly ambushed by a heavy concentration of well-armed PVA, making it impossible to proceed any further. Fox and Easy Companies took to the high ground on the north side of the road to gain better defensive positions in case of a night attack. The ground had become so hard by now that it was impossible to dig foxholes in the already frozen turf. They explored the surfaces of the hill and discovered that there were already bunkers cut into the landscape. This told them that someone had been there before them—and in large numbers. The problem was that almost all of the bunkers faced over the wrong side of the hill, so they reconstructed them as best they could to suit their own purposes.

Looking to the west, they saw movement on a distant hill. A Chinese officer in a light blue quilted coat was watching as the Marines took positions along the ridge lines. Surrounding the officer were a small group of regular soldiers in their now familiar tan quilted coats. The enemy was out of range of their M1 rifles, but the Marines fired at them anyway, perhaps just to try to scare them. The Marines, however, were still unaware of the massive assembly of PVA hidden on the reverse side of that hill.

Karlstrom radioed to the Company Commander, who came up to assess the situation.

"Call in an air strike on that hill," he ordered Karlstrom, "and make sure you have the right coordinates or they may hit us instead of them."

Soon a group of gull winged Corsair fighter-planes were spotted coming in low over the distant hill tops dropping napalm on the Chinese troops across the valley from them. The Marines cheered and waved to the Navy and Marine pilots as they flew past dipping their wings in a salute to the men on the ground.

"That'll learn 'em. Maybe we'll get some sleep tonight after all," Jimbo shouted hopefully.

The snow had been falling steadily for the past few hours, hiding the dreary sky and completely blanketing the valley, making everything glow an eerie white. The Marines settled in facing the last known enemy positions then built small fires to keep warm, heat water for coffee and thaw their canned C-rations.

"This sure as hell ain't like home," one of the guys from Florida who had been fascinated by the snow falling all around him commented as he kept inching closer and closer to the fire. The temperature continued to drop to -20 by midnight, but the Marines hardly noticed as their adrenalin surged at the sound of the Chinese bugles that reverberated off the snow laden hills, signaling the first wave of attacks by the PVA. Hundreds of Chinese massed from the base of the hill in front of them, throwing concussion grenades and firing American made Thompson sub-machine guns into the Marine lines while shouting in broken English, "Marine, tonight you die."

At first they appeared suddenly like mystical shadows on the surface of the snow. One moment they seemed to be there and the next they were gone, only to reappear again somewhere else. The confused Marines fired randomly into the suicidal mass of humanity as fast as they could reload. Then came the second wave followed by the third. Finally, the fourth wave broke through the Marine lines at several points, and Marines were there to greet them engaging in hand to hand combat while machine gun barrels glowed red hot. Marines rose to their knees, lobbing grenades into the air above the advancing enemy, creating air bursts that showered the Chinese with deadly shrapnel.

The attacks raged on during the night and then, just as suddenly as it had begun, the Marines heard the bugles again and all went silent. The Marines took advantage of the lull in the action as orders came down the line to reload and prepare for the next onslaught—but it didn't come. The Chinese had withdrawn to regroup and hide before dawns early light knowing that the Corsair pilots would be able to spot them and shower them with napalm.

This had become a brand new war with a better equipped and more confident enemy. The Marines were beginning to wonder what the high command had been talking about when they reported that the war would be over by Christmas - this Christmas or next?

The welcomed dawn seemed to illuminate the snow as the Marines walked around the hill, assessing the damages. Wounded and dead were assembled so they could be carried down the hill. On the attack side of the hill the Marines counted hundreds of dead and dying Chinese soldiers. While checking them out, they discovered the source of some of their maniacal courage. In their pockets they found raw opium.

"Smitty, come here quick," Eckles shouted.

"What's happening?" Smitty asked.

"Looks like they got Corporal Hoyt," Eckles responded.

"What do you mean they got him? Is he dead?"

"No, they captured him. See, way down there at the base of the hill?"

Looking over the side they saw two Chinese soldiers removing Billy's parka and boots. They watched as the soldiers struck him across his face then pulled him up onto his feet. One soldier tied Billy's wrists behind his back, using the rope as a long leash to keep him from escaping - while another slung Billy's carbine over his shoulder before leading him off in the direction of the distant Chinese lines.

"Who wants to go with me? We've got to get him back!" Smitty exclaimed.

"How are we going to do that with all those Chinese out there?" Eckles queried.

"We'll make ourselves look like we're Chinese, with another prisoner. It'll be dangerous, but we got to go quickly."

Eckles and Flores stripped two of the Chinese corpses of their quilted coats and hats. Eckles was much too big to fit into any of them, so Smitty decided that he and Flores would wear them. Eckles would pretend to be a captured American prisoner. Smitty and Flores left their parkas and helmets inside a bunker, hoping they would still be there when they returned.

Flanking Eckles, they proceeded down the face of the slope. Smitty was forced to carry Eckles' rifle as well as his own.

"This is nuts. We're takin' a helluva risk, Smitty. If we don't git killed by the Chinese, our own Corsairs gonna' swoop down and git us," Flores said.

"You got a better idea?" Eckles asked.

"Chut up Eckles. You choud be wearing this stinkin' coat wit' this flea infested hat, - that would be a better idea," Flores replied tersely.

"We gotta hurry, guys, or we'll get stretched out too far away from our lines and never find our way back," Smitty urged.

The Chinese already had a lengthy head start and were periodically disappearing on the stark white horizon. As they staggered along the wind kicked up the dry powdered snow ahead of them, covering the Chinese soldiers' tracks making it virtually impossible to see very far ahead. Almost an hour had passed and the only saving grace was that the Chinese were having a very difficult time getting Billy to move, so the Marines found themselves catching up more quickly than they had expected.

"When we get close enough, I'll try to signal to them to stop then we'll all sit down in the snow and let them walk back to us. Keep your face covered as much as possible. When they get closer, we'll stand up very slowly and, on my signal, we'll rush them before they can fire a shot," Smitty said.

As the Marines neared the Chinese, one of the soldiers looked back and signaled for them to hurry as they continued forward. Luckily, the other Chinese soldier looked back and Smitty caught his eye signaling him to stop. They did, but instead of coming back the Chinese decided to sit down in the snow and wait. The Marines were forced to continue to advance toward them.

Smitty watched from under his cap, which he had pulled down to his eyebrows. He nodded to Eckles and Flores as they got nearer. The two Chinese soldiers started to rise slowly to their feet. One of them seemed to sense something was wrong. Smitty charged at him, knocking him down, while Eckles took down the other with a bear hug that caught the soldier by surprise. Flores stepped on one of the rifles that had fallen into the snow before the Chinese soldier could pick it up again. Billy looked at Smitty with disbelief.

"Where the hell've you guys been? My feet are so cold I can hardly feel 'em anymore," Billy chattered through thin blue lips.

"Search them carefully," Smitty told Eckles and Flores, ignoring Billy.

Both of the Chinese were on their knees with their hands clasped together in front of them in a praying position. They seemed to be pleading for their lives as Flores pointed his rifle at them.

"Don't shoot. We don't want to warn the other Chinese that we're here," Smitty said.

"What'll we do with these guys—take them prisoner? Flores asked in astonishment.

"Hell no!—tie them up with their own rope, and we'll leave them here. Their guys will find them but hopefully not before we get back to our lines," Smitty answered.

Eckles took all their weapons, including several concussion grenades and a Thompson sub-machine gun. Flores reclaimed Billy's parka and boots then helped him put on his gear for the trip back to the Marine lines.

The return trip was an even greater challenge. Their legs were already aching from the long walk trying to catch up to Billy and his captors. The drifting snow had already covered their tracks, and all they had left to guide them back was dead reckoning. They walked for what seemed like hours, taking turns assisting Billy, who was staggering through the snow mumbling about how he wished he was back in Alabama.

"I'm hungry thirsty and cold. I just can't go any farther," Billy muttered as he collapsed in the snow.

Flores opened a small can of fruit cocktail saved from his C-rations. He had stowed it under his armpit inside his field jacket to keep it from freezing. He gave it to Billy.

"No one has any water. All our canteens are frozen solid and all of us are cold, but we have to keep going. If we don't get back to our lines before dark we'll freeze to death out in this stark wilderness," Smitty ordered.

Despite that common sense message, Billy was still refusing to move. "Just let me rest here a little longer," he implored.

"Move your ass, Billy. We can't stay here or we'll all get captured and lose our boots and parkas to the Chinese, so get on your feet—we're moving out—NOW," Smitty ordered more emphatically.

Eckles and Flores forced Billy back onto his feet.

It was getting late and the light of day was becoming scarce in the northern clime where dark of night was beginning to surround them.

Everyone felt sorry for Billy, who had previously been forced by the Chinese to walk through the snow in his stocking feet, but Smitty was right, they had to keep moving. The four would stop occasionally to get their bearings and complain about the stinging cold, but Smitty would urge them forward knowing that stopping for too long would tempt them to not want to get moving again. Time had now become their greatest enemy.

Ahead of them they could occasionally see a steep hill in the distance that looked like the one they had started from. In the frozen wind and the blinding snow, without any distinguishable land marks, the terrain appeared to blend together into a stark decolorized white blur. Being hungry, thirsty, and cold was soon being replaced by desperation as each step they took bordered on futility.

"I can't keep going like this," Billy kept repeating.

"Yes, you can. I know it's tough," Smitty said "but we can't give up. Back at Camp Catlin when I was on watch late at night I used to humor myself by counting cadence. I know it sounds crazy, but it worked. I kept myself awake that way and, as stupid as it seemed even then—it really worked. I want you guys to count along with me, and I want to hear it."

Smitty started and soon all of them chimed in. "One, two, three, four," mumbling past their frozen lips the words were quickly stolen by the wind. With each step they took they began to move a little faster than before. Soon they forgot about how ridiculous it sounded and finding humor in what they were doing helped them almost forget their agony.

"Well, what the hell is this, the French Foreign Legion?" a familiar voice interrupted. It was CJ, with Walters right behind him. They were sitting at the base of the hill where the long journey had begun several hours before.

"We asked Lieutenant Peterson if we could stay behind and wait for you guys to come back. He agreed, but boy was he pissed when he found out that you guys were gone. Although I think he'll get over it when we get back," CJ said.

"Back? What do you mean back—aren't we back now?" Billy asked frantically.

"Yeah, you're back where you started from, but we got orders to move into the valley between the Reservoir and Yudam-ni. It seems that we're totally surrounded by Chinese now. Our supply lines have been completely cut off. The Air Force has been parachuting ammunition and some food rations into the valley. Oh yeah, and get this, the Chinese have been ordering us to surrender. You can imagine what Chesty Puller was thinking when he heard that," CJ laughed.

The Marines chuckled boisterously even through their exhaustion and pain.

"Get out of those stupid Chinese coats," Walters said as he handed Smitty and Flores their parkas and helmets. "Hopefully you'll smell better now," he quipped.

"Give Billy a hand. We need to get him to the Aid Tent as soon as possible. He's probably suffering from frostbite," Smitty said to CJ and Walters.

"This could be my ticket out of here," Billy said, with the first smile anyone had seen on him in quite a while.

"Not a chance, Corporal," Walters responded. "Maybe you didn't understand what I said. We're surrounded. No one is leaving here dead or alive—unless they can fly."

There was still a little daylight left, and the snow had stopped falling as they approached the town of Yudam-ni. Off to their left they saw small clusters of smoke that appeared at first to be ground fog. Then they experienced the acrid odor of burning flesh commingled with the fumes of napalm. The smell instantly violated their nostrils even worse than the rice patties in the south. They looked to their left toward an open field that the Chinese had been foolish enough to try to cross in daylight before being spotted by Marine Corsairs. They quickly turned their heads and looked away from the ghastly scene. They could hear the Chinese soldiers screaming in agony. There were hundreds of dead. Many who looked like fourteen and fifteen year olds, lay fixed in the frozen positions in which they had fallen. For Smitty and the other young Marines it would become one more of those wartime memories they would never be able to forget.

When they reached their lines, they were told that the First Marine Division had formed a perimeter defense around the valley and the Chinese had formed their own perimeter offense completely encircling them. They grabbed some bandoliers of ammunition, hand grenades, and some C-rations before striding off to rejoin Fox Company.

CJ stayed with Billy as he limped in the direction of the medical aid tent in the valley.

~CHAPTER~

TWENTY FOUR

When the wayward Marines finally caught up to their unit, they discovered that Fox Company had already set up defensive positions along a ridge near a small farm house on the fringe of the tiny village of Yudam-ni. They were strategically positioned at the most vulnerable point of attack, from an enemy bent on breaking through the First Marine Division's perimeter defense. A fire team from Second Platoon had already been dispatched to the top of a snow covered hill to survey the situation. When they returned, they reported no evidence of enemy movement in the area—at least none that they could see.

The owners of the farm house—a man, his wife, and two children— were startled and frightened by the presence of armed men in their midst but, with great humility, they welcomed the Marines into their humble home. To keep the family safe from harm, the Marines decided to move them into their underground root cellar. It was about eight foot square with access through a trap door at ground level. The trap door was only about five feet away from the side of their flimsy plaster walled dwelling. A makeshift ladder allowed them to descend into the cellar with its six foot high ceiling that was fortified with beams of wood and earth to cover it at ground level. The room was dimly lit by a small kerosene lamp and was actually quieter, safer, and warmer than the house. The Marines shared their C-rations with the family, who were hesitantly fearful at first, but seemed to enjoy the taste of the pre-cooked canned food much more than the Marines did.

"Smitty, Lieutenant Peterson wants to see Flores, Eckles, and you – on the double," Tyne announced.

"Oh chit, we really in trouble now," Flores grunted.

The lieutenant was squatting next to a fire alongside Sergeant Collins as they patiently tried to thaw out some cans of C-rations.

"You wanted to see us, Sir?" Smitty queried.

"Yes, sit down gentleman," the lieutenant said then hurriedly went on. "Right now the enemy has us completely surrounded and more of them are joining their ranks from across the Yalu River in overwhelming numbers as I speak. We have the rest of the Fifth Marine Regiment and the Seventh Regiment forming a circle around the valley to keep them from getting inside our defense. The Army has a battalion on the east side of the reservoir and they are coming under heavy fire as well. We must hold or they will destroy us from within. Our forces are outnumbered ten to one and we have no way of getting reinforcements."

Then, he continued hastily, "We lost several NCOs in that battle last night and I'm rearranging our command structure. Smitty, I'm promoting you to Sergeant and putting you in charge of First Squad. I've already promoted Corporal Tyne to Staff Sergeant and made him Section Leader. Actually, it was Tyne who recommended you. Do you have a problem with that?"

"No, Sir, I don't. Can I make CJ my replacement as Fire Team Leader?" Smitty asked.

"Already done, he is now a corporal—and one more thing; I greatly admired your bravery for going out there after Corporal Hoyt. I found it to be both admirable and foolish; however, I'm recommending you, Flores, and Eckles for a Silver Star. But the next time you decide to do something like that you better check with me first. Is that understood?"

"Yes, Sir—and thank you, Sir," Smitty answered.

"Don't forget, Smith, it is imperative that we keep the enemy from breaking through our lines, so don't let that happen. Understood?"

"Yes, Sir," Smitty replied smartly.

"Now, pass that word down the line. You're dismissed," the lieutenant concluded looking back at his still frozen C-rations.

As they strode away, Flores playfully stuck out his chest and remarked, "I chudda got a Medal of Honor or at least a Navy Cross just for wearin' that lousy stinkin' Commie's coat and that flea infested cap." The trio laughed, probably just to relieve their tension, as Flores kept scratching his head.

When CJ returned, he was very excited to hear about his promotion, but seemed even more jubilant to hear about Smitty's rise to Squad Leader.

Billy had suffered a mild case of frostbite and was given new, dry socks to keep his feet from getting worse. Thomas and Wilson teased Billy, telling him that he deserved a special medal just for being dumb enough to get captured, but Smitty and Blake ignored them.

"Did you guys find the marker that Thomas and I set out so you guys could find your way back?"

"We din't see no marker out there," Flores replied. "What did it look like?"

"It was Thomas's handkerchief. We laid it on the ground right near where you guys went down the hill to go after Corporal Hoyt."

"What color was it?" Flores asked.

"White," Wilson answered.

"You left a white handkerchief in the snow and 'spected us to find it?" Flores scratched his head again.

"But it had Thomas's monogram on it in one corner," Wilson said.

"What color was the monogram?" Eckles joined in.

"White," Thomas answered smugly.

"Let me see if I got this right, you left a white handkerchief with a white monogram lying in the white snow. Why would anyone do something as stupid as that?" Eckles asked.

"What do you mean 'stupid'? We didn't want the Chinese to find it before you guys did," Wilson answered with a straight face.

"Chit heads," Flores mumbled as he walked away.

By now the rest of the Marines were too tired to even smile.

As the light of day ebbed closer to darkness, the platoon settled into defensive positions near the farm house. The word came down the line that the temperature was going down to minus 50 that night and would continue to plunge to minus 60 after that.

"Minus 60? Chit, if it wasn't for bad news we woun't have no news at all," Flores was heard grumbling.

Smitty sent two of the replacements who had been assigned to his squad to the top of a nearby hill to act as observers. They were ordered to fire a warning shot if they spotted the enemy. The remainder of the Marines teamed up into pairs. Flores was teamed with Eckles near the farm house. CJ was teamed with Walters further to the north, and Billy was with Doc Blake. Brutal as it might have seemed, they would all be on one hundred percent watch—meaning that no one would sleep the rest of the night.

"Too damned cold to sleep anyway," Flores chattered through frozen lips.

As daylight dwindled, the temperature began dropping rapidly. Fires were smothered so they would not attract the enemy to their exact locations.

Smoking was banned and conversations were held to a whisper. Ominous snow clouds filled the sky, and if there was a moon above it was not visible. The enemy might have the disadvantage of the darkening night by not being able to locate the Marine positions as easily but, on the other hand, the Marines would have the disadvantage of not knowing when the PVA arrived until they were right on top of them.

Evidence of a foreboding enemy was already beginning to take its toll—not the physical enemy in the form of uniformed soldiers, but the crippling internalized anxiety of not knowing when or where they would strike first. The not knowing made it a lot easier to stay awake, but the seemingly endless waiting became a lingering curse. In addition, not being able to move about freely gave the freezing cold a distinct advantage as well.

During the day, their feet were slightly warmed by just walking about and stamping them on the ground and during the day they could bang their gloves together to increase the circulation in their fingers. Now, at night, they were trapped on the surface of the snow, unable to dig into the frozen ground and unable to move or make a sound that would alert a stalking enemy.

The Marines nervously flexed their toes in an effort to keep them from freezing and to reassure them that they were still there. They kept their gloved hands under their armpits for added warmth whenever possible. The hoods of their parkas were wrapped tightly around their heads with their helmet straps buckled beneath their chin.

Smitty had selected Jimbo to partner up with that night, so that he could rely on his extensive combat experience.

"How does this compare to the Pacific Campaign?" Smitty whispered.

"Well I'd say it's a helluva lot colder here then it was there," Jimbo quipped, as Smitty choked back an outburst of comic relief.

They sat for quite a long while in stunned silence and listened cautiously, hearing only the tiny flakes of dry crystalline snow crash softly on the tops of their helmets. None of them had slept or eaten in many days, and licking the moisture-deprived snow did little to quench their constant thirst.

The long awaited breach in the peaceful quiet of the night burst upon the reverie of Fox Company just past midnight. The startling blare of Chinese bugles introduced the first charge of the PVA as they struck suddenly in wave on human wave of hostile clamor, offending the ears of the undermanned and overwhelmed Marines. The annoying bugles echoed monotonously across the valley cascading off the frozen hillsides and ravines. They served as a signal to the thousands of other PVAs that they had located the enemy and that they were on the attack. The suddenness of the initial blasts was intended to frighten their adversaries. To Smitty, the bugles constant and repetitious - tata tata -- tata ta - tata tata -- tata ta - sounded like: we are coming be afraid - we are coming - be afraid. But Thomas and Wilson agreed that it sounded more like some Chinese families had wasted a lot of money on music lessons.

For all of the Marines, the adrenalin began to course through their veins again, making them forget the ever-present sting of the crippling subzero temperatures. It was now 30 below zero and their long wait was over.

They quickly rose to the challenge, as the gates of Hell opened wide. Shouts and epitaphs filled the air, followed by ear piercing explosions and the stuttering succession of rifle and machine gun fire. Chinese concussion grenades landed dangerously close to the Marines, warning them that the enemy was within throwing distance. The incessant chatter of the Chinese sub-machine guns were responded to by intermittent bursts from the American Browning Automatic Rifles.

Out of the darkness the voice of a Marine cried out, "Corpsman!" and Doc Blake immediately charged off into a hail of steel and lead, toward the sound. Hundreds of PVA spearheaded an attempt to breach the Marine lines near the center positions held by CJ and Walters. The two answered the assault by commandeering a .30 caliber machine gun from a fallen Marine. They moved the automatic weapon to their position on the line, where the breakthrough was becoming imminent, and set up the tripod. Then, they fired deliberate, well-aimed bursts into the advancing mass of Chinese soldiers as Smitty and Jimbo rushed forward to give them support. So much was happening along the line that all the outnumbered Marines could do was hold on to the little piece of real estate they had been assigned. Loading and reloading became relatively routine even with the handicap of forcing hands numbed by the cold to perform quickly and flawlessly in the darkness.

A sudden lull in the action gave the Chinese an opportunity to regroup for their next attack. Their style was to probe the Marine lines to find weak spots, and then move heavy concentrations of troops into those areas until they punctured the lines and broke through. By now, the Marines were familiar with this tactic and they used the opportunity to reload and reassess their damages, filling the newly created gaps with additional personnel. The Marines tightened their lines and set up a squad in reserve that could fill a breach or fortify a point of attack when it occurred. Sergeant Collins scurried along the line, issuing illumination grenades with instructions to lob them far over and beyond the enemy's heads to backlight them when they made another of their suicidal surges.

The deadly silence and the agony of waiting began once more to unnerve the anxious Marines. A light dusting of new snow kissed their frozen cheeks, reminding them that the Chinese were not their only enemy. Marines whispered back and forth, renewing each other's confidence, assuring them that they were not alone. They sat and waited while under their breath they cursed the darkness and the frigid wind that held them captive – then waited some more until the waiting became another enemy.

Then as abruptly as it had begun the silence ended, introduced by the familiar calling cards of dissonant Chinese bugles and the threatening voices of a maniacal mob. The concussive sounds of Chinese hand grenades parted the arctic air and rippled along the ranks of the Marines. This time, the Marines deliberately met the attack with inaction. They were waiting for a full surge of enemy troops – and they didn't have to wait very long. In the blackness of night they saw the multiple intermittent flares of muzzle flashes ripple across the snow as they emanated from Chinese burp guns like hundreds of clustering fireflies. They fired rapidly into the advancing horde, watching as some of the flickering lights went out.

Adding to the confusion they heard the ebb and flow of the mind curdling screams of the angry mob. The Marines responded quickly with illumination grenades, hurtling them in an upward arc over and behind the crushing forces that charged toward them. The terrain fluoresced, reflecting off the snow, revealing a full force rush of humanity that bore down on the Marine lines.

It reminded Jimbo, as he would say later, of throwing the switch for the traditional lighting of the Christmas tree at Rockefeller Centre in New York City. It blinded the Marines momentarily before exposing the entirety of the massive forces that dotted the snow covered battlefield from left to right.

Walters and CJ opened up with fusillades of .30 caliber missiles. Their machine gun spit streams of light from the tracer bullets embedded in every 10th round of their ammo belt to guide the remaining rounds to their target. The clouds lit up brightly above them, reminding Smitty of the fire at Camp Catlin. Hundreds of Chinese fell, but it was like fighting the mythical Greek serpent—the Hydra. Where one once stood, there were now two, and they just kept coming. The call rang out that there was another break in the line in the area where Flores and Eckles were coming under heavy assault. Walters rose to his feet, removed the overheated machine gun from the tripod and, holding it in his gloved hands, he swept the area back and forth then back again, strafing the hordes of Chinese until he finally fell forward into the snow. CJ swiftly picked up the weapon and continued the barrage. Jimbo jumped swiftly to his feet, directing the

Marines to concentrate their fire power to fill the gaps where the heaviest points of attack were expanding.

Smitty felt a thud in the center of his chest, just above the breast bone. It was like someone had punched him with his fist, but he and the remaining Marines continued firing with carbines, BARs, and M1s stopping only long enough to reload. The rest of the Marines, who had run out of ammunition, hurled shrapnel grenades and more illumination grenades at the onrushing insurgents.

Despite their best efforts to repel the suicidal onslaught, the Chinese finally made a break through the line. The reserve squad was called in to close the breach. Tyne gave the order to fix bayonets. With enemy combatants commingling with Marines, it was impossible to shoot into their throngs without taking the risk of hitting one of their own. Combat became hand to hand and the bayonet drills from boot camp suddenly found new meaning. The clashing of body against body reminded Smitty of football, but with the deeper consequence of 'life or death.'

The battle raged for hours, until near-dawn when the exposed PVA withdrew for cover from the Marine gull-winged Corsairs flying overhead, targeting stragglers who were caught in the first traces of the light of day. The battle weary Marines staggered to their feet and pumped their fists into the air toward the pilots, cheering their saviors in the sky. The pilots waved back, pumping their fists in response to the heroic efforts of the Marines on the ground.

The battle was won, but the war was far from over.

The long awaited sun that had been missing in action for days crept stealthily over the ridge of a distant hill like a cat stalking its prey. The golden rays cast long narrow shadows along the frigid terrain as its early light revealed the scarlet snow of a blood-stained battlefield, strewn with dead and dying combatants.

The Marines were astounded as they surveyed the hundreds of already frozen Chinese corpses strewn along both sides of their lines. The enemy's successful, though temporary, breakthrough had proved very costly. The Marines hurriedly began tending to their most severely wounded.

Smitty rushed over to check on Walters and found that both he and CJ had been mortally wounded. He cradled them both in his arms and wept silently while rocking them back and forth. They both died in his arms that painful morning. CJ stared blankly at Smitty without saying a word.

Walters looked up and saw Smitty kneeling next to him, with Billy looking over his shoulder. Smitty was holding Walters hand tightly in his. Before Walters died he smiled while looking into Smitty's eyes and said,

"Do me a favor, Smitty. Take my ring and the diary inside my parka and give them to my brother Winston. It would mean a lot to him. You can read my diary if you'd like. And one more thing, be sure to watch out for Billy, OK?"

Smitty nodded affirmatively, "I will. In fact, we all will, he definitely needs looking after."

As Smitty squeezed Walters hand he heard him draw his last breath. It was then that he noticed Walters' left hand, the one that had held the red hot machine gun barrel. It was burned through the glove, deep into the flesh, down to the bones of his fingers. Smitty carefully removed the ring from his right hand while it was still warm, then he reached inside Walters' parka and withdrew the diary. With half-frozen tears still clouding his vision, Smitty grasped CJ's and Walters' parka hoods.

"I'll take one of them," Billy offered.

"No," Smitty insisted. "I have to do this myself."

Struggling under their weight, he dragged both of the lifeless bodies across the crystalline surface and into the valley below, where they were loaded onto trucks to be transported back to Hamhung. He was then dumbstruck to discover that both Eckles and Flores had been killed as well. Thomas grabbed Flores' parka hood and dragged him down the hill while Billy dragged Eckles' frozen corpse to the same awaiting truck.

To their added horror, the Marines soon discovered that the entire North Korean family had been murdered in their cellar by gunshot wounds and bayonets. Forty-seven Marines were killed from First Platoon alone and many more had been seriously wounded. Second Platoon had lost almost every man. There was no more time left to mourn as the Marines received orders to prepare to withdraw immediately back to Hagaru.

Smitty stood momentarily, staring blankly at the scarlet snow that surrounded him. And though he was devastated by the events of that morning, he knew that he was still responsible for the remainder of his squad.

"Jimbo, have you seen the two scouts I sent to the top of that hill?" Smitty asked.

"No, they must still be up on the ridge," Jimbo answered.

"I'll go get 'em and I'll be right back," Smitty said.

"OK, but hurry, we'll be moving out soon."

Smitty reached inside his parka and felt around to see if he could find the reason for the sudden impact he felt against his chest during the battle. His hand found nothing wrong. He felt no blood and no wound, just a very tender spot in the center of his chest. He searched frantically for Mama Ahue's cross but could not find it. His numb fingers fumbled to re-button his parka, and then he headed cautiously up the hill. He searched for the comfort of Nani's smiling face along the way but couldn't find that either.

All he could see framed in his mind's eye was a portrait of a senseless waste of human life lying in a field of blood stained snow; a picture that he knew would haunt him forever, just as the scene in the barn at Camp Catlin had.

~CHAPTER~

TWENTY FIVE

The snowfall during the pre-dawn hours left a fresh white blanket that covered any old tracks the two Marine lookouts might have made. Smitty decided to head straight toward the top of the ridge as the sun disappeared again behind a bank of ominous clouds. He called out frequently, stopping occasionally to listen, but there was no answer. His words seemed to be carried away on waves of stiffening winds at the higher altitude. Looking over the reverse side of the slope, he detected signs of a scuffle in the snow and numerous fresh tracks heading toward the north. He looked further north and saw the tracks disappear in the distance. He was forced to assume the worst; they had evidently been captured. Smitty gathered his wits and, slipping and sliding, he precariously made his way back down the hill toward his unit.

Suddenly he felt a sharp sting in the side of his right leg, between his knee and his hip. He collapsed back onto the snow and pulled off his glove to examine the area. He looked at his hand; it was bloody. He scanned the hillside, but saw nothing. He had evidently been hit by a stray shot that he never heard, fired by an unseen enemy. Probing the area again, he felt a lump in the center of the wound. He assumed that it had been caused by the spent shell that had penetrated only about a half inch into his thigh, leaving a small portion protruding from the wound.

He put his glove back on and decided it would be better to let Doc Blake look at it when he rejoined the platoon. Smitty stood up again and felt a stabbing pain ripple down his leg that joined, in an aching rhythm, with the numbing cold he felt in both his feet. When he reached the bottom of the hill he limped into the valley to discover that everyone was gone.

In the distance, he saw members of the rear guard moving away toward the mountain road that led back to Hagaru. Above their heads, he caught sight of a bright morning star that appeared to be guiding the Marines to their destination. Knowing that he had to catch up quickly or be cut off from his regiment he tried to move faster, but the pain intensified with every step. He didn't dare call out, fearing that he would attract the attention of the Chinese.

Just when his mind assured him that he was catching up, the Marines would disappear at a dip in the road only to reappear again as the road rose up ahead of them. He awkwardly tried to use his rifle as a cane, but could only maintain half speed no matter how hard he tried. The dreaded feeling that he might be left behind was ever present. In desperation, he tried to entertain himself with thoughts of home and Hawaii. He felt Nani inside his soul, urging him forward, helping him to fight the agony that seemed to own his leg. Occasionally, he tried to eat the powdered snow to quench his thirst, but there wasn't enough moisture in it to even wet his tongue.

To the left of him, was the frozen Chosin Reservoir, and though he knew he would not be able to find any flowing water there, he decided to chop some pieces of ice off the surface with his bayonet. He sat there for a moment sucking on a chunk of the ice that, in the frozen wind, seemed to be sucking back at him. Never-the-less, the moisture was welcomed by his parched lips and nearly dehydrated body. He rummaged around inside his pack and found two small boxes of Cheerios that were left over from his C-rations. He decided to eat one and save the other for later. The taste delighted his tongue and the sugar strengthened his aching muscles. He took out a handkerchief and loaded it with the larger chunks of ice, then tied it to the outside of his web belt so they would remain frozen. I'll need these later, he thought out loud.

Smitty stumbled forward again and, with every pain-filled step, he thought of better times. It had begun to snow again and the guiding star faded, then disappeared and reappeared only to be replaced at times by a grey overcast sky. It was just a light powdery snow, but the gusting wind made it impossible to see the Marine rear guard in the distance. At times, he felt like he had lost his course and feared that he might be going in circles.

Follow the star he mumbled to himself, over and over again. He looked back occasionally but could no longer see his own tracks, which were being covered as quickly as he made them. He began to stagger as his throbbing leg slowed his pace even more, bringing him to an agonizing halt at times.

Still, he struggled on with determination, not knowing for certain in which direction he was headed. *Follow that star* he reiterated, *follow that star.*

Evening sadistically brought with it a further drop in the already crippling temperatures. Night would soon wrap its veil of loneliness around him again. As if by fate, he stumbled into a crevice in the side of a hill and decided to take shelter from the wind. He rested his back against the hillside and stared blankly into the frozen void from whence he had come. He closed his eyes and slid down slowly into a sitting position.

I'll just rest here for a moment, he thought. Then he saw them. They were coming across a stretch of pearl white sand. He smiled and reached out to them as they smiled back. It was Nani and Mama Ahue, wearing brightly colored leis. They were carrying platters of poi, pineapple chicken, and decanters of sweet island fruit juices. He could hear ukuleles playing softly in the distance as he felt the soft warm ocean breezes sweep across his body. Then, as he reached out to touch Nani's hand, everything began to dissolve and disappear quietly into the distance. He called out to them and thought he heard Mama Ahue calling back.

His eyes opened again very slowly to see an image that appeared at first to be just another apparition. He squinted into the swirling snow. As he rubbed his eyes with the back of his gloved hand, the figure of a man who must have been following close behind appeared from nowhere. Smitty's eyes scanned the horizon and, when he was convinced that the mysterious figure was alone, he rose to his feet with his carbine cradled over his left arm and limped out to meet him.

As he got nearer, the figure raised his arms in a position of surrender. It was a Chinese soldier who appeared to be very young. After seeing that he was unarmed, Smitty beckoned him forward then signaled to him to drop to his knees. He carefully patted him down, searching for grenades or other concealed weapons. Suddenly the soldier began to giggle like a school girl and, to Smitty's surprise, he blurted out the words, "You're tickling me."

"What did you say?" Smitty asked incredulously.

"I said you're tickling me."

"Who the hell are you?"

"I'm an American," he answered.

"The hell you are, you're Chinese."

"Yes, but I'm a Chinese-American. I know what you must be thinking, but I assure you that it is true. I ran away from the Communists because I'm not one of them, and I've been trying to link up with the American army before the PVA could find me again, can you help me?"

"Follow me," Smitty urged him as he returned to his sheltered area.

"What's your name?" Smitty asked, still testing him.

"My real name is Wong Dan, but my friends just call me Dan. What is your name?"

"My friends call me Smitty."

Dan explained that he was born in the United States and that his father was a doctor who had graduated from Harvard Medical School. His family had moved to Hawaii a few years ago and from there they went to mainland China to visit relatives. To their surprise, his father was accused of being a spy, and the Communists executed him.

"I was forcefully conscripted into the PVA and made to fight for them," he added.

"How old are you?" Smitty asked skeptically.

"I just turned sixteen," the boy replied.

Smitty opened his backpack and gave Dan the box of Cheerios he had saved. Dan chomped them down like he hadn't eaten in a very long time, then Smitty handed him a piece of ice to suck on. When the darkness of night finally shrouded them like a protective shield, they both felt safe again. Smitty unzipped his sleeping bag all around and spread it over the top of their legs to hold at least some body heat inside. Together, they camouflaged the khaki color by brushing a light layer of snow over the outer surface of the bag. They were both totally exhausted, so they snuggled together in the darkness for warmth and were soon fast asleep.

The only thing that awakened Smitty from his deep sleep was the faint light of dawn as it filtered its way through the lids of his eyes. He looked up, startled; Dan was standing over him holding his carbine. To his amazement, he watched Dan raise the carbine to shoulder level. He heard the familiar click of the safety. Smitty raised his arm across his face and closed his eyes as the first shot rang out, then, to his amazement, he heard a second and a third shot ringing in his ears. Smitty rose quickly to his feet and saw three dead Chinese soldiers lying on the ground at his feet.

"Sorry if I woke you, Smitty, but it seemed rather urgent," Dan said softly in his girlish soprano voice and quickly added, "We need to get moving."

Smitty looked out and there it was - the star he had been following was hovering on the horizon as if it had been waiting for him to begin again. They pressed on, progressing very slowly with Dan helping Smitty, who was still in great pain. To their delight, it appeared that the column of Marines had also been halted during the night. The only thing the two new-found friends worried about now was that either the PVA would mistake them as Americans or worse yet; the Marines would mistake them as PVA.

Up ahead, they heard the sound of sporadic explosions and rapid gun fire that would halt the column, allowing them to catch up more quickly. Sometime around mid-morning they caught the attention of the Marines rear guard. Smitty ordered Dan to lie down in the snow then raised his carbine above his shoulders with both arms extended, dipping it left and right, hoping to let them know that he was not the enemy.

A squad of Marines approached warily. They were obviously confused by the two different uniforms. Smitty explained as best he could that Dan was OK, but they seemed uneasy and kept their weapons trained on him all the way back to the Marine column. A swarthy lieutenant greeted them as they joined his ranks.

"We got no room for prisoners, Sergeant, so take that gook bastard over to the side of the road and shoot him," he ordered.

"But Lieutenant, he's not a prisoner. He's an American," Smitty insisted.

"You think I can't see?" the angry lieutenant bellowed.

"Please, Sir, let me explain," Smitty implored.

"Make it fast, Sergeant, and make it good, I have no time for any horseshit right now."

Smitty told him a shortened but convincing story, and then allowed Dan a chance to tell his version.

"OK, Sergeant, he's all yours, so you better get him out of that chink suit and into something that at least makes him look like a Marine—that is if you want him to live long enough to get to Hagaru."

Inside a truck carrying dead Marines, Smitty removed a parka, gloves, boots, and a helmet from a Marine who didn't need them anymore. He gave them to Dan. On the back of the same truck he found a carbine, a cartridge belt, and a bandolier of .30 caliber ammunition.

"Now you look like one of us. Keep your head down and stick with me." Smitty realized that he had repeated the same words that Jimbo had said to him when they made the invasion at Inchon. He felt like a seasoned veteran now, thanks to that advice.

The column reached the narrow pass along the mountain road that they had traveled to reach Yudam-ni and the Chosin Reservoir. The going would be much slower now because of the narrow road, the heavy snow, the pesky snipers, and the mines that blasted holes in the road ahead to slow the trucks carrying the dead and wounded.

At times, the convoy would halt long enough to repair the holes and many of the Marines would sit down by the side of the road and fall asleep from their utter exhaustion. When the column eventually continued forward, many of the battle weary Marines didn't want to get back up again. Smitty joined with the squad leaders and other NCOs as they kicked the exhausted Marines awake, forcing them back onto their feet.

To their left, were the steep slopes that rose high above, hiding the Chinese snipers, who were successfully killing or wounding an occasional Marine. To their right, was the downhill side of the mountain that was becoming a graveyard for trucks and tanks that ran out of fuel or became damaged by the mines the Chinese planted in the road ahead. Smitty and Dan assumed the role of caring for the needs of some of the wounded while protecting them from frequent ambushes during the night. It was difficult to sleep even in shifts and keeping warm was virtually impossible.

During one of the daytime delays, Smitty and Dan managed to start a small fire to melt snow for drinking water, but even that proved futile; the powdered snow yielded very little moisture, even after many minutes of packing and repacking the #10 tin can they had found in the back of one of the jeeps. What they were able to collect they gave to the wounded and were content to suck on the small pieces of ice from the frozen reservoir that Smitty had tied to his belt.

During the second night, Smitty and Dan were alerted by the jabber of Chinese conversation coming from a small ravine above their heads. Dan put his finger across his lips, signaling to Smitty to be quiet. They both listened very intently. Smitty didn't understand any of what was said. He just kept his carbine at the ready until the conversation stopped.

"They're planning a massive breakthrough to separate the front of the column from the rear in hopes that they might divide and conquer us," Dan whispered.

"Where are they planning to strike?"

"Right here in the ravine above us. They're assembling up there now," Dan answered.

"Stay here. I'm going to get help."

Smitty dodged between the trucks, heading back toward the platoon established as the rear guard. His leg was still shooting stabbing pains toward his hip trying to slow him down, but the urgency of his mission superseded his desire to stop and rest. A voice ordered him to halt. It was the lieutenant who had greeted him at the rear of the column. Smitty hastily related the conversation he and Dan had overheard.

"Do you trust him?" the lieutenant asked.

"With my life, Sir," Smitty answered affirmatively.

The lieutenant assembled two squads and followed Smitty back to where Dan was waiting. The Marines took positions on each side of the gaping, snow filled ravine and waited quietly. They heard more chatter from a commanding voice above before the bugle sounded. Once the PVA started down the open slot, the loose snow collapsed beneath their feet. They couldn't stop the slide. The Marines fired indiscriminately into their ranks, killing them all. The Chinese soldiers never fired a single shot. As fate would have it, their masterful plan was foiled by a sixteen year old Chinese-American boy.

On the fourth day, the column reached Hagaru and linked up with Chesty Puller's First Marine Regiment. The Marines lined the road, greeting them with salutes as they marched into their midst standing proud and tall. They had fought their way day and night for four days over a fourteen mile stretch of mountain road—a trip that had taken less than a couple of hours on the way up. The first thing the returning Marines asked for was drinking water—the second was chow, of course.

Colonel Puller's Marines had fashioned an airstrip using bulldozers to cut into the rock hard frozen tundra. It wasn't the smoothest runway in the world, but it was adequate for delivering badly needed food, medicine, and ammunition to the still surrounded Marines. Return flights were used exclusively for the evacuation of wounded.

Smitty searched the area and found his platoon. They had been up on the ridges above the road, protecting the convoy. Smitty embraced Jimbo and told him about his trip back and his chance meeting with Dan. Thomas and Wilson were busily opening the C-ration boxes they had picked up on the way in. Billy Hoyt had removed his boots and Doc Blake was examining his frostbitten feet.

"What happened to you?" Blake asked Smitty, looking at his bloodied dungaree pants.

"You'll never believe this, Doc, but I caught a bullet up near Yudam-ni after the battle was over. I think it was a long range shot from a Chinese sniper."

Blake checked it out carefully.

"Jimbo, you and Tyne take Smitty over to the medical tent and take Hoyt over there too."

Along the way, Smitty found a chaplain and explained Dan's extraordinary situation to him, then left Dan in his care. The Marines stared in amazement as Smitty embraced Dan and told him that he hoped he would see him again someday. Smitty limped over to the aid tent to have his leg looked at. As Doc expected, it had become badly infected and it would take some time to heal. They removed the bullet, bandaged the wound, and gave him a shot of penicillin.

While he was there, he made two other interesting discoveries. A piece of Chinese shrapnel from a concussion grenade had struck the cross that Mama Ahue had given to him in Hawaii. The doctor said it had undoubtedly saved his life. An outline of the cross was still visibly imprinted on his chest. The cross itself had not faired quite as well. He found it in two pieces at belt level down inside his skivvy shirt. It explained the thud he had felt against his chest during the prior battle. The other thing he discovered was something that he had already suspected. He had severe frostbite in both of his feet. Smitty and Billy were both assigned to be flown out on the next flight to a hospital in Japan, but the ordeal was far from being over. The remaining Marines still had to fight their way back 64 miles through the same Chinese Army along the same mountainous road back to Hamhung.

"I want to stay with you guys," Smitty told Jimbo and Tyne.

"Not a chance, Smitty. No cripples allowed and, besides, the lieutenant, and Doc Blake would never allow it." Smitty and Billy limped onto the waiting aircraft. Jimbo and Tyne waved to them as they went aboard.

"We'll see you guys again in the next war," Jimbo delightfully quipped.

~CHAPTER~

TWENTY SIX

The more seriously wounded Marines on board cursed every bump as the plane bounced along the makeshift runway. For them, it seemed that every wheel hit every chunk of frozen snow and pot hole along the way.

They were traveling Marine Corps style again, in a twin prop former commercial aircraft with all the seats removed so that it could hold more cargo. The Marines, however, were not complaining about the lack of luxury. They were finally on their way out of North Korea. Smitty leaned back against the bulkhead, facing inboard. Directly across from him was Billy, who looked white and pale. The rough ride across the jagged turf caused the plane to jerk and pitch to and fro; making the brave Marines wonder if they would ever get airborne. When the wheels eventually lifted off the ground, they let out a resounding cheer accompanied by a sigh of relief. They were on their way at last.

"Wow that was scary. Wouldn't it be something if we lived through all this crap and the plane crashed while trying to fly us out of this hell hole?" Billy blurted out in relief.

"Hold off on the celebration a while longer, we're about to get a final sendoff from the PVA waiting at the end of the runway," the pilot announced over the intercom.

Sure enough the echo of small arms fire began pinging off the metallic surface of the plane—then, just as suddenly, the pinging stopped.

"It appears that they're still pissed off about the ass whoopin' we gave them the other night," a Marine sounded off.

The landing at Fukuoka, Japan was smooth as the pilot jokingly announced: "Thank you for flying with us today. Everyone please hold fast while the more seriously wounded are evacuated first. The temperature when we left beautiful downtown Hagaru was a bone chilling 55 below zero. Now prepare for a heat wave. The temperature here is 35 degrees, but it is above zero. When you plan your next trip remember us and we will be here to provide for your every comfort and safety in the friendly skies of 'Last Resort Airlines.'"

"With all the pilots in the world we wind up with Bob Hope," a Marine blurted.

When the doors to the aircraft opened, it was as if they had suddenly been routed to a tropical island, and the Marines felt very over dressed in their heavy winter parkas.

Members of the hospital staff greeted them cordially as they collected ammunition belts, grenades, and other armament gladly handed over to them by the weary Marines. The nurses tried to assist the walking wounded who were unaccustomed to such favorable treatment. Many of them insisted on limping into the hospital on their own.

Four days went by before some of the mail caught up to them. Smitty got one letter from Nani, though he knew there must be more stacked up somewhere waiting to find him. The letter was somewhat redundant, but he was grateful for every precious word that he gleefully read again and again. The sweet smell of Nani was on every page. The news she sent was that President Truman was reporting in the newspapers that the First Marine Division was surrounded and outnumbered five to one. His fears were that they might soon be annihilated.

That was the first real laugh Smitty had had in a long while, remembering what Colonel Chesty Puller had said when he was told that the First Marine Division was surrounded by overwhelming forces of the Chinese Communist Army. Smitty could almost picture the look on his stern, battle hardened face as he announced with great sincerity, "Now we got those bastards right where we want 'em."

Smitty was in a hurry to write to Nani to let her know that he was still among the living.

My Dearest Nani,

Where I have been it was impossible to write to you, but Oh God how I missed you. I am writing you now from the hospital in Japan. I was wounded in my right leg. The wound got infected as a result of not being treated right away. I also have pretty severe frostbite in both of my feet, but the doctors say that after a while I will be as good as new. The important thing is that, somehow, I am still alive.

There are so many things I want to tell you, but I guess that the worst of it is that CJ will not be coming home. He was killed because he is CJ. I know how odd that sounds, but CJ was always thinking of others. When people write about self sacrifice, CJ is exactly what they are talking about. I am alive today because of him and Walters, who was also killed. Their love for me and my love for you along with Mama Ahue's cross has made the difference. I thought about you constantly while I was in action. I promised you that I would return and, although there were many times when I felt that I would not be able to keep that promise, your love kept me safe. I am convinced that you, CJ, Walters, Mama Ahue, and the Grace of God were my special guardians. I owe so much to the five of you that I feel overwhelmed by the debt.

I remember as a boy back in grade school, during World War II, how much I worshipped my uncles and all the other guys who went into combat to protect us. Freedom meant so much to me then, and I didn't even have a clue what the word really meant - that is, not until now. Before I came over here, I often questioned whether I would be brave enough to do whatever was necessary, and it didn't take long to realize that it wasn't a question, of could I, but more of a moral question, of should I. Killing another human being isn't easy, even when you know that if you don't they will kill you or someone you love, so there really is no other option.

When I come home, and I expect to be home soon, you will find that I am a very changed person, though I pray that you will still be able to love me. Nani, my darling, I have seen so much of life and death over these past few months that it will take me a while to learn how to deal with it. I will need your help, your love, and your understanding.

I met a man in a bar in Honolulu—you know him, his name was Jerry—he was the man they arrested for the murder of those boys. He was a WWII veteran and I found it so remarkable that anyone could become so cynical about life, justice, and the law, but now I have seen some of the things that must have influenced his thinking. I too have been touched by the horror and injustice that is found everywhere in this world, and I don't want to become cynical like him.

The wonderfully beautiful Korean people from both North and South have so little to be encouraged about. They seem to have had the misfortune of being caught hopelessly between the forces of greed and power. As it is today, Korea is like the bottom of a bird cage and, unfortunately for them, it is their home. I can leave, but they must stay. I want so much to believe that what little I have been able to do to help them will lead to a better tomorrow, not just for them as individuals, but for the whole of their society. There is more evil in this world than most people—especially those who are sheltered in the freedom they enjoy today—will ever realize.

When things got really bad over there and I thought I couldn't take it anymore, my mind protected itself with thoughts of you, especially how we first met there on the beach at Waikiki. I remembered the pineapple we ate the day we toured your beautiful island and how it made our lips stick together when we kissed. I can hardly wait to hold you in my arms again.

Say hello to Lea and Kee and Joi and Mama Ahue, then give Lani a big hug for me and tell her that I am so sorry that I had to be the one who delivered the sad news about CJ.

Corporal Billy Hoyt and I both arrived here in Japan together. We expect to be moved to a hospital annex very soon. It is supposed to be for rehabilitation of guys with less severe wounds. God knows how long we will be here, but some of us expect to be going back to the front lines if things don't start looking up in Korea.

On a lighter note, I can tell you that I got promoted to Sergeant while I was here. I will write again as soon as possible.

All my love,

Smitty

Two weeks after they arrived at the hospital, Smitty saw a very familiar face. It was Lieutenant Peterson. He was being pushed through the hospital lobby in a wheel chair by a very attractive nurse.

"How do you rate the best lookin' nurse in the hospital, Sir?" Smitty asked.

"Sergeant Smith! How are you doing?" the lieutenant perked up greeting him with a smile.

"That's the first smile we've seen from him since he got here," the nurse said, "and he refuses to write home."

"Why is that, Sir? Smitty queried.

The lieutenant didn't answer.

"He lost his leg in Korea," the nurse answered for him.

Smitty heard what she said but pretended for the moment like he didn't.

"Are you taking him somewhere special right now, nurse?"

"No, not right now, we were just out for a change of scenery," she answered.

"Can you leave him here with me for a while?"

"Sure. I'll be back in about an hour. Will that be OK?" She nodded to the lieutenant, who nodded back.

"Thank you Ma'am," Smitty said.

"How were the guys doing when you left there, Lieutenant?" Smitty asked.

"We fought for several days after you left, but we all made it back to Hamhung. The odd thing was that thousands of North Korean civilians followed us out of there. It seems that all the fears the commies instilled in them about us 'white devils' turned out to be false. We had fed them, clothed them and befriended them in a way that they never experienced from their own government. We loaded them aboard our ships and took them with us when we left. As for me, they put me and several others on a plane and I wound up here yesterday."

"How are Doc Blake and Jimbo and Tyne and Wilson and Thomas doing?"

"Well, we got hit pretty hard along the road coming out of Hagaru. They attacked us every night and sniped at us from the hills above the road during the day. We lost Thomas and Wilson one evening and thought they had been killed. Everything was so confused that we didn't know where anyone really was. The next morning, the two of them showed up and told us they had been captured. They said the Chinese forced them to lie down in the snow until they could take them back to their lines. It seems they both fell asleep and when they woke up the Chinese were gone. A lot of our guys speculated that after the Chinese got to know what a pain in the ass they were they didn't want them anymore, so they pulled out and left them behind. We may never know the truth." The lieutenant chuckled.

"All of the guys you mentioned loaded aboard ships when we got back to Hamhung. They were heading back to Pusan to regroup. From there, First Division planned to start all over again and head back up the peninsula to intercept the PVA coming south. Doc Blake got wounded shortly after he attended to me. I don't know where he went after that. The regiment had so many guys get wounded that we had to unload the dead from the trucks and bury them in mass graves using bull dozers. We needed to make room for the more severely wounded guys. We marked the coordinates of the burial sites, so we can go back and get them someday. CJ, Eckles, Flores, and Walters are still there, buried in that frozen earth. Doc Blake, despite his own wounds, was still attending to other Marines. I think he forgot he was wounded too. What a guy."

"What happened to you, Lieutenant?"

"Just stupid luck I guess. First Platoon was leading the way out of Hagaru. I got out in front. They tell me that I must have stepped on a land mine. When I came to, I was on a truck and Doc Blake was pumping me full of morphine."

"The nurse says you lost your leg, Sir. Is that why you won't write home?"

"Yeah. You know how that is, don't you, Smitty?"

"No, Sir, I really don't know how that is. Only you do. I got a letter from my girlfriend and she tells me that, back home, reports in all the newspapers are that we're all dead or pretty close to it. You really owe it to the people who love you to let them know that you're still alive—minus a leg, yeah, but still alive. If you don't mind my saying so, Sir, there's a lot more to you than just a leg."

"You sound like that nurse and, of course, you're both right. So, I give up, I'll do it. I promise."

"You'll do it today," Smitty insisted affirmatively.

"Yeah, today," the lieutenant replied. "I make you a sergeant and now you're giving me orders. Stop by my room later, Smitty, I've got some papers for you to sign. I'm recommending Walters and CJ for the Navy Cross, and I need to have you sign as a witness to what they did."

"I will, very gladly, Sir. See you later and thanks for everything."

"Oh, and by the way, Doc Blake has been personally recommended for a Silver Star by the Company Commander and, of course, Eckles, Flores, and you will be receiving Silver Stars as soon as I can write up the citations," the lieutenant shouted as the nurse steered him back toward his room.

Later Smitty learned that Lieutenant Peterson died in surgery before he was able to write up the citations for the Silver Star for Eckles, Flores and himself but not before Smitty signed as a witness for Walters and CJ.

Smitty and Billy were officially informed that they would both be transferred to a rehabilitation facility at Camp Otsu the following week.

~CHAPTER~

TWENTY SEVEN

Christmas had come and gone, but the war in Korea was still raging – unfortunately, at the expense of the innocent civilian populaces in both the North and South.

It was now the end of March and both Smitty and Billy had seen enough of Camp Otsu; it had served its purpose. They were both well enough now to want a little excitement in their lives, and it had been a long time since the two had gone on liberty together.

As the train left Otsu station, headed for Kyoto, the two young Marines reminisced.

"Tomorrow we ship out of here for home, and I can't wait to get back to good old Frisco," Billy sighed. "If I'd known what I was getting myself into I never would have joined the Marines in the first place."

"That's crap, Billy. You're alive, you made it, and you're a real Marine now—just like Jimbo and Tyne. You gotta' be proud of that."

"You be proud, Smitty. I'm too busy thinkin' about gettin' my life back to normal. All I wanna' do right now is find some Jap girl, get drunk, and forget about all this Marine Corps hoopla."

"You ain't foolin' me, Billy, you love the Corps just as much as I do."

The girls they met on the street in Kyoto that evening were bent on pleasing the Marines in any way they could, and a party at their house seemed to be the best send off for two young men who would be sailing home the next morning. Billy stopped at a store and bought several bottles of sake.

"I'm taking some of it with me for the long voyage home," he smiled, winking at Smitty.

The taxi pulled up to the small bamboo structure that the girls called home, and the four went inside. They laughed and talked and drank for hours, then Billy and Michiko decided to go into her bedroom, taking a bottle of sake with them.

"You don't need any more wine, Billy, you're already pretty drunk," Smitty informed him.

Billy shrugged him off with a gesture of his arm.

Smitty and his lady friend Ami-san sat on the floor warming themselves next to a ceramic urn filled with sand and hot charcoals.

"Do you have girl friend back home, Smitty?" she asked in broken English.

"Yes I do," Smitty answered.

"Is she beeoo-tee-ful?" Ami-san implored.

"Yes she is."

"Do you ruve her?"

"I love her very much," he said affirmatively.

"Do you want to go to my room?" she asked with a wistful smile.

"Thank you, but I think we should stay here."

"You no butterfly?" she asked with a slight frown.

"I don't understand. What do you mean by butterfly?"

"Butterfly," she answered, "you know, butterfly flits from flower to flower."

"No, I don't do that," Smitty answered, shaking his head from side to side.

"You good man, I wish I had man like you. I am very sleepy. I go to bed now if that's OK with you, Smitty."

"That's fine. I'll just wait outside for Billy." Smitty smiled and gave her a quick embrace. "Thank you for a very enjoyable evening. I will always remember you and your people by your friendship and hospitality," he smiled.

Smitty wandered outside and sat down on a two-foot high brick and mortar fence that ran along the front of the house. He looked up into the night sky and thought about the journey that had brought him here. His thoughts careened from San Francisco to Walters, to Nani, to CJ, to Hawaii and Camp Catlin, then went full circle again, picking up Jimbo, Tyne, Paulo, Tedi, Blake, Eckles, and Flores along the way. But even the rice wine hadn't been very effective in helping him forget the bad times.

Smitty's reverie, which had become accustomed to disturbances, was suddenly shattered again. He heard a frantic scream coming from inside the house. He rushed back to see two terrified girls. Billy was waving an intimidating knife at them.

"Lousy Jap biches," he slurred, "I'll kill you both." He was obviously much drunker than before.

Smitty twisted the knife out of his hand, as Billy staggered backward and fell onto the bamboo floor.

"Ooriental whoores," Billy slurred again.

"Shut up, Billy. You're drunk," Smitty said emphatically.

The girls were sobbing relentlessly. "We must call police," Michiko sputtered between sobs.

Smitty calmed them down and assured them that he would handle everything.

"No need to make more trouble than there already is."

"You good man, Smitty," Ami-san said. "We be OK now. You take him and go away, OK?"

Smitty apologized, then grabbed Billy's bottles of sake, steering him outside. He sat him down on the wall.

"What kind of crap was that? We aren't in Korea anymore. You can't treat people like that—drunk or sober, Billy. You scared the hell out of those girls. Couldn't you see that they were afraid that you were really going to kill them?"

"Kill 'em? Why of course I was gonna kill 'em. A man doesn't ha'f to be in a war to want to kill those schlant eyed bastards. They're just like those worthless gooks back in Korea."

"You gotta' sober up, Billy, you're talking like a crazy man," Smitty insisted.

"Wha choo mean sober up? You sound like my ole man. He thought I din't know nothin', either. He kicked me out of the house and beat my mother black and blue 'til I had to get out of there. It's because of him that I got in trouble all the time, and the judge said I could either go to jail or join the Marines. It wasn't because of any love for servin' my country. Hell, I never cared about that servin' my country crap. He gave me a choice, and I sure as hell wasn't goin' to jail."

"That's not the story you told me when we met back in Frisco, Billy."

Billy gave Smitty a cold stare before changing the subject.

"You never killed nobody, did you, Smitty? Not really killed nobody - did you?"

Smitty was becoming seriously disgusted with Billy's drunken rambling.

"You're totally plastered, Billy. Come on, let's walk awhile and maybe you'll sober up."

Smitty had never seen Billy like this before. He took his arm to help him up, but Billy jerked away violently.

"Answer me," he insisted. "You never killed nobody - not like I did. Oh yeah, you shot into crowds of gooks in Korea. Big deal, but you never stood there and watched them die. You never saw the look of surprise or the horror on their faces when they knew they were drawin' their last breath. Hell no you din't, did you? For you, it was just a job. No joy, no passion, just doin' your duty like a good Marine. Hell, you never really killed nobody."

Billy took another long suck on his bottle, smiling a hideously blank stare at Smitty as he continued his drunken rant.

"You remember back in Hawaii when we did that special training? Yeah, you remember. That was the night you asked Jimbo what it was like to kill a man. Well, you asked the wrong guy. He never really killed nobody either, not like I did. You should have asked me. I bet you think I don't know who killed those boys at Camp Catlin either," Billy ranted on. "Well, I killed 'em. Yeah, I killed 'em both and watched 'em writhe in pain while I did it. You think I'm lying don't 'choo, Schmitty."

"Billy, you're fulla' crap. You never killed those boys. The police confirmed that whoever murdered them would have been covered with blood."

"You think I din't think of that? You really think I din't think of that? I'm a helluva lot schmarter than you or my ole man ever was. I'll bet you want to know how I did it, don't 'choo.

"No, Billy, I really don't. We gotta' get back to Otsu." Smitty answered, shaking his head.

"Well I'll tell you. I found a large set of full length coveralls in that barn and a pair of work gloves that got left behind when the Army aban'oned that dump. I pulled those coveralls over my uniform and the pant legs were so long they even covered my boots. I'm a helluva lot schmarter than you or my ole man ever was," he repeated in his drunken stupor.

"Billy there weren't any bloody coveralls found anywhere at the scene. The police searched that place top to bottom and didn't find any bloody coveralls or gloves."

"Ha," Billy scoffed. "That's cuz I stuffed 'em between the walls of that barn and pushed 'em way down inside as far as they'd go. I hoped to come back and get 'em the next time I went on that watch, but the CO made me a corporal, and I never got back on that watch again. I'm still a helluva lot schmarter than you or my ole man ever was," Billy rambled on.

"Didn't you think the police would ever find them later?" Smitty said, humoring him.

"Hell yes, I did. When they schtarted talkin' about tearin those buildings down I was worried about them findin' the camera that I hid in that same wall. That roll of film had pictures of me and those kids together. I caught 'em playing inside that building several nights before I ever decided to kill 'em. We made a game of it and I invited 'em back on nights when I stood watch. It was all a game. They trushted me. Those schtupid kids trushted me. You see, I had it all planned ahead of time. But the film in that camera was the real problem. That's when I knew I had to burn that rat's nest down."

Billy took another long drink of sake.

"Now I know you're full of crap, Billy. The night that fire started you were with me at my girl friend, Nani's house or don't you remember? We dropped you off back at Camp Catlin—after the fire started."

"Ha again," Billy chortled. "You din't really think I would set that fire myself, did you? Remember those two schlobs we met in the bar on Hotel Schtreet? Remember the lush named Kona? I got him to do it, and all it cost me was one lousy bottle of cheap scotch whiskey. I told him when, where, and how to do it. And I warned him to keep his mouth shut. That booze hound did it jus' the way I planned. The night I met him on the beach at the far end of Waikiki to pay him off he was flappin' his gums so much I knew I couldn't trusht him to keep quiet so…"

"So you murdered him, too. Is that it?" Smitty asked in astonishment.

By now, Smitty was starting to believe. It was all beginning to make sense the way Billy was telling it.

"It takes you a while, Shmitty, but sooner or later you figure it out, don't 'choo? Yeah, I killed Kona. I had to, and the world is better off without him."

"What I really need to know is why you killed those boys," Smitty prodded.

"I've tried to figure that out myself. I guess my ole man had somethin' to do with it. I always tried to trusht that son-of-a-bitch and never could. He lied to me. He hurt me so much. When I needed love he gave me hate. I became so confused that I started passin' that hate onto dogs, cats, squirrels, and other animals. I started gettin' in trouble at school by bullying kids smaller than me. It was fun. I tricked 'em into thinkin' I was their friend, then I'd hurt 'em just like I did those two little gooks in Hawaii. I enjoyed it. Yeah, that's the answer. It gave me a thrill to have so much power. I felt like I was as powerful as God, 'til I finally got arrested."

Billy took another long swig of truth serum from his bottle.

"When the judge offered me the Marine Corps inschtead of jail it was a lifeline, so I took it. It was a chance to get away from home and the ole man that I hated so much. When I met you, I thought I'd finally found a real friend, but you weren't anything like me. Then, they sent you from Catlin to Pearl and it didn't matter anymore," Billy slurred." And I'll bet you still don't know why you got transferred to Pearl Harbor, am I right?"

Smitty looked at him in even further amazement like he had just opened Pandora's Box and wished he hadn't.

"When the CO called me in he asked me if I searched around to find the killer that night. I told him that I wanted to but you were too shcared. Ain't that a laugh? Anyway he said he didn't want any Marines in his outfit like that and a few days later you were gone. I felt bad; really I did, because you were the only friend I thought I had. You were the only one that I thought really knew me."

"The Billy that I knew..." Smitty began again "...was the guy who jumped off his chair at the Kahuna Bar in Honolulu and rushed to defend a lady in distress. You busted that guy in the chops faster than I could ever have reacted. I was proud of you that night, Billy."

"You mean that barfly biche? When I saw him hit her I felt a rush all over my body. I started to tell you that night why I clobbered him then that HASP jeep and that piss ant Sergeant Urbino came rolling up. That guy hit her and I thought about my ole man hittin' my mother. If you hadn't grabbed me, I would have kept punchin' that son-of-a-biche 'til he drowned in his own blood."

"Let's get back to those boys at Camp Catlin," Smitty interrupted.

"Wait, wait—you're making me dizzy with all these queschtions," Billy exclaimed, "but that's really simple enough. I was on watch one night and I thought I heard something inside that building, so I went in. There was a faint flicker of light in there, like it was coming from a kerosene lamp. At first, I was shcared and then the fear shifted to them. They were just kids. I calmed them down. To make a long story short, we simply made a game of it. It helped me pass the time. I told them when I'd be on that watch again and invited them back. The next time they came I met them at the back fence. I was so excited. I felt like I was a kid again. We talked for hours and I would tell them lies about how I fought in World War II. They ate it up and wanted more. We took pictures of each other. We played hide and seek and guessing games. You probably wonder if I ever feared getting caught – well I did, but that was part of the excitement. One night, the Commander of the Guard came rolling up to the gate as we were coming out the door. I checked my watch and it wasn't time for the changing of the guard, so I pushed them back inside. He never suspected a thing, and that made it even more daring. I grew to hate those little bastards. They had everything I ever wanted out of life. I planned to kill 'em the next time they came. I had everything organized and everything planned. I guess I could compare it to goin' huntin' when I was a kid. The thrill of the hunt made me feel ecstatic. I could barely wait to see their faces when the game became real."

Smitty could see the wild look in his eyes as Billy seemed to be reliving the moment.

"I separated 'em, then I tied 'em up and gagged 'em before I put on the coveralls and gloves. I picked the skinny kid first and held him down with my knees, while I undid the front of his pants. He knew by then that it wasn't a game anymore and I knew by the helpless look in his eyes that he was very frightened. I jabbed him in the chest and face with my pen knife just enough to make him hurt and cause some blood to flow. Then, I put tiny slashes across his chest and arms. It was…"

Smitty couldn't take his eyes off Billy's face as it contorted with every word he spoke. Billy stopped long enough to take another drink before he continued.

"It was like bein' drunk. No, it was even better than that. It's hard to explain to someone like you, Schmitty, but God how I loved it. You should have been there to see it."

"Yes, I have wished many times that I could have been there, Billy."

"You don't understand, Schmitty."

"You got that right, Billy. I sure don't, and I pray to God that I never do."

Billy ranted on, completely oblivious to Smitty. It was as if he were his own audience, greatly enthralled by his own performance. "When I stuck that knife in his chest and very slowly pulled it down to his pelvic bone, I watched his eyes roll back inside his head. Then, I watched as blood and guts oozed out of his body. It was like dressin' out a deer. Yeh that's what it was, like dressin' out a deer."

Billy's hands moved constantly, going through the motions of his actions. As he spoke, his eyes filled with excitement.

"I waited 'til he drew his last breath, then I grabbed the lantern and rushed over to the other kid. When he saw me, he seemed to know somethin' was wrong. I'd been gone too long, and he was wheezin' through his nose, schtrugglin' to breathe and free himself at the same time. He must have seen the blood on the front of the coveralls, and that created an immense panic in him that gave me a super rush. When I finished with him I was totally exhausted. It took me awhile to recover. I removed the gloves and coveralls, turning them inside out, being very cautious not to let any blood get on me. I stuffed them inside a hole in the double wall near where I had hidden the camera. I carefully wrapped the knives in one of the torn shirts and then I ran to the back fence and threw 'em on the ground. That was when I came looking for you. Forgive me for saying so, but I almost burst out laughing when I saw you at the gate, but I knew I had to play my role of being shcared and innocent." Billy laughed an eerie laugh.

In the moonlight, Smitty could see that Billy wore an evil smile on his face as he spoke the words. It appeared that just talking about that night brought Billy's hate flooding to the surface of his persona.

"Did you ever ask yourself why you did it?"

"No, I never asked myself anything, but I'm sure it was for the exhilarating power that I felt. I was finally in control, and I had absholute power just like my ole man had over me. Yeah, that was it—power over another person's life—it's a wonderful feeling to have, Schmitty, but you'll never understand that."

As the train stopped at the station, Billy was still so drunk he needed to be helped on board. They sat across from each other as the empty train car left the station, headed back to Otsu. Although, Smitty felt that he had already heard too much, there were more questions he needed to have answered. They sat there in silence for a while until Smitty finally broke the ice.

"There is one thing you haven't figured out yet, Billy. How do you know I won't tell the Honolulu Police when we get back? Are you going to have to kill me too—now that I know?"

Billy appeared to be totally unfazed by Smitty's comments.

"You won't tell 'em shit because, first of all, they would never believe you. And what's more, if you did tell 'em, I would involve you in all of this. You were there that night—remember? And besides, right now, those schtupid 'Keyschtone Cops' believe they already got their murderer. No, you won't tell 'em, much as you think you'd like to. And there's a lot more you don't know yet. Yeah, about Flores and Eckles," he mumbled before passing out.

Smitty just sat there, staring at him in total disbelief.

It wasn't ending quite the way Smitty thought it would, but there was some bittersweet victory in knowing that at least the mystery of the dead boys was solved. Eventually, Smitty would need to know what Eckles and Flores could have had to do with any of this, but at this moment he felt overwhelmed by what he had heard so far.

Smitty pressed the side of his face against the window of the speeding train. He looked out at the beautiful countryside as a panorama of trees and farms sped by. It had been an entire year now since the murders of the two boys and Smitty had finally met the phantom of his worst nightmares. He looked back to his left and, there he was, seated directly across from him.

When he got back to Hawaii he knew there would be the matter of Gerald Needham to deal with - but how?

~CHAPTER~

TWENTY EIGHT

The next morning the ship sailed without fanfare, but the Marines didn't care. They were going home. Some of them manned the rails for their last look at the Japanese coastline. On board, they were officially informed that the rumors were correct, they would be making a stop in Hawaii. Some of the more seriously wounded would be dropped off at Tripler Hospital for special therapy and advanced trauma treatment.

Most of the Marines sought out places below deck to start the usual shipboard games of pinochle and poker. Smitty, however, lay below to find solace on his rack. He would spend many hours that day, and in days to come, just trying to make sense out of what Billy had told him. The more he thought about it the more convinced he became that what Billy had said was undoubtedly true, though so impossible to believe. What worried him most was that he wasn't convinced that anyone else would find it believable either.

Billy, he always thought, had been his trusted friend. What was worse was that Billy was a fellow Marine. Smitty believed all along that Billy had always shared his sense of honor. What Billy had portrayed to him since San Francisco were the same ideals and devotion to duty that led him to respect the Marine Corps values of 'Honor, Courage, and Commitment.' Now, that dream had been shattered in the worst possible way. He had to choose between what he knew to be right, by turning this information over to the police in Honolulu or living the rest of his life knowing that a maniacal murderer would still be on the loose. And then there was the other possibility, that perhaps they had already convicted Jerry Needham.

If so, that might be impossible to undo—especially if twelve jurors were already convinced that he was guilty.

But there was more to it than that. Billy was right. It was quite probable that, even if Smitty did tell the police, they wouldn't believe him. After all, without Billy's confession there was no proof of anything, not even what Billy told him about the fire and the death of Kona. A psychiatrist would think Smitty was nuts. And, unfortunately, Smitty was occasionally beginning to entertain that possibility himself.

Sometimes, in the dark, he thought he heard the scrambled voices of Chinese soldiers with bugles blaring. He would often be suddenly awakened, finding it impossible to return to sleep again. Drinking to forget hadn't helped and there were times, even in his waking hours, that he thought he heard Billy's voice calling out, "Smitty, over here, by the fence." He couldn't seem to shake off an endless parade of nightmarish thoughts.

He lay on his rack for days, never venturing any further than the mess deck or the head, occasionally even missing a meal. He heard the other Marines coming and going through the sleeping quarters, but never spoke to any of them. He was in his own world—a world of pain and confusion. Truth and conjecture had become so intertwined that he couldn't make sense of anything. He had to do something and he needed answers to the hellish questions he was afraid to ask. His worst fear was that the justice he had sought for so long might truly be dead.

After several days at sea, he overheard Marines talking about Hawaii. They were saying that the ship was nearing the coastline of Oahu and would probably make landfall by early morning. That statement seemed to rouse him back to his senses. He rolled out of his rack and headed up the ladder, toward the main deck. He stopped and then peered over the rail. There was a sudden gust from a refreshing coastal breeze that cleared his nostrils, reminding him of Nani. He gulped breath after breath of the clean fresh air to replace the pervasively stagnant air that had clogged his lungs in the tight and cramped sleeping quarters below deck. He stood on the deck alone. The only sounds he could hear were the waves washing alongside the ship as it knifed its way through the calm sea. Everyone, except the crew inside the enclosed bridge near the bow, was probably below deck sleeping.

It was very late at night, and the light from a friendly moon guided him aft toward his favorite spot aboard ship. He stood there looking over the rail again as the sea behind the ship quietly swirled and churned, leaving a wake that glinted in the bright moonlight. The rising moon, lingering low on the horizon, seemed to hold its fixed position directly ahead as if it were guiding the ship like a beacon toward the Hawaiian Islands.

He was alive, but he felt like he shouldn't be. Walters and CJ, Flores, and Eckles should be here—not him. He momentarily entertained the thought that it would be so easy to slip over the side into the deep and placid waters below; to drown his anguish forever in the depths of the bottomless ocean, but he knew there were important things he needed to do.

He stepped back quickly and rested his shoulders against the aft deck superstructure. From there, he slid down into a sitting position. He stared hypnotically at the rippling waves created by the ships propeller. The image of the moon reflected brightly on the surface of the water behind the ship. He closed his eyes and tried to conjure thoughts of Nani and of home. For awhile he dozed off. Before long, however, he was abruptly awakened by a familiar voice.

"I thought I'd find you back here," the voice said.

Smitty blinked a little, adjusting his eyes again to the sudden light. It was Billy, and it was obvious that he had been drinking.

"Do you mind if I sit down? It's been kind of difficult making new friends since we left port," Billy said.

"I can imagine," Smitty answered sarcastically as he caught a blast of Billy's foul breath.

Billy held a half full bottle of sake in his hand.

"Care for a drink?" he asked Smitty casually.

"I'll pass," Smitty responded, "but I would like to talk to you."

"About what, Schmitty?"

There it was again, that annoying drunken slur.

"When we were on the train going back to Otsu you mentioned Eckles and Flores before you passed out. It seemed that there was something else you wanted to tell me."

Billy took a long drink. "You sure you won't have some?" he said, holding the bottle out to Smitty again.

"I'm sure," Smitty answered.

"I don't remember much about what I said that night, but Eckles and Flores, yeah," Billy began slowly, while deliberately looking away from Smitty. "Now that you know everything else, I might as well tell you about them too," He hesitated. "I killed them both." He hesitated again. "I had to Smitty. I really didn't want to." Billy looked at Smitty, perhaps to get a reaction, but now Smitty was no longer looking at him.

"It was because of that gook family in Korea. You see, after Doc Blake ran off to help someone calling for a corpsman, I was left there by myself. It was cold, you know that, and I was shcared and alone. Hell was breaking loose all around me. I crawled over to the hatch near the farm house, shlid it off, went inside, put the hatch back, and went down the ladder. It was quiet and so much warmer down there. I was shcared and so tired I guess I fell asleep on the earthen floor for a while. I woke up and saw two kids, huddled together, sleeping near me. The ole man woke up. He saw me hovering over his kids with a bayonet in my hands. He lunged at me. I grabbed my rifle and shot that gook bastard right between his shlanted eyes. His wife sat there, staring at me in the dim lantern light. She was an eerie sight with that frantic look on her face. It haunted me. So, I shot her too. Then I bayoneted both of those noisy little brats to shut 'em up and I sat there and watched 'em die—yeah, and I admit I loved every minute of it."

Billy went on and on like a broken water spigot that you couldn't turn off. The sake was numbing his senses again, and now he seemed bent on telling everything—no matter what it was.

"I knew I had to get the hell out of there, so I shlid the hatch back and saw that it was near dawn. As I replaced the cover on the hatch, I heard a booming voice that sounded like it was coming out of a cloud—and, no, Schmitty, it wasn't God. It was Flores. Him and Eckles were shootin' at a bunch of chinks and Flores called to me to come and help them. I din't wanna' get killed. I wanted no part of that damn war. Bullets were flying all around, so I scrambled back further behind the line. I knew I had to do something about those two because they saw me come out of that cellar. I knew they would tell someone so, during the heat of the battle, I shot 'em both. Simple as that, I had too. You undershtand, don't 'choo? I knew when they were found everybody'd think the chinks did it."

"So you shot them in the back," Smitty murmured disgustedly at the sinisterly evil form silhouetted against the moon.

Billy took another drink while Smitty sat there in stunned silence, not wanting to believe what he was hearing and not wanting to hear anymore. He thought he had already heard the worst but this was becoming even more grotesque then he could bear. Smitty's mind was in a fog, overwhelmed by truth that sounded more like fiction.

Smitty did recall that it had been during that battle that Flores and Eckles positions were overrun, and the PVA had broken through the lines. What Billy was saying explained everything bad that happened that night, including the deaths of Walters and CJ, who had moved up to close the breach.

"So, now you're wondering if I would kill you too, Schmitty. Well, I can tell you quite honeshtly that the answer is no. You can truchst me, we've always been friends."

Billy was again trying to find acceptance from the only person who he had ever thought to be his friend.

"What a strange thing for you to say, Billy. Can I trust you? After all, those kids in Honolulu trusted you; Kona trusted you; that family in Korea trusted you; Flores and Eckles certainly trusted you; and those Japanese girls trusted you too. And now, you tell me I can trust you? What a joke, Billy. You go against everything that I've ever believed in. To you, trust is only a vehicle that allows you to exploit your victims' weaknesses. You go against all the values of the United States Marine Corps. You're a misfit, and now I regret thinking that you were ever my friend."

Smitty hesitated for a moment, just to catch his breath.

"Do you realize or even care that a man has been accused of your crimes and may have been convicted of them already - or that he might go to prison for what you did?" Smitty asked.

"Yeah sure, you mean that dumb drunk at the Kahuna Bar. That's really a laugh—him and his useless drinking buddy—they're just scum bags that barely existed anyway. Like I've said before, the world will be better off without either of 'em.

Smitty buried his face in his hands before he spoke again.

"Billy, there are some things you've told me that make it impossible for me to understand, but there is one thing that haunts me more than all the rest." Smitty hesitated. "How could you possibly justify murdering Eckles and Flores, who, just the day before, put their own lives in harm's way to save yours? Was that a feeling of power too?"

Billy took another long drink from his bottle of sake and then he expelled a long, foul sigh before giving Smitty an answer.

"That's a tough question, Schmitty, but you have to understand that I was on the spot. Like I said, those guys would have told someone that they saw me coming out of that cellar. I was just doing what my father always used to say. In fact, I can hear him saying it now, 'Billy, in this dog eat dog world a man has got to look out for number one.' So, I killed a nigger and a spick. What's the big deal about that?"

Smitty was completely stunned. He opened his mouth to respond, but the words just wouldn't come. He suddenly realized that there was no way to reach a conscience that didn't exist.

"Just a few more questions, Billy. How many North Korean soldiers did you kill?"

"I don't know. None, I guess." Billy answered hesitantly.

"And how many Chinese soldiers?" Smitty continued angrily.

"None," Billy admitted.

"A killing machine like you, and you wasted all that opportunity? Why?" Smitty prodded.

"I discovered back at Inchon that if I shot at them, they'd shoot back and the more I lay back the safer I was. That makes sense, doesn't it?"

"To you it does, but not to me," Smitty shuttered, "and the night you got captured, you dropped back behind the lines supposedly to get more ammunition, didn't you?"

Billy didn't respond.

"And some Chinese who got behind our lines picked you up and took you down the reverse slope, didn't they?"

"I guess so," Billy replied, "but so what? I'm still alive, ain't I?"

"I wonder if you really are," Smitty answered, "but, if you are alive, it's because of guys like Flores and Eckles. So, why are you telling me all of this? Did you actually think I would understand? Did you think that I could have empathy for someone who had no empathy for anyone but himself? Did you think that I would accept what you have done, then forgive you and look the other way?"

"You caught me with those Jap biches," Billy slurred. "I would have killed them both. You knew that, didn't you? I was drunk, and I guess I thought I could trush you to keep your mouth shut. But I know now that I was wrong. I couldn't trush my ole man, and I sure as hell can't trush you either—can I?"

"No, Billy, you can't. Walters had you figured out all along."

"Yeah, Walters, Walters, Walters. He had me figured out alright. You remember the morning he died? You remember what he said before he died?

"You mean about his ring and his diary?"

"Yeah, that too, but do you remember what he said about me?"

"Of course I do. He asked me to look after you."

"No he didn't. What he said was, 'Watch out for Billy.' You thought he meant look out after Billy. Do you remember now?"

"You're right. I do remember now. And later I remember wondering why he suddenly had become so concerned about you when he never really liked you."

"Now you're getting it, Schmitty. He was trying to warn you about me. He had seen me behind the front lines when him and CJ were setting up that machine gun and he tried to get me to move up and join the battle, but I was too schmart for that, so I drew back even further. I was standing behind you that morning, waiting to see if he was going to tell you about that, but thank God he died before he could finish."

"Thank God? What God are you talking about, Billy? Walters and CJ saved all of us that night no thanks to you or your 'god' whoever he is. You helped to get a lot of our Marines killed. I've struggled with my decision, but now I know that you have to be stopped before you ever kill again. Maybe the Honolulu Police will believe me, and maybe they won't, but I have to take that chance. I also have to take the chance that you'll try to incriminate me along with you. If that's the case—then so be it."

Billy sighed and took another long drink from his bottle. "I knew it. I knew you couldn't keep your mouth shut. You sure as hell ain't my friend and never have been."

"So now, Billy, what do you think? Are you going to kill me? That seems to be your answer to everything that stands in your way," Smitty said.

"I'm not ready to give myself up yet. People like you have their own wishy-washy, perverted sense of justice that leaves no understanding for people like me, so you're gonna' have to go too," Billy said with a silly smirk, like he had one more secret that Smitty knew nothing about.

Billy finished the bottle and threw it over the rail of the ship. Within a moment, that secret was revealed. A gun, that hadn't been there before, suddenly appeared in Billy's hand.

"So what's your plan Billy? You don't mind telling me, do you?"

"I'm gonna' kill you—of course. It's as simple as that. Then I'm gonna' dump your holier than thou ass overboard. Nobody will hear the shot, nobody will hear the splash, and nobody will miss you. Does that shound like a plan to you, Shmitty? Guys turn up misshing all the time during wars. You're gonna' be MIA. It's what they call the fortunes of war."

"You're going to shoot me with that gun?" Smitty chuckled, incredulously. "Let me guess, Billy, you got that gun from Eckles' body when you dragged him down the hill after you murdered him. Isn't that right?"

"Right, Shmitty, you're shmarter than I thought. Now stand up and move over to the back rail," Billy ordered. "Let's get this over with."

Smitty obligingly stood up and walked over to the rail. He turned around with his back now facing directly aft. He looked forward toward the bow of the ship and saw the top of the main mast with the yard arms extending to the left and right. With the bright moon backlighting them, it looked a lot like the cross hairs of a sniper scope, perfectly centered on the alabaster moon. The longer he stared, the more it reminded him of the cross Mama Ahue had given him in Hawaii.

"I've got some bad news for you, Billy, that gun doesn't work."

"Don't give me that Hollywood movie crap, Schmitty. It's loaded; I checked it myself."

"Did you test fire it, Billy?'

"Why would I need to do that?"

"Well, if you had, you would've realized that it doesn't work. It has a faulty firing pin. Eckles showed it to me while we were aboard ship in Korea. Do I need to tell you again? It doesn't work!" Smitty said more emphatically.

"That silly crap doesn't work with me," Billy said angrily.

"OK. Then go ahead and shoot me. Like you said, nobody will know. Go ahead and shoot."

"Goodbye, Smitty, I'm sorry that it had to end this way, but like I said, nobody is going to mish you—not even me."

Smitty smiled. "It's really strange, but occasionally the things you say make perfect sense. Semper Fidelis, Billy," Smitty added sarcastically.

Suddenly, the words of Gerald Needham, the ones he had so eloquently expressed back at the Kahuna Bar in Honolulu, ran through Smitty's mind, *"If there ever was any justice in this cock-eyed world, it died a long time ago."* Then, Smitty's mind shifted to the words of Mama Ahue, *"You must promise me that you will wear this cross at all times so that God's Grace and Mama Ahue will be with you wherever you go."*

Smitty's hand fumbled around in his dungaree pants pocket searching for the broken pieces of the cross. When he found them he clutched them in his fist then leaned back against the ships rail and waited.

Billy hesitated only momentarily. His hand trembled slightly as he raised Eckles' gun to eye level, pointing it at the center of Smitty's chest. Then there was an almost inaudible click immediately followed by an outcry, "DON'T!"

A single shot rang out that was swallowed up by the roaring of the gathering waves behind the ship.

On the other side of the horizon a new day sat quietly and patiently, waiting to be born.

~CHAPTER~

TWENTY NINE

Nani and her family waited anxiously at the pier. Captain Corwin had received official word that a ship loaded with wounded Marines would be arriving at Pearl Harbor that morning. They were hoping Smitty might be aboard. The more seriously wounded Marines and those in need of special treatment were the first to be unloaded and transported to Tripler Hospital.

Nani paced nervously as the Marines assembled at the quarter deck then began ambling in a steady line down the gangway onto friendly Hawaiian soil. The line grew shorter and shorter, trickling down to a few stragglers. Nani stopped some of the men coming off the ship to ask if they knew Sergeant Smith, known as Smitty, but they just shrugged their shoulders and moved on. Nani waited and watched well after the last Marine came down the gangway. A couple of hours passed and Lea was becoming more anxious to return to the parking area, but Nani pleaded with her to wait a little longer.

After several more minutes without seeing any more Marines on deck, Nani relented and the entourage headed back toward the car with Mama Ahue bringing up the rear, her arm surrounding Nani's waist. Nani expressed her disappointment by allowing a few teardrops to roll down her cheeks. Captain Corwin explained that during the coming weeks there would be several more ships coming through Pearl on their way to the States.

"We must not leave, child. Smitty is here, I feel his spirit nearby," Mama whispered to Nani.

"Oh Mama, I hope you are right. I miss him so much," Nani sobbed.

Nani stopped suddenly and listened, thinking she heard a distant voice calling her name. She hesitated for a moment then heard it again. She quickly did an about face and started running back toward the pier. There, at the bottom of the gangway she saw the face she had been longing to see for so many months. She ran to him, hugging him and kissing his mouth, like the love struck teenager that she was. They held each other tightly, spinning in a circular dizzying motion, until they almost dropped from exhaustion.

"Are you alright?" Nani asked as her tears began to flow again.

"I am now," he smiled at her, looking deeply into her eyes. "I am now."

"We waited and I thought you were not on board," she said. "I prayed that you would be here today."

"Something happened aboard ship last night and I had to write up an 'Incident Report' for the Executive Officer. That's why I was late coming ashore. I'll tell you about it later."

For the next few moments they acted as if there was no one else there, while Lea, Joi, Doc Corwin, Lani, and Mama Ahue stood on the periphery, feeling like they were mere spectators watching a romantic movie.

Finally, Lea broke the spell and introduced herself to Smitty as Mrs. Lea Corwin.

Smitty hugged Lea and congratulated the captain. "That would make you Nani's stepfather then, wouldn't it?" Smitty added with a grin.

Smitty turned and embraced Lani and whispered into her ear, "You and I and the rest of the world have lost a great friend, and I wish with all my heart that he could be here with us today."

"I do too, Smitty. I do too," Lani repeated.

Smitty held her very tightly while Lani struggled to hold back the tears that were beginning to form in the corners of her eyes.

"I've been volunteering at Tripler Hospital." Lani said nervously, needing to change the subject. "You should try to stop by later today, if you can."

"I will," Smitty assured her." Then, he turned to Mama Ahue. "You'll never guess what happened to me, Mama."

"Mama Ahue knows what happened, Smitty." She held out her hand to him at the same time that he held his hand out to her. In his open hand were two pieces of a broken cross. In her hand was a new cross with a beautiful gold chain attached.

"How do you do it, Mama Ahue?" Smitty asked incredulously as Nani hooked the clasp around his neck.

"No one knows—not even me," Mama said with an impish grin, "and I know something else too. Last night I awoke from a dream. My grandson Tedi visited me and warned me that you might be in danger. Mama could feel your spirit coming closer to her island. I went outside and saw a full pearl white moon rising overhead and suddenly a great black bird flew across its surface with wings outstretched. It was a sign of death. I prayed all through the night. Then, suddenly, a great weight was lifted from me."

Smitty hugged her tightly. "I understand Mama and I feel like a great weight has been lifted from me as well," he said to her.

"You're going to be staying with us until your ship sails out again," Nani said emphatically.

"I was hoping you would say that," Smitty smiled. "I have my duffle bag with fresh clothes and shaving gear right here," he said, holding the bag up so she could see it.

As they strolled back to the car, Smitty asked Joi about Kee, and she told him that he had joined the Marines and was at the Marine Corps Recruit Depot in San Diego, California.

"I can't wait to see him again," Smitty said.

"Me too," Joi smiled back at Smitty.

At the house, Lea told Smitty about the trial of Jerry Needham.

"Mama Ahue and I attended both days of the trial. The first day was like a three ring circus with so many people trying to get into the crowded courtroom. Many were turned away. Mr. Needham came in wearing the same shabby clothes he had been wearing since the day they arrested him. The prosecutor had a smug look on his face. He strode around the courtroom, giving his opening argument, professing his assurance that they had the right man. He told the jury about Jerry's homeless status in the community and added that they had witnesses who would prove his guilt. He put a lady on the stand who claimed to know Mr. Needham quite well. She gave her name as Ruth Wanabe and said that she first met Jerry at the Kahuna Bar on Hotel Street. He was a bad one, she told the court, and he hated cops. He wandered the streets of Honolulu with his friend, Kona. After an hour of her testimony, her hand began to tremble and the court took a short recess. When she returned the trembling had stopped, but Mama and I swore that we caught a faint hint of alcohol on her breath as she walked past us to retake the stand. She remembered distinctly, she said, that the night of the incident he left the bar, saying he was going to meet some friends out near Camp Catlin. Jerry's court appointed attorney never asked her a single question."

Mama Ahue nodded her head approvingly as Lea continued.

"After lunch, the prosecution brought a detective named Voss to the witness stand. He pointed directly at Jerry and said that he had suspected him right from the beginning. He claimed that Mr. Needham's answers were evasive and that Jerry couldn't remember where he had been that night. He too, professed that he was convinced of Mr. Needham's guilt. The next day, Jerry Needham appeared in the courtroom clean shaven with a military style haircut, wearing a new blue serge suit, a white shirt, a dark blue necktie, and new shoes—all compliments of Mama Ahue who, after that first day, became totally convinced of his innocence."

"Was he found guilty?" Smitty asked with a worried look on his face.

"No," Lea answered, "he was acquitted. The jury felt that there wasn't enough evidence to convict him. None of our family ever believed he was guilty, and we got a chance to tell him so. The entire case against him was purely circumstantial at best."

Smitty let out a sigh of relief. "I need to see him—today if possible. We'll be shipping out again day after tomorrow for Frisco."

"He's gone Smitty," Lea said ominously.

"Gone where?" Smitty asked with a wrinkled brow.

"Gone, gone, Smitty, he killed himself just three weeks ago. It was in all the papers. After he was acquitted, a lot of people thought that he got away with murder. They cried out for justice and vengeance and people badgered and taunted him constantly until, I guess, he couldn't take it anymore. They say he got drunk one night and went down to the beach where they had found his friend Kona's body. Mr. Needham hung himself on a nearby tree. The rumor was that he left a short note that said: 'There ain't no justice in this cock-eyed world, so I'm going to another place to see if I can find it there.' It wasn't until after his death that an autopsy discovered he had a withered leg from wounds received during WWII. There was no way that he would have been able to climb the chain link fence at Camp Catlin. That fact was never brought out at his trial. We also discovered that his court appointed attorney had never handled a criminal case before. He practiced civil law and had two lucrative cases he was handling at the same time as Jerry's trial. Mr. Needham's death was very sad and many people, even those who had at first thought he was guilty, attended his funeral. There were hundreds. The American Legion, the Disabled American Veterans, and the Veterans of Foreign Wars paid for his funeral. They buried him at Punch Bowl Cemetery with full military honors and placed a beautiful marker at his grave site."

"I need to go there, Nani," Smitty said.

"Would we be able to use your car this afternoon?" Nani asked her mother. "Smitty wants to visit the cemetery and we wanted to go over to Tripler Hospital for a while. It shouldn't take long."

"You can have it all day," Lea assured her.

~CHAPTER~

THIRTY

All the way to the Punchbowl Cemetery, Smitty sat in the passenger seat in rapt silence. He had assumed that his pain and guilt had ended aboard ship with the death of Billy. Now, this new surprise was dumped on him. He was convinced that as long as he lived he would have to carry the memories of all those senseless deaths inside his head. For him, none of it would truly be over. His eyes stared out the front windshield, but all he could see were gory reruns of the past.

He was suddenly startled back to reality.

"We're here, Smitty. Have you been sleeping?" Nani asked.

"I'm fine," Smitty replied.

The Punchbowl seemed to be a more solemn place now than when he had visited it before. Probably, he thought, it was because he had a more personal understanding of the sacrifice made by those who occupied these sacred grounds.

Nani escorted Smitty to Jerry's gravesite, then politely excused herself saying, "I'll go over and visit my father's grave, and you can meet me there when you're ready to leave."

Smitty removed his cover and knelt by the plaque that identified Mr. Needham's final resting place. He searched for words and fumbled through his mind before he began to speak quietly to Mr. Needham.

"When I first met you, Sir, I didn't understand how a man could become so cynical, but then I hadn't experienced life through your eyes. I wish that I could have changed all of that for you. Now I know that each man has to play the cards that he has been dealt, and you were dealt some really lousy hands. I want you to know that I have had my own doubts

---

and, many times, justice seemed to be extremely difficult to find. I know now that what little justice we have comes to us compliments of Walters and CJ and guys like you who unselfishly sacrificed themselves to preserve it for others. As you know, Billy Hoyt won't be doing any more killing. He inadvertently sealed his own fate. Ironically, justice for Billy Hoyt has finally come, thanks to a great lady named Mama Ahue and the grace of God. Sadly, for you, justice came a little too late. I hope now you will find the solace that you deserve. I, for one, will miss you, and I'll always be grateful for the sacrifices you made for me when I was too young to understand. God bless you, Jerry Needham. May He give you the justice that you could never find in this world."

It was only after he finished that he realized there were tears rolling down his face. Some of them were for Jerry and some, he realized, were for himself. For a long time, he had feared that Jerry's philosophy about justice had been dragging him down as well.

The ride to Tripler Hospital was very quiet and somber. Smitty stared blankly out the window as if he were in a trance. His mind was on a journey to elsewhere. It was as if the knowledge of Jerry's suicide had reopened the floodgates and all of the events of his recent past were let loose to prowl freely within the labyrinth of his mind.

"We're here, Smitty," Nani was saying. But Smitty wasn't here, his mind was somewhere else.

"Smitty, we're here," she repeated. Nani sat there, staring at Smitty. His eyes were wide open and fixed. He appeared to be staring at a distant point. She looked out ahead of the car to see if there was anything there to attract his attention. She saw nothing but a vacant area beyond the parking lot.

"Smitty," she said, "Where are you? What are you staring at?"

Without moving Smitty said, almost unconsciously, "Don't you hear them?"

"Hear what?" she asked, wrinkling her brow.

"The bugles," he replied without hesitation.

"What bugles?" she asked.

"Those bugles, the bugles blaring in the wind. Hear them?" he replied with the same stare.

With a puzzled look on her face, she shook Smitty's shoulder. "Smitty, where are you?"

"Oh, I - I'm sorry, honey, I was just thinking."

"About what?" she asked.

Smitty hesitated for several moments. "Oh nothing, just things, it's not important," he finally responded, with an almost apologetic smile.

Standing in front of Tripler Hospital, he allowed his eyes to scan the landscape below. It was a new perspective, one that had never been available to him before. The hillside still bore traces of the wild Plumeria blooming on the downward slope. Beyond that, he could see the full layout of Camp Catlin with Marines moving about in the distance like tiny soldier ants. And there, in the open space, was where it had all begun. It seemed so long ago.

Inside the hospital, he saw doctors, nurses, and aids scurrying about, tending to the new arrivals from the ship. Nani led the way down the corridor to the main floor nurses station. From there, they were directed to the ward were Lani was working.

"I have definitely decided to become a nurse," Lani told Nani with great exuberance. "Definitely," she repeated, "and I want you to meet one of my patients. He tells me that his name is Corporal Woodrow Philip Jackson the third. Isn't that a mouthful?" she laughed. "He's quite a guy and he's well enough now to be going back to the States on the same ship as you, day after tomorrow, Smitty."

Much to Lani and Nani's surprise, the two men embraced each other like they were long lost brothers.

"We know each other, Nani," Smitty said.

"I see that," she replied with a bewildered look.

"How are you doing, Woodrow? I see you survived. And you're a corporal now?" Smitty laughed.

"This guy saved my tail from HASP down on Hotel Street one night," Woodrow said to Lani.

"Yes, and Woodrow here probably saved a lot of guys lives on a hill in South Korea," Smitty responded.

The four of them had been chatting for a while when Smitty saw another familiar face on the ward.

"Who's the guy over there wearing that white smock?" Smitty asked Lani, wrinkling his brow.

"Oh, you probably don't know him. His name is Dan. He's Chinese and a volunteer here," Lani answered.

Smitty rushed over to Dan and, after a few words, embraced him.

"This is getting to be more than a little strange," Nani said to Lani.

Smitty briefly explained to the girls how he had met Dan and how odd it was that they were seeing each other again so soon.

"It sounds like all three of you guys have got a lot to talk about," Nani said. "Lea is having a welcome home dinner for Smitty tonight at our house. I'm sure she wouldn't mind a couple more guests."

"That's a wonderful idea," Lani said. "I'll clear it with Doctor Doug and I'll bring them home with me when I finish work."

Nani excused herself. "I want to visit with Doctor Corwin for a while," she explained.

She went down the hall and directly into Captain Corwin's office.

"Have you got a few minutes? I have something I need to talk to you about," Nani began.

Captain Corwin looked up at her, giving a nod of assent.

"Smitty's not the same," she continued. "I've caught him twice today, just staring into space. When I asked him what he was staring at, he mumbled something about 'bugles in the wind.' He has moments when it's as if he's not aware of anything or anyone else around him. It's really scary and I'm worried about him. Is there anything you can do? I think he needs help."

"I'll arrange to have him talk to a specialist. We'll see what he thinks."

Nani returned to the group, this time with the Captain.

"Well, Marine, I was hoping to see you again before you left. I've got someone here with me that I'd like you to meet. His name is Doctor Gillespie, and he's a specialist," Doctor Corwin said to Smitty.

Lani and Nani went along the ward, visiting with other wounded GI's, while Smitty and Doctor Corwin disappeared down the hallway.

Smitty sat in a comfortable overstuffed chair and stared at the man in the white cotton jacket sitting across from him.

"Don't tell me, Sir, let me guess. Doctor Corwin called you a specialist, but I'll bet what he meant was a psychiatrist, didn't he?"

"Bulls eye, Smitty, but you needn't worry. Neither of us thinks you're crazy. A lot of guys come back from battle fields where they have experienced an excess of mental trauma. Doctor Corwin thinks you may have experienced more than your share. I'd like to help you, but you need to help me. I want you to tell me what's bothering you."

"I don't think you've got enough time for that, Sir," Smitty replied.

"Try me, Sergeant, and don't leave anything out. It might be very important."

Smitty knew that he needed help, but he felt uncomfortable talking to anyone about his experiences. Although hesitant at first, once he started, it was like a dam had burst, flooding the room with the debris of sorrow and guilt.

He told him about what had happened to Tedi and Paulo and how that led to the killing of Kona, Eckles, and Flores; about the fire that killed two people who were there to fight the blaze; the atrocities he had witnessed in Korea; his grief about the loss of CJ and Walters; about the Korean family in the cellar; his confrontation with Billy aboard ship and his plan to throw him overboard. By the time he finished, he was almost exhausted. He capped it all off by telling him about his nightmares, his feelings of depression, and the ultimate suicide of his friend Jerry Needham.

"That's a lot of baggage for one man to carry, Sergeant Smith. I'm going to pass my report on to a doctor at your next duty station in the States."

~CHAPTER~

THIRTY ONE

At the house that evening, everyone sat transfixed, as Woodrow's story unfolded about how he and Smitty had originally met on Hotel Street and how that meeting led to another chance meeting at Inchon. Smitty told everyone how Woodrow single handedly assaulted an enemy machine gun nest and earned both a Purple Heart and a Bronze Star medal for bravery.

"I must have been nuts. It just happened. I don't really remember much. I guess, at the time, it seemed that it needed to be done, so I just jumped up and did it. I was really scared later when I thought about it," Woodrow said shyly.

When it came time for Dan to tell his part of the story, Smitty became more interested, listening to hear how Dan had been released and returned to Hawaii so soon.

"The chaplain that Smitty left me with looked after me and had Division Headquarters verify that I was an American," Dan said. "Division arranged to ship me straight back here after they verified my story."

As the evening wore on, Smitty eventually got to spend some quality time with Nani. She told him that she had decided to become a teacher.

Smitty took the opportunity to tell her that, when he got back to the States, he would be assigned to a new duty station and that he was going to visit CJ's folks and probably Eckles', Walters', and Flores' families as well.

"Then what are your plans after you get discharged?" Nani asked.

"Well, I think I'm going to join the Merchant Marines and spend the rest of my life sailing around the world," he answered, with a straight face, before he broke out laughing. Nani slapped him on the arm.

"I'm coming back here to spend the rest of my life with you—if you think you'll be able to tolerate me," Smitty said.

"I might be able to do that," Nani smiled.

"Actually, I want to go to college on the GI Bill and study law," he said. "And that reminds me, I need to go talk to Detective Earl Voss, with the Civilian Investigation Department in the morning."

"I can take you there if you'd like," Nani said, "but first I'd like to know why you were so late getting off the ship at Pearl Harbor.

"Oh yes, I haven't told you about that yet have I? It all began back in Japan. You remember Billy Hoyt, of course. Well, he got really drunk one night when we were on liberty and he got so plastered that he confessed to me that he killed the two boys at Camp Catlin. Of course, I didn't believe him but he tied everything together so neatly that I became convinced he really did it. I told him that when we got back to Hawaii I would have to report him to the police. On the ship coming back, he decided he would have to kill me too. Billy and I were alone out on the back deck of the ship. It was very late at night. He pointed a gun at me that he had picked up in Korea. I'd seen that gun before, so I knew it wouldn't work; it had a faulty firing pin. I told him that, but he wouldn't believe me. He seemed disappointed that he couldn't trust me to keep his secret—if you can imagine that. He decided to shoot me and throw my body overboard. I was told later that a sailor aboard ship had seen him drinking and acting erratically. A Marine told that same sailor that he saw Billy playing with a pistol that he had concealed in his sea bag. The sailor told the Chief Master-At-Arms, and the Chief strapped on a 45 caliber semi automatic pistol. He followed Billy around the ship waiting for him to do something stupid so he could lock him up. It didn't take long and it turned out to be something stupider than the Chief had expected. The Chief came up behind Billy, who had his gun trained on me. He obviously believed Billy was about to shoot. The Chief hollered, 'DON'T.' Billy was startled. He whirled around with the gun still in his hand. The Chief evidently wasn't taking any chances. He fired one shot into Billy's chest, killing him almost instantly. I saw the look on Billy's face as he lay there staring up into the morning sky. It was one of complete surprise and horror. I'll never forget it."

"Do you feel relieved now that you've told me all of this?" she asked, holding his hand.

"Yes, actually I do," Smitty told her. "But I haven't told you the one thing that really relieves me more than anything else. You see, it almost didn't end the way it did. I knew that night on the back of the ship that there was no way I could take the chance of having Billy get away with those horrendous crimes. I knew I could tell the police, but I doubted whether they would have believed me. After all, the police had no more tangible evidence against him than they did against Jerry Needham. It would have been my word against his. If the police didn't believe me, he would be back on the streets again murdering more people. I feel a little guilty telling you this, Nani, but when he pointed that gun at me, I knew in that instant that I was probably going to throw him overboard. Thank God the Chief showed up when he did or I would have carried the murder of Billy Hoyt with me for the rest of my life. And yet...."

"What?" Nani implored, seeing that the thought of Billy's death disturbed him.

"Billy was lying there on the deck with a startled look in his eyes, staring blindly up at me. He seemed so pathetic. He raised his open hand toward me as if..." Smitty stopped speaking again and then continued. "I, I didn't feel a thing. It was as if I had witnessed the death of a rabid dog. I felt relief, but no compassion, no pain, no joy, no sorrow, no anger, no loss, and yet....he had been someone I would have given my life to protect. It was warm that night, yet I felt a cold chill come over me as I stepped over his lifeless body and walked away."

He told her the whole story, including Kona's involvement in the fire at Camp Catlin, and how Billy murdered him to keep him quiet. But Smitty deliberately withheld information about the murders in Korea. He felt that it wasn't relevant to her or anyone but himself.

"There is one more thing I'd like to do. Woodrow and I wanted to go over to Hotel Street one more time before we ship out. It's just an old times thing. I asked the Captain about it and he granted Woodrow a Cinderella Liberty."

"Which means what?" she asked.

"It means he's got to be back to the hospital by midnight."

All the other guests had left, but Captain Corwin was just arriving as Woodrow and Smitty were leaving. He had worked very late with all the new arrivals at the hospital.

He pulled Nani aside. "You were right to tell me about Smitty," the Captain stated emphatically.

"Doctor Gillespie told me that he is suffering from extreme remorse, anxiety, and guilt from the war and the loss of so many friends. He actually feels that it should have been him that was killed instead of them. There is a lot that he probably isn't saying and may never tell you, and he is probably going to carry some of this baggage with him for a long time. The good news is that, with time and some expert counseling, he will get better, but it's going to be a long road. What you saw when he was staring into space was what we call 'the thousand mile stare.' He may have been replaying gruesome scenes from his experiences in the war. These will fade away in time, but he will need a lot of love and understanding, even at times when you don't really know what he's feeling. He's been through a lot in a very short period of time. Doctor Gillespie has made arrangements for him to get some counseling when he gets to his next duty station."

When Smitty and Woodrow arrived at Hotel Street they found that it was the same old place they both remembered so well. The Kahuna Bar was just getting warmed up for a big night of action, but Smitty and Woodrow had only one beer and then left. The street was dotted with prostitutes and wayward GIs. The two walked down toward the YMCA, as Smitty told Woodrow about how Walters had punched Urbino's lights out before they had left for Korea.

"You would have loved Walters if you had gotten to know him better. He was quiet, shy, and unpredictable – a lot like you – and you could always count on him to do the right thing. Its guys like him who make a big difference in this crazy world. You may remember that he was the guy who paid your cab fare the night you had the run in with Urbino. Unfortunately, Walters was killed in Korea at the Chosin Reservoir."

They stopped at the 'Y' and had a cup of coffee before heading back.

"Do you think we've made a difference?" Woodrow asked Smitty.

"Only time will tell, but I sure hope so."

Across the street, a soldier sat on the curb with his head bowed between his legs. He was obviously drunk. As they started to cross the street, to see if they could help him, two jeeps pulled up to the curb. A big guy, wearing three stripes on his sleeve, got out of the first Jeep and approached the dazed soldier.

"That sergeant looks familiar to me," Smitty said to Woodrow.

The sergeant tilted the young man's head upward and asked if he was all right. Then, he pulled him to his feet and straightened his tie and cap. He then led him over to the passenger side of the jeep and sat him down. The sergeant reached into the back seat and got a thermos. He poured some coffee into a cup and gave it to the young soldier to drink.

Smitty approached the Sergeant First Class in the second jeep.

"What is that sergeant's name?" Smitty asked him, inquisitively.

"That's Sergeant Urbino," he answered, "but most GIs around here know him as the 'Guardian Angel of Hotel Street.' He looks after all the guys and tries to make sure they don't get into too much trouble and wind up in the stockade. Would you like to meet him?"

"No, Sergeant. Thank you, anyway. He just looked a lot like someone I

218

once knew," Smitty answered. Then, he and Woodrow continued walking down the street.

"Is that the same Sergeant Urbino that you saved me from?" Woodrow asked, scratching his head. "He doesn't seem to be all that bad."

"Yes, that's him and he's the first pleasant surprise I've had in a long time. He must have had an epiphany. He certainly isn't the same guy he used to be—but then, neither are we."

~CHAPTER~

THIRTY TWO

Smitty knocked on the door bearing the name "Detective Sergeant Earl Voss, CID," freshly painted on the frosted glass window. The detective, wearing the same old wrinkled suit, opened the door and invited him in.

"I've been expecting you, Smith. The Navy Department sent me a report saying you would be coming to see me today. I see that you're a sergeant now too, congratulations."

"Thank you, Detective Voss. I see you've shined your shoes since last I saw you," Smitty quipped sarcastically.

"Actually, they're new. Do you like them?"

"Very becoming, but now you might have to change professions, Sir."

Voss smiled. "You haven't changed a bit, Smith."

"Actually I have, Sir," Smitty responded confidently, "and please call me Smitty."

"I just finished reading this investigative report from the executive officer of the ship you sailed in on yesterday, and it seems to verify everything I have always known about this case."

"Everything you've known about this case?" Smitty queried. "That probably explains why you prosecuted Mr. Needham then, doesn't it, Sir?"

The detective nervously cleared his throat and continued, ignoring the implications of Smitty's response. "It says here in the report that Corporal Billy Hoyt confessed to you that he was the one who killed those boys, and it says that he confessed all of this to you while he was drunk."

"That's correct, Sir. I didn't believe him at first until he explained how he did it. It's all in the report. And, sadly, it all adds up."

"Then he tried to kill you to shut you up. That must have been scary?"

"Indeed, detective, indeed." Smitty replied.

"Very interesting, Smitty, well, now I've got this case wrapped up," the detective said smugly as he rubbed his hands together.

"Yes, very good job, Sir," Smitty said facetiously. "I'll bet the next time I see you, you'll be a lieutenant. Then maybe you'll be able to afford a new suit," Smitty added with more sarcasm as he left his office.

Nani smiled at Smitty as he got back into the car. "Is everything OK?" she asked.

Smitty nodded affirmatively.

By afternoon, it was a full page story in a special edition of the newspaper with a picture of Detective Earl Voss on the front page in what appeared to be a brand new store bought suit.

Thousands of Islanders huddled around their television sets that evening as Detective Voss expounded his theories about the case, explaining how Billy had been his main suspect from the very beginning. Lea had a full house as her family sat spellbound around the small screen of their television set.

"There was something suspicious about him right from the get-go," Voss said quite sternly and emphatically. "A good detective can sense things like that. I suspected all along that he was probably guilty. It just took a while for me to gather enough evidence to prove it."

Voss never mentioned Smitty—only that Billy had confessed and was killed by a security officer aboard ship while trying to escape capture. It was all very dramatic to hear him tell it.

Earl wrapped up the broadcast with the words, "Solving this heinous crime has been the shining moment in my long and distinguished career."

Mama Ahue looked over at Smitty and gave him an all knowing wink, but Smitty was deep in thought.

Lea reached over and turned off the television set. "It sounds like he might be running for a political office in the future, doesn't it, Smitty?"

Smitty didn't reply.

Mama Ahue put her arm over Smitty's shoulders and led him out into the courtyard.

"I need to talk to you before you go, Smitty," she said.

"Sure, Mama," he smiled as they both sat down at the picnic table.

"Nani tells me that she is worried about you. She tells me that you are kind of sullen and distant sometimes. It's because of the war, isn't it, Smitty?"

"Yes, Mama," Smitty answered. "I lost many of my friends. Guys who deserved to live more than I do."

"Who is to judge things like that? God that is who." She said answering her own question. "Smitty, not you or me, but only God. We must accept His decisions. When Paulo and Tedi were killed, I suffered greatly but I knew it was His plan. Mama Ahue does not understand all things, but she knows that God does. You must remember what Mama told you about the tiny oyster and how he makes beautiful pearls out of irritating grains of sand. Certainly, we humans are smarter than the oyster. We can take ugly, irritating memories and replace them with pleasant thoughts. Mama thinks about the wonderfulness of Tedi and Paulo and their lives become beautiful memories instead of the agonizing memories of their untimely deaths. You must do the same. We must mourn the losses of our loved ones by celebrating their lives—so look at the good side of all this, Smitty."

"Good side? Mama, how could I find a good side to any of this?"

"What you and your friends have done in Korea will probably bring freedom to the beautiful people of South Korea and that is something that they and their ancestors have not had for hundreds of years."

"And what about Paulo and Tedi?" Smitty replied.

"Think about it, Smitty, because of you, Billy Hoyt will never kill again," Mama smiled up at him.

The Marines who had stayed ashore were excitedly assembling on the dock, preparing for the last leg of their journey back to the States. Lea's entire family was there to give Smitty and Woodrow a proper send off.

Lea handed Smitty a book.

"This is a new book that was just published. The author is a guy named Ray Bradbury. I think it is the type of book that your friend Walters would've loved to have read. I just finished reading it before you got back here from Japan."

"Thank you, Lea, what's it about?" he inquired curiously.

"The title is, The Fireman, but don't be fooled, it's science fiction, and it's about a future that we hope never comes. It's about burning books—the precious things that George Walters loved so much. I hope you enjoy it as much as I did."

Smitty looked puzzled but clutched the book tightly in his hand. "Maybe you just need to read more books," Walters's words echoed inside his head.

Smitty gave Lea a hug and thanked her again.

"I still have some unfinished business when I get to my next duty station. I promised CJ, Eckles, and Flores that I would visit their families if anything happened to them. It will be very painful, but I gave my word. Most importantly, I need to visit a young man named Winston Walters to deliver his brother Georges ring and the diary he had written since they had gone ashore at Inchon – and, of course, to tell him about his brother's great courage and sacrifice.

Smitty extended his hand to Captain Corwin and his arms to all the ladies. He saved the best for last and gave Nani a lingering kiss.

"I love you very much Nani Tyler. I miss you already, and I can't wait to complete my tour of duty so I can come back to you."

"Aloha nui, loa." Nani said to him as Mama Ahue placed a Lei around his neck.

"I created this lovely garland of very special Island Orchids just for you, Smitty," Mama Ahue smiled. "You will smell very good when you get on board the ship and the other Marines will be very jealous," Mama laughed. "Be sure to remember that when the ship gets out to sea at a point where you can still see land, you must throw it over the side. It will return to our shores on a friendly wave just as you will return someday too. Aloha, Smitty."

"Aloha to you, Mama, I will be back, and I will think about all of you often while I am away."

The sky that day was a rich Hawaiian blue from horizon to horizon.

Smitty smiled before beginning his ascent up the gangway. Halfway to the top he stopped, faced aft toward the flagstaff, and saluted the American Flag that was floating freely on a gentle breeze. With his head bowed slightly, he paused, entertaining fleeting thoughts of the fellow Marines he had left behind.

Then, he continued up to the Quarter Deck and saluted the Petty Officer of the Watch, requesting permission to come aboard. From there, he walked over and leaned against the rail and waved farewell to his new family standing on the pier below.

He saw Nani quietly weeping. Mama Ahue put her arm around Nani's shoulders and whispered in her ear.

"Don't cry, child, Smitty will be coming back soon. Mama Ahue knows these things."

His journey had come full circle now. He was on his way home. Nothing had turned out to be what he had expected when he first arrived on the Island of Oahu. It was as if he had lived out a dream - a constantly changing dream over which he had no control. Someday maybe I'll write a book, he thought, but if I do I'll have to label it fiction because no one will believe that any of this could possibly be true.

Smitty remained standing by the rail as the ship sliced its way through the crystal blue Hawaiian waters heading out into the Pacific then, while he could still see land, he cast Mama Ahue's beautiful orchid lei over the side. He stood there for a long time reminiscing and watching as it rode toward the shore on a gentle wave before disappearing from view.

He stood their spellbound for a while then went below and found that his same bunk, the one he had spent so much time lying in on the trip from Japan, was still available. He stowed all his gear with the exception of the diary Walters had asked him to deliver to his brother back home. Then he ascended up the ladder again and standing on the main deck he took deep breaths filling his lungs with the fresh ocean air.

Smitty paused momentarily pondering the incident with Billy on the way from Japan then he headed back to the fantail. He braced himself against the aft deck superstructure and slid down into a sitting position. His thoughts of what had happened there were unmarred by the death of a scoundrel who had no place in his Marine Corps. The churning waters that he loved to watch lulled him into a peaceful silence. He opened the diary deciding that he could read it now in the sanctuary of his place of solace. Inside, he found an unsealed letter addressed to Walters' young brother Winston.

Smitty withdrew the two soiled and weathered pages from within the envelope and began to read quietly to himself feeling a little bit like a voyeur invading someone's privacy.

Dear Brother Winston,

After dad was killed I crawled inside my books in an attempt to escape reality. I guess you might say that I became bitter and anti social. I found it easier to cope with my grief that way but as time went on I came to realize that interactions with people are important and that they have needs just like you and I do. Since that time I have discovered firsthand the evil that is born from having too much power. I saw it in Hawaii in one of our military policemen who got carried away with the power that was given to him. I saw it in the murders of two young boys who were senselessly killed by someone they had obviously trusted. Now I am seeing it in Korea where a power hungry government is killing its own people just to maintain their power. I remember reading a phrase that read, "Power corrupts and absolute power corrupts absolutely". It is sadly very true. I am certain now that our father knew that when he joined the Marines and later when he died protecting the rights of absolute strangers. Do you recall our discussions with dad regarding why the world is always in turmoil over things that we often viewed as petty crimes centered on power and greed? I have thought about that a lot since I have observed so many deplorable atrocities here in Korea and it appears to me now that it is all just an endless journey. Just as the bible states, 'the poor will always be among us', so to, will wars.

Why then do we, as a nation, become embroiled in other people's wars? In the final analysis I can only conclude that we are definitely our brothers' keeper. We fight for other people's brothers just as I would fight for you and hopefully you for me. We fight for their freedom or risk losing our own. The stakes are high my dear brother – but freedom, unlike the air we breathe, is not now, nor will it ever be free.

It ended there as if he intended to continue writing more at a later time but these were certainly the words of the very thoughtful and philosophical George Walters who was willing to defend his beliefs even if it could cost him his freedom and ultimately his life.

Smitty rested his head back against the ships superstructure and watched as a myriad of rippling waves trailed behind the ship – each carrying a memory of the adventure he sought so eagerly when he left home so long ago. Memories now captured by the wind at a God forsaken place in North Korea.

His mind drifted, swarming with stories he would never tell, and soon he was asleep.

EPILOGUE

How does that look?

The voice startled the elderly man back to reality.

He opened his eyes and saw his own image staring back at him from inside the mirror.

"Not bad—but could you make me look a little younger?" he smiled at the barber.

"If I could I'd have to charge you more" the young man replied with an impish grin.

As the man fumbled inside his wallet looking for money the barber noticed a black and white picture of a beautiful young girl with a Hawaiian lei draped around her neck and shoulders. Beside her was a teen aged, baby faced boy dressed neatly in a Marine uniform.

"Your girl friend?" the barber responded questioningly.

"My wife" he answered. "I returned to Hawaii after I got discharged and we got married. She passed away about five years ago."

"Sorry to hear that." The barber responded

"And that is you, sir?" the barber said pointing at the picture.

"Yes that's me," the elder man replied

"Tell me sir were all the guys you served with in the war as young as you?"

"They still are," he answered.

The barber gave the elder man a puzzled look. "Why do you say that?" he queried.

"Because many of them were killed and the rest I haven't seen since then, so they live inside my mind and stay young while I grow old. It's the price you pay for living too long, son."

As the old man turned to leave he heard the barber call out, **"Next!"**

227

CHOSIN STAR

Synopsis

This novel could best be described as historical fiction since it is based on actual events which the author experienced firsthand during the year 1950 and uses both real and fictional characters as well as real and fictional events.

Following the second 'war to end all wars' a group of young men stationed at Pearl Harbor, Hawaii find themselves in a virtual land of enchantment. Though not exactly a murder mystery, the book begins with the investigation of the murders of two young boys which takes place at a now defunct military base, Camp Catlin on the island of Oahu.

The narrative follows the exploits of these young marines who eventually get caught up in an unexpected war in an unexpected place. There is mystery, romance, humor, camaraderie, deceit, betrayal, dilemma, death, hardship and pain as the book shifts from Part One, in the tropical splendorous "Heaven" of Hawaii to Part Two, in the frozen "Hell" of war-torn South and North Korea.

If you enjoy adventure filled with twists and turns this is the book for you.

ABOUT THE AUTHOR

The author, John Smith, is an 83 year old United States Marine who served before and during the Korean War. He was wounded in the battle of the Chosin Reservoir at age 18 in North Korea and was awarded the Purple Heart medal. After his discharge from the military in 1952, he finished high school, and then went on to receive a BS degree in Public Administration at the University of Detroit on the "G.I. Bill." He worked for a major computer manufacturer during the 1960s and later became Assistant to the President in Public Relations at Siena Heights College in Adrian Michigan. Also during the 1960s he was awarded 5 daughters and eventually numerous grand children. John retired from Central Michigan University in 1991.

In 1998 he formed a unit of U.S. Naval Sea Cadets (a youth program) dedicated to teaching the importance of respect, courtesy and commitment in which he was the Commanding Officer for 15 years. In 2014 he formed another local group designed for youth emphasizing drug demand reduction and is presently the Unit Commander of the Central Michigan Young Marines in Mount Pleasant, Michigan.

In addition he is a proud member of the VFW, the DAV, the American Legion, the Military Order of the Purple Heart and the "Chosin Few".

GOD'S CHOSIN FEW

Draw near my friends and listen closely,
And hear – yes hear – my tale unravel,
Bout those who made an epic journey,
On roads that Angels dared not travel.

Somewhere, out there in northern climes,
Where even the wisest feared to tread,
You will hear the sounds of frozen silence,
Whispered softly by our honored dead.

T'was in God forsaken North Korea,
A country torn by strife and war,
Where Iron Men took up a challenge,
At a place they called the Reservoir.

As they arrived at Yudam-ni,
The temps quickly dropped to 60 below.
Greatly outnumbered by soldiers from China,
They relentlessly fought in the blinding snow.

Against all odds these stalwart men,
Guided by a star that shone on high.
Endured cold and hunger, and sleep deprivation,
Undauntedly determined to do or to die.

The names of these Heroes will ne'er be forgotten,
As so many died far from their hometown.
There was: Hamlin and Balog, Walter George and Faith,
Windrich and Collins and Sweet Jesse Brown.

Courageous men - most now forgotten,
Who gave their lives when the battle seemed lost.
Their heroism speaks for all Men of the Chosin,
Who stood their ground no matter the cost.

Ten thousand had entered that Valley of Death,
To do for us all, what no others could do.
They confronted the demons of power and greed,
And accepting the challenge became "God's Chosin Few".

So I dare you to listen, on cold winter nights,
When whispers are echoed on winds that are frozen.
You'll hear cursing and swearing, born of valor and pain,
But only the wind can be heard whining at Chosin.

231

Printed in the United States
By Bookmasters